Smoke and Fire

KATIE CROSS

KCW

To Cory Carlson.
From the women of the mountain.

Chapter One

DAHLIA

The growing plume of smoke on the horizon did *not* give me warm fuzzies.

A wildfire in the mountains north of Pineville was not how I wanted to start the week. Nor did it lend hope for a low-key day. That's all I wanted—something quiet, calm, and filled with time to research my new life. I'd make cappuccinos, enjoy the quiet purr of life in Pineville. Maybe sit in the sunshine outside my RV at the end of the day and pretend like I played in the ocean.

Simple arithmetic.

Or was it?

To that end, the romance book splayed open on the counter behind me also did not give me warm fuzzies. No, far worse. It gave me butterflies, hope, thrills, and a dramatic sense of *oh my gosh will they ever?*

"Fantastic," I muttered darkly.

The last thing I needed was a romance novel that I liked. They only made my wary attitude toward relationships worse. To make matters even worse, the water heater in my RV failed this morning. My sleep-deprived state didn't help either. Yet again, I'd stayed up *way* too late reading.

I blamed Lizbeth.

Dahlia Finau did *not* do mornings. This girl was a sleeper.

Yet, work at the Frolicking Moose Coffee Shop didn't care if I wanted to sleep or not. Just like that book didn't care, either. Thanks to a deranged Lizbeth on a book bender, I'd fallen face-first into this romance novel and forgotten to buy groceries yesterday. My alarm erupted twenty minutes late, so I barely managed to stumble into work on time. The whole smeared-mascara-messy-bun appearance had to cut it today. Still felt totally worth it.

The book was *that* good.

I spun around and eyed the waiting novel. The cover had frayed edges, well-loved from use. No doubt, Lizbeth had conned other people into reading it, too. *Life is a Freaking Dream.* What a weird title. The second book, *Love is a Terrible Nightmare* felt far more apropos. It waited in my purse at the very, verrrry bottom where I could ignore it a little easier. Not much easier, just a little bit.

But what an amazing book the first one has been, sang my inner voice. The one that I occasionally spoke to out loud and deeply confused people that heard me. I mentally hushed her now. She always got in my way.

"Romance doesn't have a place in our life right now," I replied. "We're recovering from the break with Jakob and can't be trusted to jump into anything like Amalia and Rodrigo."

Inner Me rolled her eyes. *We've been "recovering from the break up" for the last six months. How long do you need?*

I ignored that *and* her metaphorical air quotes. The only other thing to think about was the book that I hated to love. Or the new fire outside, but I definitely didn't want to think about that.

Two days ago, I—very stupidly—confessed to Lizbeth that

I'd never picked up a romance novel before. Within an hour, she brought twenty romance novels into the store.

"Take this series as a strong suggestion for you to get started in the romance genre, Dahlia," she'd said.

"What does that even mean?" I'd mumbled.

She glared at me. "It means you're going to read all twenty novels because they're that good. Try me. If you aren't totally addicted by the end of the first book, I'll take them all back. But, c'mon. We aren't cave people here. We recognize romance as a powerful force in this world, so get reading already. Jess will change. your. life."

I'd cracked a tolerant smile that slowly deflated, like a dying balloon, when I realized she was serious.

"No one knows who Jess is." She'd prattled as she hoisted all twenty books past her pregnant belly, then placed them in straight, stackable lines. "Jess is brilliant. She doesn't write with a last name, never appears anywhere in person, and almost tops the romance charts with every launch. She came *so close* to number one last time." Lizbeth pretended to faint. "I'm holding out for the next one. She has twenty novels in one series and I've made it through the first eight for the tenth time in the last four days. Start at the beginning with *Life is a Freaking Dream*."

In the present, I pulled myself out of my thoughts and eyed the book warily. In all fairness, at least *Life is a Freaking Dream* didn't have a cover with giant, heaving bosoms and a man with a chest so chiseled it looked like a painted sculpture. The subtle, text-based font had stylistic scrollwork that was a mixture of contemporary and ancient which drew my attention. The whimsical, yet masculine feel made me want to snuggle it.

Lizbeth had been right, darn her.

Life is a Freaking Dream was a fabulous first book. When I finally collapsed to sleep at three in the morning, I desperately wanted to keep reading but couldn't keep my eyes open. Now that an opportunity to read had presented itself, I wasn't sure it would be wise to pick it up. No work would get done and I'd dissolve into a puddle all day.

"What," I murmured with a frown, "am I going to do with you?"

The sweet, endearing moments of the book still had my heart. When Rodrigo really *saw* Amalia. When their love was just budding and everything felt fresh and new and exciting. A touch on the small of the back. An unexpected smile. The terrifying wait of a kiss. I'd once had that with Jakob.

For sure.

At some point.

In some distant, faraway history.

An uncomfortable feeling grew inside me, like itchy wool lined my stomach.

"Sorry," I whispered to the book. "I'm sorry. I want to love you, but I also *don't* want to love you. You're not real and I don't want hope. Hope sucks. I'm not so good at forming my own path, you know? I fall into the first guy that shows me romance and I let them take over my life . . ." I shrank smaller, poked the book with my index finger, and said a gentle, "Sorry."

Love is a Terrible Nightmare folded back together in protest of my rejection and sat there with a silent huff of annoyance. My gaze slid back to the ugly column of fire yet again. Speaking of *actual* powerful forces . . .

Should I call Bethany and ask what was going on up there? The fire blazed somewhere in the canyon between Pineville and touristy Jackson City. What would Bethany be able to do about it? Nothing. If anything, I should call the fire department.

Really smart, Inner Me drawled. *Cuz they can't see that*

towering pillar of destruction smack dab in the middle of the sky.

The hairs on the back of my neck stood up.

Fire.

Blech.

In the evergreen mountains that wrapped around Pineville like long, lush arms, fires were portent to disaster. At least, that's what my favorite male cousin, Sione, said a few weeks ago. Pineville had only been home for a little over a month. No, my stopping point. Right now, there was no home until I figured out where my life would go next.

And that was just fine.

I pointed to the smoke with a firm growl. "You stay over there." I jabbed a thumb to the espresso machine, where I stood behind the coffee shop bar. "I'll stay here. We're square. Got it?"

The plume ignored me, but the book stared while I bustled around. I absolutely did *not* think about Amalia and Rodrigo. Or whether Rodrigo would return home from the war an altered man, but one willing to understand the real depths of Amalia's love for him. I mean, how could he not?

"By heavens, Rodrigo!" I cried, unable to help myself. "She bloody loves you, man. Get over your own pride!"

Unable to avoid another moment without knowing their fate, I snatched the book off the counter. Within moments, swirls of unrealistic romance captured me. Reluctant reader or not, I couldn't peel myself away from the pages. To make matters worse, no one wandered in for a coffee, so I sipped my own and devoured each and every word.

Twenty minutes later, a green bus-like truck parked near the edge of the lot. The words PINEVILLE HOTSHOTS were painted across the top in blocky black letters. The fire department lived next door, and with it, a building that held the crew of fire workers in the summer and their office in the winter.

"Ominous," I sang as I peered at the truck over the top of my book, thoroughly distracted from the hunky men in the book for the potential in real life.

Thought relationships had no part of our world right now? Inner Me chimed in.

"Looking," I murmured, "does not a relationship make."

Outside, grungy men spilled out of the bus in matching yellow jackets, green pants, and haggard expressions. They huddled together in a meeting while the bus hissed and turned off. With a sigh, I shoved a napkin into the pages and set the book aside. Rodrigo and his fiery kisses would have to wait. Now, I could play my favorite game.

Match the drink with the drinker.

"Cappuccino for that guy." I eyed a tall, lanky figure with a scraggly beard. Had it been set aflame on one side? "Espresso for Mr. Scruffy next to you, sir. Black, no creamer, and one sugar for Mr. Short-and-Scrumptious."

The concoction game amused me until one guy stumped me. I frowned, straightening. Broad-shouldered and tall. He had messy blonde hair and a thick beard, with piercing eyes and skin tanned to a golden hue around his neck and face. Hints of chest hair peeked out of the neckline of a sooty yellow shirt.

Plain black coffee?

Meh.

He seemed like he'd have a sweet tooth. Definitely nothing too sweet, like a frap. Maybe a macchiato, but that didn't fit either. Before I could peg him down, the hotshots grabbed heavy bags and headed toward the fire department.

Bemused, I forced myself away from *Love is a Terrible Nightmare* to do the maintenance log on the fridge and a few checks. I would not be caught derelict on duties while reading a romance novel.

I had my pride.

An hour later, the crack of the door brought me out of my reverie. With a squeak, I whirled around and shoved the book to the side.

"Welcome to—"

The words died on my lips.

A pair of stormy eyes peered at me from an angular face. One of the hotshots—the one I couldn't quite peg.

A rough beard streaked with brown and hints of blonde drew my gaze to his strong neck and shoulders. The smell of smoke entered the room with him. None of that startled me. Not even the obnoxiously yellow shirt, muted by layers of grime and filth, or the dark green pants.

The expression of panic in his eyes, despite his haggard mein, stopped me. That strange, glazed terror wasn't normal, certainly not in such a strapping face. What could possibly have a man like him look terrified like that?

"—the Frolicking Moose," I finished lamely.

He shifted, revealing a computer under his left arm. A backpack strap rested lazily on the other shoulder. When he spoke, it rumbled in his chest.

"Internet."

I tilted my head to the side. Wait . . . what? What was that? A caveman request? It wasn't even a question. *See?* I told my inner self. *Men are the same everywhere.*

Not true. In direct contradiction to your point, Jakob never caveman-requested.

Peeved now, I countered. "Coffee shop."

He frowned. His gaze dropped to the countertop, as if seeking something, then landed on the books. The muscles around his lips tightened.

I bristled.

Great. He was going to judge me to be a simpering woman that read romance novels at work. That would put me into a label without him knowing me at all. A true label, unfortunately, but that was besides the point. The judgment already built up in his gaze, like a gathering storm. Oh, that's *exactly* what I saw in his a-little-too-attractive face right now. Condemnation.

Judgment.

Or, maybe, just an extension of his strange fear.

On an average day, I liked everyone I met. It's why a coffee shop in a small mountain town for the summer ended up being an ideal job. It gave me space to plan my next move, enough work to not feel utter terror over my lack of direction, and connection with people so I didn't get lonely. Something about *this* tough guy, however, set my teeth on edge. Definitely wasn't that masculine appeal.

Nope. Not that.

He scowled and shifted the backpack strap. "I would like to use the internet, please." His voice purred like a lazy cat now.

"Okay."

Utter silence followed, and I felt his annoyance deepen in the weighty pause. A little guilt for my own intensity trickled through me. My cousin Pele told me I could be a *tad* defensive, even before anyone said something, and I had a feeling I'd just done that here.

"If you are asking," I drawled in response to his obnoxious quiet, "if we have internet, the answer is yes. Hot and cold running water too, if you like that kind of modern upgrade, but the outhouse is out back if you need it. Password is on the board."

If possible, his frown deepened. Ooookay, that attempt at humor certainly didn't work, which only intensified my frustration.

Tough crowd.

I slapped on my brightest smile. The kind that almost crackled. He seemed to notice the edge of frustration as well because his gaze darkened.

"What can I get you to drink?" I asked.

"Coffee. Straight," he turned to head toward a table, then added over his shoulder, "and protein."

I opened my mouth to clarify, but decided not to. He probably operated life using less than twenty words per day. No reason to force him to outdo his quota.

I grabbed a cheese-and-sausage bagel sandwich and tossed it on a plate. Then I reached for a mug off of our wall collection with a picture of a scowling cat on it that felt deliciously passive-aggressive, and slung coffee into it. By the time I worked my way to his table with the requested nourishment, he had his laptop open. Within minutes, he'd sunk deeper into his own foul mood.

Whatta happy pair.

I set the food down, eager to sneak away without a word, but he grabbed my wrist. The gentle burn of his skin zipped straight to my bones. I didn't know his name, his face, or anything about him.

But with his hot touch that burned like fire, I knew that everything in my life had just changed.

Chapter Two

BASTIAN

Words blurred on the screen as I read them. Unable to focus, I rubbed my eyes with the heel of my hand and navigated away.

Bastian,

We need to talk.

You're fighting fires in the forest like a crazy person and have limited availability—I get it. But your career is knocking on the door. It's time to answer. As your agent, I'm on this ride with you. Your success is my success.

Interview requests have been pouring in from several different avenues. Podcasts, TV stations, some online influencers. In anticipation of launching book #21, we've seen sales and traction rising. Your marketing team is actually doing its job, now you need to do yours too.

The stock photo we put up as an author profile photo is soon going to be discovered as not *you. Eventually, readers will learn that Jess is a single, thirty-something male. I calculate a 62% chance that your hidden career is about to unravel right before we launch into a bestseller slot.*

I don't like those odds.

Growing unrest is noted amongst some of your normally most popular message boards as well, might I add. Only made worse by the constant silence from Jess on social media this summer.

Your goal to push to a #1 spot on the charts for release could happen, but not if you're hiding in the woods.
I know you want to remain anonymous, but we need to get ahead of what could be a massive issue.

—Priyanka

Once I finally understood it all the way through, I scooted lower in the booth and closed my eyes.

This was a bad idea. I came to read Priyanka's communications at the Frolicking Moose because I knew I'd ignore them when I returned home. I'd crash on the couch for eight hours, wake up exhausted, throw some laundry in, and crash again.

This place smelled like vanilla and the heady, thick smell kept me from falling asleep. The original coffee shop had nearly disappeared under all their renovations. I remembered it when it was still a fishing place, when Bethany's dad still owned it. Proof that life always evolved and sometimes surprised all of us.

With a sigh, I turned back to the onslaught of emails that awaited.

Punctuating my private inbox, where readers couldn't

reach me, awaited financial correspondence. Bills. Bank updates. Interest amortization schedules on a mortgage I was just about to pay off on Dad's behalf. The usual.

The other email, my author one, gushed with words from sincere women that loved my books. Requests for podcast interviews, video interviews, appearances at conferences, and book signing forms dotted the landscape there. The landscape that I had always ignored. Gradually, it had started to get worse and worse.

How my career as an author hadn't absolutely tanked from sheer lack of involvement with the readers, I'd never understand.

Nausea welled up in my stomach at the thought of tackling two weeks' worth of emails. The tab shrank into the ether as I navigated away from that disaster, ignored the messages on my phone from Pri, and found myself staring at a blank white page. The open expanse of the computer canvas just *waited* for more words.

I had none.

My fingers stalled on top of the keys. Two weeks away on the fires, and all I could think about was getting words out of my brain that whole time. Now I sat here, and my mind filled with snow.

This wasn't the ideal time to write. Laundry awaited—so much laundry. Had to feed the cat. Sleep. Get some food in my too-hungry body, amongst other things.

Priyanka's words of warning waved like red flags as I drummed my fingertips on the keys. I reached into the back of my mind. Sometimes, I had to search for words. Find them left in the crevasses and shadows of my creativity.

Writing emptied my brain, like I had an allotted number of things that I could hold in my head to share with the world. The words filled back up over time in a slow trickle.

Especially when I spent time in the forest, hacking at trees, filling my lungs with smoke and my body with charred scars. Like all summer, the words didn't come. I couldn't dredge them free. Wasn't sure I wanted them right now anyway.

I navigated back to the inbox, focused more on Pri and her not-so-gentle warnings.

Interviews.

Podcasts.

We need to talk.

The words carried more implication than anything else. Pri wasn't wrong. We did need to talk. Since last year, my sales had been expanding like a slowly inflating balloon. The lines bumped up and up on my reports, sometimes stabilizing at a new plateau. An advertising push would raise them again now that the marketing team had proof that people wanted my work. Rarely did sales drop drastically, although the days popped up and down in any normal pattern.

Then . . . they exploded.

A few strategic influencers on Instagram got a hold of Rodrigo and a wildfire of fandom began. Jess raced like a freight train toward new popularity this summer. Social media growth became exponential. Fan groups popped up in book clubs, online, at conferences, romantic gatherings. Invitations to speak at conferences, talk with experts, and meet fans flowed in constantly.

With the launch of my twenty-first novel, I stood to break my own record—and maybe some others—in sales.

If you're serious about this career and the money that you want to make, Pri had said before I left last time, *we're going to have to reveal Jess.*

Of course I was serious.

Protective-younger-brother serious.

The building plume behind the mountains drew my gaze,

and I stifled a frustrated head shake. We just finished a two-week rotation on another fire and had forty-eight hours off to do laundry, recover some sleep, and pretend like we didn't overuse our bodies on a daily basis. Food would be paramount. So would rest.

Certainly not answering fan mail.

That plume would likely be the next assignment for my hotshot crew. The fire had been named the Pinegulch fire. It was probably ten miles west of the highway between Pineville and Jackson City and originated from a lightning strike start, I'd wager. Might have smoldered for a few days before conflagrating, because the only lightning storm in this area passed last week. Aside from a sprinkle here and there, weather reports had been dry all summer.

A beep drew me out of my thoughts. I glanced over to the counter where it originated, then quickly back to my computer.

For whatever reason, the saucy little barista had rattled me. First, I'd wanted to wrap my hand around her wavy black hair and feel it between my fingers. Something about her sparky, dark brown eyes caught my attention, and I had a feeling it was her wit. Second, I wanted to lay a kiss on those full lips. It had been a while.

A *long* while.

In the same breath, she also spurred an idea of a totally different nature. A far more acceptable nature, anyway, than how soft she'd be in my arms. Spurred by the idea, I turned back to my email.

Computer keys finally rattled under my fingertips after I navigated onto a fresh email.

Pri,

Sorry about the delayed reply. What will happen if we continue to do no PR work? Or what if I hired someone to pretend to be Jess and do the appearances?

Those are my two preferred options.

—Bastian

Damn, but I sounded like a total ass.

Still, that's where reality lay. I never misrepresented myself to Priyanka, and I wouldn't start now. No work—which is what I'd been doing for the last couple of months—or someone *else* does the work. It's all I could offer.

After I sent the email into the void, I leaned back against the seat with a sigh. So, there went that, the worst idea ever. Someone else be Jess? Probably too stupid to follow up on. Privacy issues abounded, not to mention who would do it? What would happen if we were found out?

I toyed with those questions all the time anyway.

With any luck, Pri would be at her computer, probably frustrated that I hadn't responded in two weeks. My lack of a decision would compound her emotions over the topic and she'd probably advocate harder for me to reveal myself as Jess. Then I'd push back and . . .

A truck roared by outside and the sound drew me out of my deepening spiral. I sucked in a sharp breath and looked up as a plate clinked in front of me.

The girl behind the counter—her name tag said Dahlia— avoided my gaze as she set a coffee mug down. A long lock of hair, almost to her elbow, slipped off her shoulder. She began to retreat, but I didn't want her to go. Not yet.

I grabbed her wrist.

My movement happened so suddenly, it startled me also. She stilled immediately. I released her, feeling like a total weirdo. Nothing said *dangerous* or *idiotic male* quite like grabbing a complete stranger.

"Sorry." I folded my arms against my chest. The response came out gruffer than I intended. "I didn't . . . I didn't mean to grab you. I was going to ask you—sorry. Never mind."

Her eyes narrowed to slits where I saw more curiosity than fear. She didn't step back or send me a dirty look or curl away. Maybe I wasn't too scary. Or maybe she was about to punch me in the face. The look in her eye said she'd only be moments away from protecting herself, given the opportunity.

"Thank you for the food and the coffee," I said.

"Anything else?"

Her voice had an edge, but not too much. If anything, she sounded kind.

"Can I get the coffee to go?"

"Sure."

She grabbed the mug, spun on her heels, and walked away, her hair swaying around her back. A sweet scent remained in her wake. Nothing pungent, yet I couldn't put my finger on it. For some reason, I thought of sunshine. With a growl, I grabbed the sandwich and tore into it.

Time to get out of here.

* * *

Dad's home lay under a thick blanket of guilt and shadow.

The air smelled stale. Only two weeks had passed since I'd last opened the windows, but they creaked like old ghosts when I threw them open. Dad never believed in air conditioning, which meant a fetid air lay in the rooms. He hadn't even installed ductwork in the walls for a furnace when he'd built this place.

Flipping on lights and laying all my smoky gear on the

table livened the atmosphere. My bustle breathed life back into it.

My eyes ran along the pictures populating the walls. Almost too many, if you asked me, but maybe just right. The clutter felt like the comforting chatter of family gathered around a table.

Vague, but nondescript.

My thoughts fractured into ribbons as I yanked clothes out of my bags and shoved them into the tiny room at the back, where the stacked washer and dryer waited. The smell of burnt wood lingered in the air like char. I hardly smelled it out there on fires. Here it seemed stronger than ever.

Mail waited on the table, along with a note from my neighbor Mrs. Cortez that said, *Bought more cat food. She's doing fine.*

As if summoned by thought, a distant tinkle of sound preceded the swish of the cat door opening. A hearty purr, like the roar of an engine, announced a dainty, calico cat from the shadows. A tiger-like design of black and orange decorated her face, giving way to the white, soft fur of her body.

Unbalanced, Dad had always said, *but perfect.*

With a crouch, I extended my hand. Calluses hardened my knuckles and fingertips, but Psycho didn't care. Did cats assign blame? Feel emotion? Sometimes when she ignored me, I thought she punished me for taking Dad away. After these long breaks, she was desperate enough for human interaction to tolerate me, but I think she actually missed him. My sister, Inessa, for sure.

Psycho deigned to show me affection and butted her head against my hand with a gentle rutting sound. I petted her for several minutes, until she turned her back. Hair littered the floor, but I'd sweep it up later. Her Highness hopped on top of the couch and made herself at home.

By the time I finished sorting the laundry and the initial

batch started, the sun had settled toward the edge of the sky. My stomach growled, so I threw pasta on the stovetop and hunted for marinara. Lacking ground beef that wasn't frozen solid, I tossed frozen maple sausage links on next. Not exactly a symphony of flavors, but the calories would be good.

Finally, I sat down at the table. The envelopes stacked in piles weren't unanticipated. More stuff always gathered at the end of the month. Dad had been classic that way. Didn't like the online route. Preferred everything in paper so he could see it, file it away, and pull it out after seven years to tut over in disgust for tax law.

After I sorted through the mail, I flipped the sausage and opened my computer. The girl at the coffee shop moved to the front of my thoughts. Something about her had a vague . . . undeniable quality that I couldn't let go of. It bothered me, lingering uninvited.

What did it mean?

How did I write that undefinable something into a book?

I yanked an envelope toward me, sent from nearby Jackson City. The front of it said *Memory Care Services*. It caused a familiar gut clench. Beneath it lay another envelope, another round of bills. *Adult Care Services.*

With a sour stomach, I shoved them both away to dive into later. A text caused my phone to jump to life again.

Hernandez: You back?

I glanced at it while rolling the sizzling sausage in the frying pan. The water had started to boil, so I flung the pasta inside and grabbed my phone off the counter.

Bastian: Just arrived.

Hernandez: Dinner tomorrow, my place. Dagny's cooking, so you won't die.

Bastian: Thanks. See you then.

Relief swept through me. Hernandez always gave me a few hours of alone time to set my life back to rights before he had me come over.

He always invited me for dinner in between fires, though. He must watch for the obnoxiously green buggy parked in front of the fire station, because he always knew when to text.

Fire season felt like living along the edge. I could dodge whatever life threw at me, but it left a vague sense of running away behind. Not to mention the worsening fallout when I returned to utter, ignored chaos.

Hernandez: How's your sister?

Bastian: Getting what she needs.

Hernandez: Dad?

Steam billowed out of the rolling boil of water that cooked the noodles. I flipped the knob on the stove a little too force-fully when I turned off the frying pan and the knob dropped onto the stove top. I frowned at it. I replaced the knob with a roll of my eyes, then slid the hot pan onto an empty coil.

Slightly calmer, I returned to the phone.

Bastian: Same. Worse.

Hernandez: Sorry, brother. I'm always here.

I grabbed the sausage, dumped it on a plate, then poured a

can of uncertainty-aged marinara sauce into the noodles I'd just drained. While I ate, I completely avoided my computer and the blinking, giant red strobe lights in my brain.

Must. Do. Something. Now.

Disasters waited in my inbox. Bigger disasters than I wanted to admit. I would take care of them, just not right now.

Tomorrow would have to be soon enough.

Chapter Three

DAHLIA

Red hair appeared in the doorway of the coffee shop the next day, seconds before the door tinkled open. I hummed and bopped to a song when Lizbeth shuffled inside. A basketball-sized belly preceded her.

She smiled wearily.

"Hey."

Instantly, I hustled over. "Sit down, Mama. You look tired."

She sighed, seemed to think of protesting, but obeyed. Her hands-on-the-back-shuffle waddle killed me. Adorable. Utterly miserable. Whatever you wanted to call it, late pregnancy looked like it totally sucked. Once she settled, I grabbed another chair for her to put her feet on.

She smiled.

"Thanks. You always seem to know just what I need."

"I got you, sister. Vanilla frap with extra whip cream and two cherries on top?"

Lizbeth grinned with all her teeth.

"*Exactly* what I wanted."

I fist pumped. "Nailed it."

She fell quiet while I bustled behind the counter, prattling about anything *but* the Jess books. Hands folded and perched atop her adorable almost-ready-to-pop belly, Lizbeth peered out the window and toward the smoke stack with the same smudge of concern I'd had.

"You heard anything about the fire?" she asked.

"Not yet."

Her brow formed into wrinkled lines.

"Huh."

"You?"

"Not really, just that they sent a fire crew up there yesterday. Has the loft rented out yet?"

Her voice lifted with a moment of hope, and I hated to dash her dreams. Bethany and Maverick had decided to use the loft of the Frolicking Moose as a HomeBnB instead of leasing it out for months at a time. Lizbeth had spent the last couple of weeks throwing together Pinnable boards, then bringing them to life up there. In between local antique stores and bargain shopping, she'd created a whole new esthetic.

"Mountain chic," she'd said. "It's a new thing."

The whole apartment was put together in a charming, mountain-esque suite that I constantly wanted to live in. A cozy leather sofa. Queen bed made from rough slabs of timber. Pillows so fluffy I could sink into them for hours.

Despite a busy tourist season, renters had been minimal. I suspected Bethany and Maverick kept forgetting to update the listing or set it live or something. Several times they'd forgotten to tell me to expect someone, and renters had come to the Frolicking Moose seeking keys.

Small disasters.

"Ah, no," I said to Lizbeth. "Not that I've heard of, anyway."

Lizbeth's hopeful expression dropped into a frown.

"Huh. Did you ever get a hold of Jada?"

I wracked my brain to remember who she meant until I recalled the local doctor. Jada was a middle-aged woman that ran the clinic in town and trained horses on the side. A gentle woman with a dazzling smile and full lips. She always looked like a million bucks. Rumor had it her legendary gumbo could cure all ills.

"Ah . . ." I hedged to buy time. Lizbeth and Jada were bibliophiles and close friends. Lizbeth had offered to introduce me to Jada when I expressed an interest in becoming a nurse. Further research into the idea turned me away. Blood, guts, and squalling babies?

Not my thing.

My previous job as a manager of a hardware store lent me more to a paper-oriented career, not a bodily-fluids one.

"I sort of moved away from the medical field as a route for my next thing," I finally managed. "A little too . . ."

"Gross?"

"That's it."

She laughed. "I agree. Jada's also a horse trainer, too. If you wanted to look at that route."

"Animals definitely appeal to me. I put a call into the local veterinarian office to see if I could shadow them for a day but haven't heard back. Isn't there a town attorney, too?"

"Kinoshi, yes. He's brilliant."

The sheepish feeling of being a bit too old to be doing this overcame me again. Most people ran through life options at seventeen, not twenty seven. Settling into a relationship with Jakob at twenty-two, then letting his life absorb me, is exactly why I was only a decade or so late.

Late, Inner Me said, *is better than never.*

"Truth."

"What?" Lizbeth piped up.

"Oh, nothing," I called, cheeks burning with embarrassment. "Just about done."

While slinging her frap together, my mind drifted back to Mr. Mysterious the hotshot, who'd stayed like a rock in the same position for ten minutes before he wolfed down his sandwich, slammed his computer shut, dropped twenty dollars, and left the shop with coffee in hand.

I definitely hadn't thought about him while laying on my bed in the RV last night, the cool wind whispering through my hot trailer. Definitely didn't smell smoke and think of him. Or mutter over how frustrating his silence had been.

Or accidentally juxtapose him over the top of the love interest in the second book, Rhashaad, so that I inadvertently spent all night thinking about Mr. Hotshot.

Okay, all that happened.

I'd never see him again, so why did he haunt me? No, that was probably a lie. I'd see him again, and that was the exact thought that made my heart flutter. He clearly lived here, at least for the summer. With the fire still building in the mountains, I'd probably see him soon enough.

Lizbeth sighed, looped her fingers over her belly, and then eyed me while I swept around the counter to deliver her drink. I wouldn't give into her silent pressure to talk about Rodrigo or Rhashaad. No, I'd keep myself together and remain composed, the way any self-respecting woman would do. No way would I simper and exclaim and lose all my self-respect over a romance novel. Mom would be so proud of me.

"So?" she drawled.

"SHE LOVES HIM!"

The words burst out of me as I melted bonelessly into the chair across from her, head in my hands.

Way to keep it cool, Inner Me muttered. I silenced her as Lizbeth tilted her head back and laughed.

"I knew it! You were suckered into the books!"

"Rhashaad is a beautiful idiot. Playboy he might be but

idiot he is not. Rhashaad and Amy Grace are going to end up together. Mark my words."

She squealed.

Like a monster, I kept going. "Amy Grace loves him more than anything she's ever had on this planet. Why can't he just accept that he's broken and let her heal him?"

Lizbeth held up both hands. "I KNOW!"

Frustrated at my less-than-two-seconds capitulation, I sighed dramatically and leaned back.

"I hate you for how much I love them."

Lizbeth shook her head with a sigh. "I know. Jess has *got* it. I can't tell you how many romance novels I've read, but never have they affected me like these."

My nose wrinkled. "Does any other author you know have a single name?"

She shrugged. "Probably, but I also don't care. Her books are phenomenal and you've only read one."

"And a half!"

"And a half," she conceded with a quick grin. "There are eighteen-point-five others waiting for you. Plus another one launching in just a few weeks. Book twenty one of the series, *Wanderlust is a Battle,* is very highly anticipated. Jess left a huge cliffhanger with a beloved character at the end of twenty and we—meaning her fandom collectively—have been dying for this to come out."

A squeak/groan combination escaped my throat. Was I happy or sad about that news? Delighted, in some forms. Aggrieved in others. At the heart of all these stories were relationships I wasn't ready to dream about again. Not so soon.

Six months, sang my voice.

Not long enough, I sang back. She rolled her metaphorical eyes.

"So." I straightened. "Tell me about the baby and the swelling and the many eternities that are pregnancy. My cousin, Pele, has four kids and tells me all about how terrible it is every chance she gets."

"Active." She let out a raspberry. "So active. I've loved pregnancy, to be honest. It's really fun! People help me out at the store more often, and open my door more, that kind of stuff. It's like you get a free pass! But I'm ready to just . . . have my body back."

"How many weeks left?"

She fake sobbed. "Twelve!"

"Drink your frap." I nodded to it. "Maybe the cold will shock time into moving faster."

"I hope so." Her gaze drifted around. "I'm supposed to meet Bethany here. She hasn't popped in yet?"

"Nope."

"We're planning a trip to see Ellie out in North Carolina with the baby in the spring." She grimaced and repositioned. I nudged her drink a little closer, and she had a sip. "Thanks."

"Sounds fun. I miss Ellie. Is she still happy over there with Devin?"

Lizbeth grinned. "So happy. Devin has always completed her. She's homesick and struggling to find a job, but it's only been a month since she arrived there. Besides, Devin's love counters all of that."

The temptation to snort nearly overcame me. *Devin's love counters all of that* was comically cheesy. *Yet,* came my inner voice, *you are filled with envy.*

"Silence," I muttered.

"What?"

"Nothing!" I chirped. "Ah . . . how are things for you and JJ?"

Lizbeth blinked, gazed around, and sighed. "Fine. Maverick told me about the overbooking disaster last week. I'm so sorry that happened. I might be able to help pick up some hours here if you need it."

My grimace couldn't be helped. A children's birthday party and a very serious Bunco club showed up at the same time. Bethany had accidentally overbooked a slot for the back room, and the fallout had been ugly.

"Yeah," I drawled. "Those old ladies were pretty intense."

Lizbeth's eyes widened. "I'm sure. Bethany needs a manager. Someone to take inventory, do the ordering, coordinate hirings and firings, and all that other boring stuff. If I didn't have a princess coming, I'd manage it. But I already do that for the bakery and my online business still needs some love."

The Frolicking Moose definitely needed someone to smooth things out. Bethany and Maverick had both been so busy, I rarely saw them. The offer for me to manage the Frolicking Moose hadn't come and hopefully wouldn't. I didn't want ties to Pineville.

Not yet, anyway.

Maybe I'd land here and stay awhile, but I didn't want to make that decision so soon into my adventure. Besides, I hadn't been here very long. Two months. Long enough for Ellie to train me then take off for North Carolina. They hadn't even hired another barista since Ellie left, which left me running the place. When I didn't work, the shop wasn't open.

Their space to cater events booked out every weekend in the summer, and parking lot parties had started to spring up, which required drink and food catering. In a word, things had risen to disaster-level this summer. The forest wasn't the only thing on fire.

Lizbeth tapped her fingers on the side of her frappuccino, gaze narrowed. A thoughtful expression filled her freckled face.

"Leslie would be perfect for the job. She managed a house with four boys, a husband that didn't believe in romance, and now a divorce."

The phrase *a husband that didn't believe in romance* rang in my head. "What does romance have to do with their divorce?"

"10%, I'd say."

"What?"

"Leslie and her ex-husband's lack of romance contributed about 10% to their divorce, if we divvy out the causes."

"That's ridiculous."

"But true." She shrugged. "Romance may not be everything to a relationship, but it is something. They had a deeper lack of connection, but the lack of romance certainly didn't help."

A little too much defensiveness stained my tone when I said, "Romance isn't the only indicator of a relationship."

She popped out of her chair with surprising agility for someone that pregnant. With her drink in hand, she grinned.

"I know. But it's an indicator of the good ones. I'm going to see Leslie and feel out if she needs a job or not. Thanks for the frap! Tell Bethany, if she even shows up, which I doubt, that I'll stop by with dinner tonight. JJ made homemade croutons and salad dressing, and I am *here* for it."

My brain dulled as I watched her head toward the door, her words still whipping through my mind. *It's an indicator of the good ones.* Maybe she wasn't wrong. Why else did I love Rodrigo and Rashaad so much? Still, it made my chest heavy. Sad, a little. If there was one thing that Jakob and I didn't have when we parted, it was romance.

There was some at the beginning, Inner Me said a bit whimsically.

"But not much," I murmured.

Lizbeth paused halfway out the door, the bell on the handle jingling as she stood there. "You believe in romance, right?" she asked.

"Sure," I said.

Because what else was I going to say?

That you desperately miss it, said my inner voice in a sound like a sigh. *That you thought you had it once, but now you see it wasn't really there. That it makes you unaccountably sad. That you invested years in something that, in the end, may not have been that great.*

Yeah, I thought sadly. *That.*

Lizbeth tilted her head to the side. "Have you been in a relationship before?"

"Just got out of one a few months ago."

Her expression softened. "I'm sorry."

"Me too."

She gave a little smile, a wave, and wafted out the door. I watched her go, heart slamming against my chest. Dark emotions aside, it felt like a win. Saying *a few months ago* was the first acknowledgment of Jakob and the demise of our relationship since I arrived. Words made it real. Words out loud made it irrefutable.

It's in the past, Inner Me said. *Where it belongs. Time to turn forward again.*

"Right," I muttered. "It happened. It was real."

Now it's time.

With a long breath out, I returned behind the counter and grabbed *Love is a Terrible Nightmare.* If nothing else was going to present itself for a drink, might as well dive back into Amy Grace and Rashaad.

* * *

The big lug of a wildland firefighter showed up later that day, computer under his arm like a hidden wing.

Such a small computer, against such a wide set of shoulders, created an odd juxtaposition. He stood at the counter with a frown that I had the feeling he didn't know was there.

This time, he didn't smell like smoke. More like soap. Man soap. The kind that smelled like good deodorant too, and made me want to walk closer to anyone with it. The kind that I'd sniff when I walked through the soap aisle, before I reminded my heart that it was still healing.

Which happened just yesterday.

"Is it okay if I stay for a while?" he asked. His voice had a raspy quality to it, and depth in the words. Seeing him sent a thrill through me, because all I could think about was powerful Rashaad.

"Definitely not," I quipped.

He blinked.

I fought back a smile. This guy had *no* idea how to have a good time. "Just kidding." I held out a hand. "Of course it's okay. Do you want something to drink?"

His shoulders relaxed a little. "Same as yesterday." He turned on his heel, but stopped to add over his shoulder. "Thanks."

I took *same as yesterday* to mean straight black coffee and a sandwich, so I set to work. My gaze wandered to where he sat. He glared at his computer screen with a furrowed brow again. Did he think it would open up and eat him? The intensity of his expression made me wonder.

I grabbed a mug that said, *I'll smack the grump off your face*, and took it over steaming hot. He glanced up, saw me there, and kept my gaze.

"Thanks."

"Sure."

Once I set it down, I paused. *Gonna grab my arm again, big guy?* Inner Me taunted. Because I definitely-kinda-sorta wanted him too. His eyes arrested those thoughts. Ocean blue. The sort of color that didn't mess around. Nothing robin's-egg about this shade of sapphire. No, this guy was oceanic. I sensed an old soul in those eyes.

"What's your name?" I asked.

"Bastian."

"Good to meet you. I'm Dahlia."

I held out a hand. He paused for a moment to regard it—apparently, a barista had never introduced herself to him before—and eventually accepted. The warmth of his long fingers against mine felt like sliding on a hot-from-the-dryer-on-a-cold-day glove.

"Same."

"The fire?" I nodded outside. "I'm assuming you and all those guys in the parking lot yesterday know something about it."

"Not much."

"Are you going to go fight it?"

"Maybe."

"Well, you're a barrel of helpful words." The comment from Inner Me escaped before I could stop it. My eyes widened and I sealed my lips together in a thin line. The corner of his mouth twitched, which I took as either amusement or forgiveness. I flicked my fingers in a beckoning motion. "Give me something, brother. I don't like fire. Imma water girl."

He leaned back a little. A sliver of amusement appeared in his eyes. "The fire is north and winds are west."

"Which means . . .?"

"Pineville is fine. For now," he tacked on.

"That's good news!" I cried. "Isn't Adventura summer camp east of the fire?"

"Yes."

"So does a west wind mean it's blowing to the west, or to the east?"

"East. West to east."

I frowned. Was Sione safe? "That's not good news."

He shook his head. I waited, but he didn't say anything

else. His voice appealed to me though, so I'd have to keep the conversation going myself. No problem. I'd tackled more difficult challenges before, like live karaoke and Pele singing just after me. I propped my hands on my hips.

"So are you going to fight it?"

He shrugged. "Maybe."

"Do you have the day off today?"

"Yeah."

He stared at me, as if mentally preparing for the next question. I bit back an aggravated sigh and said, "Good talk," before I spun around to leave.

I secretly hoped he'd call me back or grab my wrist again, but no such touch or call came. Egads, this man wouldn't know how to converse if I provided a flow chart. For the next twenty minutes, I tried not to think about the intensity of his expression or the simple, one-word answers that left me still wanting more.

Duuumb.

When he appeared at the counter, money in hand, I tried not to jump out of surprise. His computer remained on the table, along with an open backpack that appeared bulky, as if it had several books inside.

"What's up?" I asked.

He slid a twenty across the counter, then his cup. "Another coffee, please. Keep the change."

"Sure."

We remained quiet, and I kept my eyes oriented on the task at hand. Meanwhile, I could feel his gaze studying me. I had the absurd thought that, if this were a movie, he would burst into rapturous song. Birds would twitter overhead. The sky would change to a sunset, and glitter would spontaneously combust out of everywhere at once.

Instead, that weighty study remained behind.

"Here you go."

I slid the coffee back across the counter, suppressing the urge to do it bartender-style the way Hernandez liked. He ignored the drink while I dumped the leftover change in the tip jar. The charged air forced me to look up, even though my entire body wanted to flit away and pretend like I didn't notice his attention.

His gaze had narrowed. "Do you like people?" he asked.

"Yes, for the most part. In manageable doses."

His brow grew heavy over his eyes. He pulled his bottom lip through his teeth. His gaze had dropped to something just beyond me as he moved into deeper thought, and I couldn't help but wonder what gave him such a deep expression.

Yesterday, he'd looked terrified. Today, there was a hint of panic in the way his arms remained tense at his side. His finger tapped the top of the coffee mug. Try as he might, that gentle panic hadn't once relaxed.

What did he have going on?

"Do you get stage fright?" he asked.

I scoffed, which turned into an inelegant snort, then cleared my throat. "Ah, no. Not at all."

An unintelligible, deep rumble came from his throat. Was that supposed to be a response?

"Why do you ask?" I asked in a failed attempt at nonchalance. There wasn't enough time in the day for games like this.

Instead of answering, he asked, "Do you like romance books?"

My hands twitched, ready to grab *Love is a Terrible Nightmare* and fling it under the counter. Too late. He'd already seen the bright, turquoise cover.

"No," I drawled, then scoffed. "C'mon. Romance books?"

"Liar."

He said it softly, but without judgment. If anything, I detected amusement in his eyes, somewhere beneath the layers of stress and concentration.

"Fine." I sighed. "I've read exactly 1.85 romance novels and I've been absolutely obsessed with them so far. In general? No."

"Same."

"You've read 1.85 romance novels?"

This time, he almost smiled. "No, but in general I don't like them."

His quick agreement startled me, but I kept going because my name must be cleared. I hooked a thumb toward the book.

"But this author is . . . really good. Like *really* good. Lizbeth sort of cornered me into reading her and . . . look, I'm not a romance junkie, all right? I deal with reality. I just . . . Rodrigo is an idiot and it took him too long to come around! Rashaad is at least more self aware but so stubborn." I held up a hand. "Please, don't get me started on Rashaad because there are not enough hours in the day."

He held up both hands, palms in the air.

"No judgment. Just wondered."

Too late, I realized I'd escalated faster than I needed to. A tell, for sure. Why it mattered what this guy thought, I had no idea. My shoulders relaxed back. The general tension in the air faded.

"Right. Sorry. Why are you asking?"

He tapped his teeth together and studied me, as if attempting to decide whether I would be worthy of a great secret. For half a breath, I thought I'd be found wanting. He'd spin on his heels, march back to the table, then disappear out of my life. And while I wasn't honest about myself with everything, I at least knew that I didn't want him to leave.

Not yet.

There was something to be said for looking at someone who was easy on the eyes, but that wasn't the reason I wanted him to stay. Plenty of attractive people came and went and I never remembered them. But they never had the same mixture of terror and hope as this guy. I had to know his demons.

The words he said next caught me by surprise.

"I need help."

I blinked.

Wait, Inner Me me said. *What?*

"Help?"

He nodded with a bleak sigh. A balloon had deflated inside him, and everything that once held him up had disappeared. The one phrase that would remove my reservations about Mr. No Words was the quietly uttered *I need help.*

I swallowed, trapped now.

"Help with what?"

"Something that I think you'd be perfect for, if you like people, money, and can work independently."

Color me intrigued. Not only had he just given me a sentence with more than ten words, but his mention of *work independently* clued me right in.

"What is it?"

Those sapphire eyes turned downright wary. He stepped back and motioned to the table with a nod.

"It will take a while to explain. Have a seat. I'll buy you a drink."

Chapter Four

BASTIAN

As far as first dates went, this wasn't my least smooth.

Definitely my weirdest.

If you could even call this a date, that is. Dahlia sat across from me with her right shoulder back, her head tilted to the side. The wary purse of her lips made her look like a diva about to pounce, her cheeks tense in warning. What made a girl her age—probably twenty-eight, just a few years younger than me—have that expression?

My plan whirled through my head, but all the meticulous details and pieces fell into a mental heap. For several moments, I could only stare until I managed to wrench three words free.

"I write books."

Dahlia's eyebrows rose, but she didn't comment on the awkward start.

"Books?"

"Books."

"Okaaaay," she drawled. "You need help with that?"

I ignored her question—it would be answered in a moment—and stayed on the track that my train of thought barreled down.

"I'm also a wildland firefighter." A hand rose to gesture vaguely to the plume of smoke that had ebbed in the morning, but would grow as the afternoon progressed. "In a day or two, I will most likely be assigned to work that fire with my crew. We get forty-eight hours off after every two week assignment. That's why I came back, but I'll need to leave again soon."

Her mouth opened, but closed. She gestured for me to continue. This is where things got rocky and would likely go downhill fast.

My mind wandered back to the way she'd blushed and attempted to justify reading a romance novel. Her expression had been open and bright, but now it looked straight suspicious. I tried to explain, but words failed me. Never mind that I could knock out a 10,000 word sprint in two hours when I needed to, but I couldn't find two words to put together now.

Dahlia took pity on me. "What does writing books have to do with you being a firefighter on an assignment?" she asked.

Her arms folded across her chest, reminding me of a wary cat. Bristled and ready to strike, but not yet threatened.

Back away, common sense stated. *This is doomed to fail.*

My hastily-scrambled-together plan never had much chance of success, but it gave me a slim margin of hope. I'd lived on thinner chances before. My throat bobbed as I swallowed, my mouth so dry I could have spit cotton.

"I'm a very popular author and I have a book launch coming up in a little over a week. When it launches, I'll be on a fire and out of reach. I need to be present—or at least appear to be—for the reader's sake. There's already been some complaints that I'm not visible enough."

The edge of her brow lowered. Maybe she understood that whatever came next wouldn't be normal. I plowed on. No way out but through.

"My agent says that we're on track to break records for launch numbers and sales, which is . . . whatever. Great. Don't really care about that as much as I do the income that comes from it. I'm glad for the success, but it's brought a lot of work with it. Emails, social media posts, interview requests, that kind of thing." I rushed to add. "I don't do the interviews, but maybe . . . maybe someone should."

She grazed right over my last, tentatively-stated line to ask, "Do you write thrillers?"

My stomach clenched. Here is where the downslope began.

"Ah, no."

"Murder mysteries?"

"Nope."

Her nose wrinkled. "Don't tell me you write fantasy."

"None of that."

The skin around the edge of her eyes crinkled in confusion. "Then what do you write and what does it have to do with me?"

My body tightened as I braced myself for the judgment. The shock. The disbelief. The inevitable disappointment or exclamation of *are you weird or something? Why would a guy write romance?*

Because I'm damn good at it, I always wanted to say. I never had to, because I'd never had this conversation before. Only Priyanka knew.

"Ah . . ." I cleared my throat again. I really needed to stop doing that when I was nervous. "Romance."

Her brows shot up. A grin spread across her face, and then she giggled. Her girlish delight lit her face up like a chandelier, all sparkling facets, movement, and light. She appeared to be a totally different person.

Captivating.

I had to suppress the urge to reach over and touch her cheek. Could that sort of brightness be shared? Could she illuminate the dark places in me? I folded my fingers into my palm and tried to ignore the perfect teeth in that brilliant smile.

"Romance?" Her laugh grew as she tilted her head back and laughed. "You're kidding! That's a pretty good one."

I dropped my gaze from the attractive column of her throat. Several long moments passed in silence before her hilarity calmed. Her lips dropped. My teeth worried my bottom lip so hard I thought I'd break skin.

What to say now?

"No?" she whispered. "You . . . you write romance novels?"

"No, I'm not kidding. I write romance novels."

"The sexy kind?"

"There is sex in it, yes." I shrugged. "But it's not erotica."

She blinked. Astonishment filled her gaze in a slow, easy wash. "You're serious about all of this?"

Fantastic, I thought with growing despair. She didn't even know the half of it yet, and already I'd floored her. Before I could answer, she shook her head.

"No, of course you're serious. You don't seem like the kind of guy that uses one more word than he'd have to."

Oddly spot on.

Her gaze tapered. "You're a guy. Writing romance. That's . . ."

"That's what?" I asked.

Her teeth clacked together as she fell deeper in thought, then gestured to me with a sweep of one hand, clearly dismissing that topic.

"Never mind. Let's just . . . I . . . back to the main point. What does writing romance and launching a new book while you're on a fire assignment have to do with me?"

I straightened.

"Let's not ignore anything because this *is* the main point. I don't want to continue if my being a male author in the romance genre is a problem for you."

Her eyes widened, and I realized a defensive edge had come to my tone. My chest expanded in a deep breath. I let it back out.

"Sorry."

"Don't apologize." She held out a hand. "I should be the one apologizing. As far as responses go, that wasn't my best. It was . . . presumptive and wrong. I'm sorry. I'm more curious than anything and I'm sorry if I came across as sexist. Please." She nodded. "I'd love to hear more."

The sincerity in her tone spoke to me. If nothing else, she clearly had a professional side, which only raised more questions about her. I sent the questions away.

"The novels I write are under a female pen name. I've never used an image, a detail, or anything in my pen name that would lead back to me in real life. No one knows the truth except my agent, which makes it easier to maintain my privacy. Before this year, it wasn't a big deal. Recently, my popularity has grown. The launch of my latest novel could explode that even further. But . . . I need to be available to respond to emails, social media questions, and interviews. That sort of thing. If I go radio silent during this launch, it will stir up more questions. It will stunt the launch."

She blinked.

"Oh."

"I need someone to become me. I mean . . . my author pen name."

Her brow furrowed into grooves. "What does that mean?"

"I want someone to be her. To show up for interviews and act like they're the ones writing these books."

Her lips turned down. "You want me to pretend to be a female author? Like at interviews and stuff?"

I hesitated. Priyanka had warned me that this was a bad

idea over email, but I hadn't listened. Dahlia's open air had suddenly shunted to something far more suspicious.

"Well, maybe. Maybe not." I ran a hand through my hair. "I just . . . this career can't die yet. I need to give more to it, but I can't. I don't want to sacrifice my privacy and reveal who I am, but I also need the income that such a big launch would bring in. My publisher takes a cut and so does my agent, which means the royalties don't go quite as far. I have very strong reasons to make as much money as I can."

"You need money, okay. But . . . you want me to *be* you? That's a lie. I'm no actress. I can't just . . . what if my family saw? What if Jak—"

She leaned back, pushing away from the table. Panic coursed through me, but I kept myself from reaching for her.

"Then not that," I said quickly. "If you didn't want to act like her, then you could run my behind-the-scenes PR, basically. It's all online, all text. Answer emails, watch social media, that kind of thing. No personal appearances anywhere."

Her body relaxed back against the seat. I drew in a deep breath. She hadn't bolted. That meant something.

"You want me to help you respond to emails and social media?"

"Yes. Even that would be so much better. Right now it's all just a building disaster. I've been ignoring it for too long."

She waved a hand in front of her.

"Why me?"

"Because you're bright and bubbly and funny and *here.*"

"We said maybe fifty words to each other before you proposed this. Clearly, you thought this out last night after meeting me for the first time. How could you even know who or what I am?"

"I stand by what I said."

It wasn't an answer to her question. At least, not really.

But it was all I had right now. Her nose wrinkled in an expression I couldn't hope to read.

Nor could I stand the silence.

"And," I continued, "you read romance novels. If you can open a web browser and type on a keyboard, you could figure the rest out."

I set that comment down as a test. She hadn't been very excited about me knowing her love for Jess's books yesterday. How would she react when I *really* broke the news? If she'd giggled at me being a romance author, she might faint when she found out that I was Jess.

"Doesn't mean I'd be good at what you need," she said.

"Would you?"

She bobbled with a response before letting out a soft raspberry. "Yes," she replied, with just a touch of arrogance. "I'd kill at it. Could I do it on my own hours?"

"Of course."

"You would trust me to do it while you're on a fire and probably out of reach?"

"Yes."

She eyed me. "What do you pay?"

"$30 an hour."

Her eyes widened for half a moment, then returned. "Acceptable," she said, slightly strangled.

What did she make at the coffee shop? I'd probably shot too high, but I'd be paying her for more than just social media responses and email coordination. This woman held my privacy in her hands.

"Being an author isn't an endgame for me. It's the means to an end," I said, feeling shaky. "I need this to work. Honestly, if no one ever knew that I was Jess, then I'd die a happy man. She's going to stop writing books at the end of this thirty-book series anyway, if all goes according to plan. And if things work the way I want, this launch is what will make my outside goals happen. Then I won't be a slave to my computer for the rest of my life."

As I spoke the words, I felt the cowardice in them all the way to my bones. They weren't true. Maybe parts of them *were* true, but put together like that? Not at all true.

Writing was one of the only things I'd ever been fully honest with myself about. I loved it. It thrilled me. The quiet of a room and the clack of keys made everything fit.

Dahlia had gone oddly pale. Too late, I'd realized my slip.

"Did you say Jess?" she whispered.

Hesitantly, I nodded. "Yes. My pen name is Jess."

"One name, Jess?"

"Yes."

Her voice lowered to a whisper. "The *Jess* of the book I was reading when you came in last night?"

I sucked in a sharp breath.

"Yes."

"And this morning?"

Several moments of shocked silence passed. Clearly, the reality of what I'd just said began to click in her mind. By the time her brain caught up, she glowered. Why it was so much worse knowing my pen name, I had no idea.

"You're not joking?"

"Do I seem like the type to kid around?" I asked calmly.

"No, not at all. You are Jess? Jess . . ." She trailed away, voice faint. "The originator of Rodrigo and Rashaad and . . ."

Hearing their names on her lips sent a weird feeling through me, like a shot of lightning. Did she like that? Did I care if she liked them?

I did.

My pride certainly gained some power from her adoration of Jess when I strolled in. Now, it worked against me. Dahlia shot to her feet. Her fingers trembled as she shoved hair back behind her ear, then swallowed hard. Her throat bobbed.

Why so nervous?

So . . . panicked?

"Listen," she said, "you've created a super tough situation for yourself and I get that you need help. But this is . . . I can't do this."

"Oh."

"You've got the wrong girl." She stepped back. "Lizbeth Bailey is down the canyon. She's already read all your books and if you want someone to step into the shoes of a romance author and live it to the fullest, that's your girl. Not me. I don't even . . . it's not . . ."

With that, she turned and strode out of sight.

Chapter Five

DAHLIA

Sometime in between me running away from Bastian and ten minutes later, he'd quietly departed.

My retreat to the bathroom to slap cold water on my face and pretend our exchange hadn't happened didn't restore any courage.

My thoughts grew at an alarming rate, nearly tripping over each other as I returned behind the counter. Central to the theme was one main point: Bastian had to be insane. At least partially.

Why were all the cute ones unbalanced?

I shook my head to clear my thoughts, but they held on with tenacious regard. No matter what part of the shop I cleaned or paced or reorganized, the only thing that filled my head was the panic in Bastian's gaze.

I need this to work.

He'd avoided saying why such a need was so important to him. Obviously, it had roots in money. He'd mentioned as much, anyway, but not what he'd spend it on. He didn't strike me as the buried-in-debt kind of guy, nor a big spender. No ring on his finger, so it wasn't a wife and kids, I'd wager. He might be dating someone. He could be gay.

A thousand scenarios streamed through my mind. I pushed a pot of coffee onto the warmer and prayed for someone to order something and save me from myself.

Besides, who made a request like *can you pretend to be my pen name* anyway?

I leaned back against the counter, tilted my head back, and closed my eyes. Deep in my gut, I could already feel it. The regret. The curiosity. Beneath the roiling emotions, my inner voice quietly said, *you've felt that way before too.*

The constricting panic born of having nowhere to go. Hemmed in by decisions that went awry, even when they weren't supposed to. I'd responded to his sincere plea for help out of fear.

Fear of *him*, for heaven's sake.

What are you afraid of? Inner Me asked.

"You know what," I growled.

You're afraid that you'll fall for him. Hard. Because you already are crushing on him and you think that relationships can't be trusted. You think you're not ready.

"I know it, don't I?" I muttered. "I totally botched my own life with Jakob. I invested too much in another person because it felt so good at the beginning. Then I fought to get that back for too long."

No. That's not what you were supposed to learn from Jakob. That's not what's real. It's what you're telling yourself. There were other problems with Jakob. A total lack of connecting ground, for one. The only thing you had in common was a shared love for raisin cookies.

My inner dialogue only made my quagmire worse, so I shut it off. Regret for turning Bastian away swooped in on swift wings. Why should I regret saying a very normal *no, thanks* to such a crazy offer?

Because . . . because.

My life and circumstances had been crazy once too, and others had stepped in when I needed them. Maybe I hadn't asked them to pretend to be a romance author . . . but even that didn't seem so bad now that his blue eyes weren't staring at me.

"Dagnabbit," I muttered.

Customers had mentioned Bastian's name before. Hernandez, I thought, mentioned his best friend, the hotshot. Something vague about a father and sister lingered in the background of my thoughts, but disappeared before I could recall anything solid. My next thought came with unfortunate clarity.

How do I find him?

That moment, I knew I wanted to say yes. The ridiculous hourly payment would be nice, not to mention seeing more of Bastian. It would provide an alternate career route I'd never thought of before, and help me not feel a sense of wallowing in my current position. Inevitably, we'd have to speak again and I liked that thought.

Too much.

So much that I couldn't turn away an opportunity to help him, even if relationships were scary. Nothing *had* to happen between us, and likely nothing would. Not with the way Jakob still thrived in my head. This would be a baby step in the right direction. The direction away from Jakob and into my new, uncertain future.

If Bastian strolled through that door right now, I'd take the job and slice the panic right out of his life. My gaze zoomed outside where the mountains cut a sharp slope up. The smoke pillar had thickened today, but not drastically. It only made me think of him more. I chewed on my bottom lip, lost in thought. No, I wouldn't wait.

I had to go after him.

He couldn't be that far away. The man apparently walked everywhere because I had yet to see a vehicle. With a growl, I flipped the closed sign on the shop, turned the lock, and rushed outside.

Time to say goodbye to Jakob's lingering influence.

Chapter Six

BASTIAN

Stupid. Stupid. Stupid.

The words battered my brain with every step down the street. What had I been thinking?

I didn't know Dahlia beyond the curious looks she leveled my way the less than thirty minutes we'd been in the same room together. Of all the people to approach with such a wild request, I'd given it to the one person who'd say no.

Self sabotage at every level.

Panic made my chest tight as I headed down the street, toward the neighborhood where Hernandez and Dagny lived. Pineville was so small it wouldn't take me long to get there. My bag hit my back as I walked, thoughts in a spiral as I thought about what to do next.

Lizbeth? Would she work for me? Unlikely. I already knew Lizbeth, but not personally. Her obsession with books and the local book club made her a Pineville legend. Besides, she managed a business with her husband.

Didn't she have a baby coming soon?

Dagny . . . no. I wasn't ready for Dagny, and then Hernandez, and then all three of my high school best friends—collectively called the Merry Idiots—to know my secret. Dagny was busy with the construction company that just hired her on after she graduated college last year anyway. Not a good fit.

My steps to Hernandez's place slowed. I still needed to go to the store, stock up on blister stuff for my kit, some new laces, and protein bars. So many protein bars. But not yet. Now I needed to call someone that I'd been avoiding for too long.

With a sigh, I headed back toward Dad's house. If I didn't call Pri now, she'd strangle me later.

* * *

After I returned home, Psycho butted her head against my leg while I sat at the table and listened to Pri prattle in the background.

A tingling sensation pervaded my hands as I tried to hold my phone. I put it on speakerphone when my thumb went numb and set it on the table. My muscles and tendons ached as I stretched them out, swollen from all the chainsaw work on our last fire.

"Your anonymity as a person isn't really the problem with Jess, is it?" Pri asked and pulled my attention back to the moment. "I mean, I don't want to circle the wrong tree here."

Despite occasionally grouchy emails, Pri had a gentle nature. Her quiet way of speaking and easy demeanor had first drawn me to her. It bled into her voice now, as if she nudged a box of eggs toward a precipice. Calmly and with painstaking care. Regardless of delivery, however, a precipice was still a precipice.

"It's about the money," I said. "We're both aware that my intentions aren't exactly the purest. This isn't some higher calling. This is how I save my family."

"But you're so good at writing romance, Bastian," she cried. "There's some inner romantic in you that's dying to get out. Why else would you have written a romance book? You could have gone straight to a culturally and historically more masculine-dominated genre, like mystery or thriller."

"Because romance sells. I studied the markets before I wrote the book."

"You saw the book through and you wrote twenty others, so there must be something in you that likes the subject matter."

"I like taking care of my family."

She sighed. A resignation if I'd ever heard one.

"Okay, I give up." I could practically hear her shrug. "Regardless of motive here, you'll still make money after people figure out that you aren't a woman named Jess, which takes us back to the original point. This really *isn't* about a man being Jess because you'd still make money. There's something else that's pushing your career decisions, and I think you should figure it out."

I scowled at the wall. She didn't even know what she meant. How long had she been talking in circles over this? At least ten minutes. How was I supposed to understand her if she didn't fully get it or herself? Or maybe I didn't want to understand.

That made sense.

"Many readers will be loyal to your books no matter your gender," she continued, "now more than ever. Some readers will drop out, but most won't even care. Some might even read more books to make a point. If anything, it'll definitely get you publicity and probably sales. It's certainly one method of getting your back list to sell, I'd wager. Besides, a lot of readers won't ever know about the update . . . unless you make headlines," she added, almost as an afterthought.

That afterthought is what made my teeth grind at night.

"Face it, Pri. Jess turning into a thirty-something-male would make the headlines, and not in a transgender kind of way but in a this-author-lied kind of way. It looks terrible."

"Probably, yes."

"And that is the last thing I want. People will descend on my life and I'd really rather avoid that."

"I know. It would be such a fantastic opportunity to call out some prejudice, though."

Priyanka had an advocate's soul and had long wanted to call out and tackle the hypocrisy that could follow the announcement that a man wrote such gentle romantic novels. Then again, maybe this news wouldn't hit in such a big way. The unknown is what held me back the most.

I'd definitely misrepresented myself when I used a female pen name. Any reader would be right to be upset and have broken trust. I didn't want that either. But some of them could be aggravated enough to find out more about me. To really abuse the revelation to get some sort of revenge.

The paths of how a reader could find out my real identity were slim and few, thankfully. If a reader came to Pineville, caught me writing, and outed me on it, we'd have a problem. Without that very unlikely possibility, there were only two ways anyone could link me to Jess.

1. Pri.

2. The Merry Idiots.

Neither of those gave me true concern.

For all of our differing opinions on whether I should announce or not, Priyanka 100% respected my decision. So far, no one had outed us from her end. One day, there could be an intern that worked her slush pile, or someone in her office that might snoop and then spill, but it hadn't happened yet.

The three other Merry Idiots knew nothing about Jess, as far as I was aware, so they weren't a real concern now. One day, they could figure it out, or I might spill the secret. That day hadn't come, so my identity was locked fairly tight.

I tilted my head back to stare at the ceiling.

"We're back to where we started, Pri. This whole thing is about money and privacy. You know I don't want my life out there."

"Because you're ashamed of writing romance?"

"No."

She waited. *But yes,* I quietly tacked on. I sifted through all the things her statement brought up, but felt only a giant ball of ugly in my chest.

In truth, I didn't know why I wanted to stay so deeply anonymous. Nothing felt safer than privacy. Down the road of *come clean* waited a whole lotta not-privacy. That didn't feel good. In fact, it felt downright terrifying.

Flashes of the Merry Idiots appeared in my mind like fireworks. Jayson, whom we called Hernandez, Grady, and Vikram. The guys figuring out my secret? Big whopping no-way-in-hell.

The thought of their laughter and ribbing after they found out would be unbearable and would follow me for the rest of my life. But I still couldn't credit them with that much power in my life. No, Priyanka was right. Something else lingered below the surface.

Just . . . didn't know what it was.

Technically, I could hide behind the computer for however long I wanted, but it would impact sales eventually. An impact in sales meant a bigger impact on Dad and Inessa. I wasn't about to allow that.

"Let's focus on deeper meanings later." I rubbed the back of my neck with a heavy sigh. A bell announced the dryer was finished. "For now, what do you need from me for the launch of *Wanderlust is a Battle*?"

"What I *need* and what I *want* are two different things, so

I'll stick with what you requested. I need you to keep up on fan mail and not disappear. You don't have to have your voice or your face attached to anything, but a few live messages wouldn't kill you. Neither would an updated post or five on social media saying you're excited about the launch or something. Readers can't rally around an author that doesn't care."

"I care."

"Do you?"

"Yes! I'm just . . . I'm at max capacity right now."

"That's fair. You have a lot going on."

I stood up to pace. My fan mail inbox totalled in the thousands after my summer in the mountains. The email drama was the result of a low-level cliffhanger ending in the last book. This current launch would satisfy the clamor for more. Women all over the world had been messaging about *Wanderlust is a Battle*, and Pri had started to get interest from *Hollywood types,* she called them.

Asking for more visibility really wasn't unwise.

"Okay," I said.

"Can that happen?"

She spoke crisply, and I didn't doubt it was because she already knew the answer. No, I couldn't be present to live message or respond to emails or hashtags. In less than twenty hours, I'd be back on another assignment for two weeks, and the launch was just over a week away. My only option had just backed away like the opportunity burned her.

"Someone can be present," I said firmly. Just who that *someone* would be, I had no idea.

"With pictures?" she asked.

"How can we post pictures without outing me?"

"What if it was just pictures of the book and a coffee mug, or a bit of hair, or something?"

"That will only grow the interest behind who Jess really is. It's like teasing the readers. That doesn't seem very fair."

She scoffed. "You are twenty-one chart-topping novels into this mess, Bastian. You are beyond teasing the readers. Give them *something*. Yes, there's intrigue and mystery behind these vague pictures. Yes, that may only grow interest. Interest is a good thing. You're just about to launch a #1 bestselling novel with preorders alone. That's incredible. Let's see it happen."

Turmoil responded, but I thought of my latest paycheck. My publisher paid every three months, and I'd got a whopping $78,457. Enough to set aside a disconcerting amount for taxes, pay off a few monthly bills, another chunk of Dad's mortgage, and tackle the savings account I'd set up for Inessa and her bills. It had been my biggest payout yet, but I'd need several more of those to keep my family in the clear.

Not to mention, at some point, live my own life.

"I'll figure it out."

"Okay," she drawled. "I choose to trust you and the person that you hire. Best of luck, Bastian."

"Anything else?"

"Stay safe, please?" A note of pleading entered her tone. I softened beneath it.

"Always."

The phone cut off, going to a dark screen. I stared at it with a welling feeling of despair. How on earth would I make this happen?

The numbers stacked in my mind, but I shoved them back. No, this would be fine. If I kept churning out books and the novels topped the charts, then I'd have a great head start on unknown financial situations.

Given time, there would be enough money in both savings accounts that I wouldn't have to worry for at least a few years. Wildland firefighters made $15 an hour, and only had work for a few months. Given the amount of overtime we worked, I could store away the extra like a squirrel and live happily through the winter by myself. With Inessa and my father on the line?

Not happening.

I stood, stretching my fingertips and forearms as I headed into the back for laundry, round six. A few more and the clothes would be washed and ready to go. No amount of soap removed the grime or the scent of smoke, but at least I wouldn't be oily and stinky.

Unbidden, my thoughts drifted to Dahlia. Right now, I could go for a coffee, mixed with the scent of caramel and the hiss of a machine. Coffee shops were soothing. They were a reminder of life and noise and people, but without required interaction. Being around falling, burning trees, quiet forest, and filthy hotshots had a way of creating a bubble.

In that, Priyanka was correct: I definitely hid from something out there.

Also here.

Just what it was, I hadn't yet figured out.

My mind skipped around, probably because I didn't want to focus on this new problem. The day after tomorrow, I had to assemble with the hotshot team in the morning at 0500. We went back on active status and would no doubt get the fire assignment that loomed right in front of me. Not only was this fire in our region, it was in our town.

I glanced at my watch.

Which meant I had one day to figure out who would keep my career and my family from spiraling into a fiery crash.

* * *

"B-b-bastian!"

A pair of warm arms looped around my waist as Dagny walked straight into me. She didn't even welcome me off the porch, just stepped into my space. With Dagny, I didn't mind, but few people held the honor.

Hernandez materialized behind her with a broad smile and shiny, still-wet hair. Just finished a shift and a shower, no doubt. He clapped my shoulder when Dagny finally extricated herself.

"Good to see you safe, my brother."

We slammed chests and pounded each other on the back. Hernandez motioned me further into his house with a tilt of his head. He left the front door open for a cool breeze through the screen.

"C'mon. Dagny just finished dinner, and it's going to blow your mind."

The air lay thick with the scent of roast beef. The thought of mealy potatoes, hot and cracking open with the touch of a fork, made my mouth water. My body craved protein and carbs. On my two days off, I could rarely eat enough to satisfy the deficit created by weeks of whacking my way through mountains on a fire line, or hitting my way through project work in the national forest.

"S-s-simple stuff," Dagny said with a wink, "always t-t-tastes the best."

She shut the door as Hernandez led us toward the kitchen. Hernandez had a small house, but Dagny had taken it from militaristic-male-deputy life to a homey place after they married in the spring.

"Smells wonderful," I said.

Without looking like a creep, I attempted to study the way they finished assembling dinner and quietly spoke with each other. What words quantified such warm expressions? How did I write the way watching this felt?

Without my computer under my arm, I felt restless. Naked. A bit unnerved, as if I didn't know how to belong without my words. The written ones. Those flowed like water.

Verbal ones were like stuck honey between my tongue and the roof of my mouth on good days.

Plates and a simmering pot roast waited on the table. Dagny had thrown a simple white tablecloth down, folded napkins over utensils, and had soft jazz music playing in the background. The warmth of the kitchen gave me an instant pang of jealousy for Hernandez. Did he return home to this every day?

Lucky dog.

Maybe I didn't want to get married, but a warm greeting at the end of the day would be infinitely better than a cold house and a needy cat.

"Have a s-s-seat." Dagny nudged me toward the far chair. "It's all ready to g-go. Just b-barely tabled it."

Hernandez pressed a hand to her back as he slipped behind her, then pulled her chair out. She shot him a smile full of adoration that I tried not to study too obviously. When thoughts of Dahlia interposed over Dagny, I shut them down completely. We settled into steaming pot roast that fell apart at the touch, and potatoes that steamed when I cut them open with the edge of my fork.

My ravenous stomach nearly doubled over in anticipation.

"How are things here?" I asked.

Hernandez shrugged. "Not bad. Pineville is the same." His gaze darted to me. "Except for, you know, a raging forest fire. What's up with that, amigo?"

"Not sure yet," I said.

Hernandez raised an eyebrow. "You going on it next?"

"Probably. Just depends on what assets have already been assigned. I'll spend the day with Inessa in Jackson City tomorrow, then go to active status with the crew the next morning. We'll find out then."

Hernandez whistled low. "Short break, my friend." He sliced into a carrot that fell apart on the plate. "Hope you're close, but I don't want you in any danger. We're tracking things just in case evacuation status comes, but they're already anticipating a pre-evacuation going live."

I nodded. Sounded about right.

Dagny studied me as she grabbed a salt shaker. "How ab-b-bout you, B-bash?"

"What about me?"

"You d-doing okay?"

"Yep."

She eyed me with a gleam that meant she noticed something. Did she see my cagey energy? Could she tell that the weight of the world pressed on me?

"You still keep track of the Frolicking Moose?" I asked. Her inquisitive expression altered a little. She nodded. I leaned back. "The new girl. Dahlia. What's your take?"

She blinked. "Oh. W-well. She's really n-n-nice. Quick on her feet, learns fast, d-d-does things correctly. From what I understand, she's been eager to t-take work, so that helped B-b-bethany and M-maverick transition out of Ellie leaving. Sh-she's the only one th-there."

Lifelong stutter aside, Dagny had graduated with a degree in construction management at the beginning of the year and taken on work at a local construction company. In the middle of all that, she'd married one of my best friends and made him the happiest deputy on the planet. All that change pushed her out of working at the coffee shop, but in such a small town, no one could entirely disappear.

"Her c-c-cousin is Sione," Dagny continued, "the guy r-running Adventura Summer C-camp now. They're p-p-pretty close."

I nodded. Sione I didn't know, but I'd heard rumors that Mark Bailey had turned over the operation of his summer camp to one of his trusted counselors. He worked on business from his cabin, with his wife, Stella. Mark and I knew each other out of sheer reputation. He and JJ had paved the path for the wild antics of the Merry Idiots. We'd looked up to him and his twin, JJ, in the weirdest ways possible.

Dagny tilted her head to the side.

"You know her?" she asked.

"Ran into her yesterday."

And today, I mentally added, *when I botched absolutely everything.*

"Everything okay, B-bastian?" she asked again, and broke apart my thoughts. I shook my head to clear my head.

"Yeah. Fine."

A dubious expression followed.

"Lizbeth Bailey," I said next, unsuccessfully keeping the desperation from my tone. I shoved some translucent onions onto a triangle of potato. "What's she up to these days?"

"New baby in a few months," Hernandez said. He leaned back in his chair, the tips of his fingers toying with a sweating cup of milk. "Staying in a place in Jackson City. The bakery she started with her husband has been doing well."

I swallowed hard.

Damn.

Confirmed details were hard. Everyone had a life. Inessa would soak up my day tomorrow, so there wouldn't be time to search then either.

Were there online job postings I could search? Could I trust someone with my secret that I didn't at least have eyes on? I knew Dahlia as much as any stranger on the internet, but at least we shared a common town. That built a little trust and safety.

The emails from Pri stacked in my mind, and the tightness in my chest started to return. Upcoming end-of-the-month bills. Dad's update. Messages from the doctors that I'd been slowly listening to on my voicemail. News from Inessa's nurse. I missed my family.

"How's Vik?" I asked in a last-ditch attempt to distract myself.

The question came out a bit garbled. I cleared my throat and reached for my milk. Panic over my writing career gave way to utter terror. Would I have to out myself right now? What would Hernandez say? Did Inessa miss me?

The lack of control boiled.

Hernandez studied me. "Vik is fine. He talks about going to South America again soon, but he's too much of a disaster to travel anywhere. You're in charge of the retreat this year. Any great plans?"

"Not yet." I swiped my lips with a napkin and avoided his gaze. I'd completely forgotten about the yearly Merry Idiot retreat. "Just getting through fire season, then I'll tackle it."

He nodded, as if to silently say, *fair enough.*

Words revolved around my head like whirling fire sirens. *Priyanka. Book launch. PR. Readers. Must decide.* I'd dug myself into a deeper and deeper hole. Before I left on the next assignment, I'd have to tell Pri that I couldn't find help. Emails would build through the launch and readers might think I abandoned them. My next manuscript was underserved—I hadn't even started because the words felt like glue on my fingers. I needed to get it rolling soon.

The obligations stacked higher and higher and higher.

"Hey, man." Hernandez's voice cut through the swirling cloud of anxiety. My head lifted to look at him. Concern filled both their expressions. Dagny had set down her fork and regarded me with eyes full of love and worry. Hernandez leaned forward, brow furrowed.

"You good?"

Too late, I realized my hands clutched the cloth napkin so tight that my knuckles were white. My throat felt thick, my head boozy.

No, I'm not okay. I can't take the weight. I can't take the pressure. It's all going to fall down.

A moment before I could reply, a knock came on the screen door. Through it floated a lyrical voice that set a spasm of shock all the way through my body.

"Dagny, it's Dahlia. Is Bastian here?"

Chapter Seven

DAHLIA

A face full of wary uncertainty met me at the door.

Bastian peered through a lowered brow, as if he didn't know what to make of my arrival. I didn't either.

Behind Bastian, Dagny wore a perplexed expression. Out of sheer nerves, I'd refused her offer to join them at dinner and fidgeted with the edge of my shirt on the porch while Bastian walked to the door. A lovely, late-summer day unfurled at my back, interrupted only by the growing smudge of smoke out on the horizon.

"I'll take this," Bastian said to Dagny. "Thanks."

Dagny filtered back into the house, unspoken questions in her eyes. Hernandez hung back, but gave me a head nod. I returned it with a smile. Bastian shut the door behind him and tucked his hands into his pockets.

"Hey." I cleared my throat. "Sorry. This is . . . sort of stalker-ish."

A shadow passed over his expression, then disappeared. He opened his mouth, then closed it again. A shrug came next, and I figured it's as good as I could expect. All words fled my brain. Like stepping onto a stage and forgetting the lyrics.

"Look, I just . . . I felt like I made the wrong move back there. You really seemed . . . panicked, like you need help. And I felt bad for freaking out on you a bit. In full honesty, I just got out of a tough relationship six months ago and I'm still recovering."

One of his eyebrows twitched. He studied me with unusual intensity. His weight shifted.

"Does my job offer somehow remind you of the guy?"

"No."

He blinked, clearly perplexed. Heat flared in my cheeks. How could I explain that I didn't want to be this near him because I was on track to a massive, walloping crush my heart wasn't ready for?

It is so ready for him, Inner Me whispered.

"I want to help," I said to him, just to shut her up. "Can I take it back?"

A long silence lay between us.

"I really like your books," I finally admitted. My gaze lifted to peer at him through my eyelashes. "Too much, maybe. I don't want to like them, but I do. That's what took me by surprise. To be Jess . . . I just . . . I can barely reconcile these books with being you. It just seems so far-fetched. And yet . . . why would you make this up?"

My tone sounded far too much like I still had to convince myself. He leaned back against the house, all casual ease despite a burning hope in his voice.

"If you could help me manage the launch of this book, that would be . . ." He let out a long breath. "Very appreciated. You don't have to become Jess. Even answering emails would be helpful."

"Can I answer them as your assistant?"

"Of course."

I opened my mouth to reply, but stopped. I hadn't

expected a quick capitulation. He clearly wanted me to help him.

"Okay," I whispered. "I'm happy to help."

"Why?"

Somehow, I knew what the question encompassed. Why would I help a total stranger? A huge name in the publishing world that terrified me to even think of knowing in person? My general lack of knowing him? My uneasiness around the topic of relationships in general?

All of them could be answered with one single reply: I had a gut feeling about this guy, haunted terror and all.

"Because I'm here in Pineville to try to find myself after said relationship crashed and burned earlier this year," I said. "And this seems like an unexpected path worthy of exploring."

His shoulders deflated like a balloon.

"I'll take it. Give me half an hour to finish up here and I'll meet you back at the coffee shop to show you what to do."

* * *

Not a single person showed up to buy coffee and distract me from what I had just done. The void of something to do left me to fidget behind the counter with nothing but my own thoughts to help me pass the time.

Had I just made a huge mistake? No, the mistake wasn't in helping Bastian. The mistake was picking up those blasted romance novels in the first place. If I hadn't read them, I would have happily said *yes* and all this turmoil about Jakob wouldn't have followed. My mind wouldn't have already been thrilled by fantastic love stories in the first place.

Thirty minutes passed in between my acceptance and his appearance, and every minute felt like a lightning storm. Fraught with moments of terror, but more often with a general sense of uneasiness. Thoughts of this going awry plagued me, but I backed myself out of those. I couldn't predict the future, and even if I did, how bad could it be?

Moments before he appeared in the parking lot with that long stride, computer under his arm, I had finally settled my nerves down. This was nothing but assistant-level work, done on a computer, from the privacy of the RV. Not a path I'd ever seen for my life, but it was going to be just fine. Pineville had been an exploration into the new and unknown. So far, it hadn't disappointed me.

"This is okay," I whispered as he stalked toward the shop. My voice turned to a squeak. "This is totally fine."

The bell jangled as he let himself inside. My gaze darted to his second romance novel splayed on the counter. The strange dichotomy of a man like him writing books like *that* struck me. Lovely romance. Not even the hot-and-heavy, although he had moments of that too. His women were imperfectly strong, his men were out-of-the-box but not creepy, and somehow the whole thing felt like walking through a park with Jane Austen. Minus the dresses and societal expectations and overabundance of caution around the opposite gender.

Which I could also use more of, perhaps.

I couldn't blame his uncertainty around revealing himself as Jess, now that I thought about it. What would I have thought if Lizbeth tried to convince me that a wildland firefighter like Bastian had penned Rodrigo? I would have laughed and laughed and laughed, then told her to knock it off. And, in essence, I had done that right to his face.

Was it ridicule he wanted to avoid?

The spotlight?

If so, why?

These were questions that bubbled restlessly inside, but I wouldn't ask them. Not yet, anyway.

Bastian's gaze caught the book in front of me as well, but I couldn't read the expression that followed. Was it amusement?

Uncertainty? Not sure. If he'd really been hiding behind Jess's name, did he ever get feedback on his novels? Or did they just sprout fully formed from his mind?

With eyes that stormy and beguiling, I didn't doubt magnificence came to him unaided.

"Hey," he said, and I realized I'd been staring at him for an awkward amount of time. I shook the last of my thoughts free and managed a smile.

"Want anything to drink before we get started? Black, straight, decaf?"

He nodded.

Nailed it, my inner voice sang. My intuition had never let me down.

After pouring the coffee in a mug that said *I'd rather a book, thanks,* I joined him with a bottle of orange juice at the table. No one lurked in the parking lot and a bell would ring if someone approached the drive through, so I sat across from him. The Frolicking Moose wasn't usually open this late, but things had been so slow I wanted to give it a little more time to pull in money.

Bastian opened his computer, typed in a password, and turned it to face both of us. His gaze met mine.

"You ready?"

I made a beckoning motion with my hands.

"Bring it."

For the next thirty minutes, he reviewed a surprisingly simple set up. One email account for Jess, and then a private one. I'd have access to the one for Jess. Over 1,000 unread emails already populated the main inbox. Haphazard attempts at organizing the messages seemed apparent, but never followed through.

"Jess has done some AMA's and a few other online forum appearances, but nothing physical," he said. "No podcast interviews, videos, conferences, or book signings.

Nothing that would assign a voice, picture, or physical trait to her."

His habit of referring to *Jess* as a third person intrigued me. Did he see himself as two people? Is that how he separated his life in his mind? I pushed those aside to ask, "AMA's?"

"Ask-me-anything. They're an hour long question-and-answer session where people can write in questions, and Jess would respond to them. They're all online. You can just type AMA into my email search and pull up the ones she's done. That'll help you know how I respond to questions that readers write in, since you and I really don't know each other all that well."

For some reason, his admittance of the fact felt incredibly vulnerable. Our eyes met for a quick touch, then skated away again. In it, I felt a burn I couldn't deny. Was it because I didn't want it to be true that we hardly knew each other? Or because everything about Bastian felt . . . different?

Like playing with fire.

"Then how is she selling?" I asked with a little clearing of my throat.

"I wrote a lot of books fast." He shrugged. "Wrote the first four, then pitched to agents. Pri helped me find a mid-sized publisher that put it into the world, where it did well. As more books were released quickly, traction grew. I kept writing, they kept publishing.

"Around book sixteen, a few influencers got a hold of the series. They started to spread the word. Traction grew, so I kept going. When more success came, more marketing dollars funneled to me from the publisher. My name grew big enough it created more opportunities for the publisher, so they continued to fuel Jess. The books carry themselves from a rabid fandom now. You should see the social media group that's formed."

The buried warning in the words made me want to gulp. I

thought of thousands of Lizbeth's hidden behind a computer screen and felt a new version of screen fright. *Rabid fandom* was a new phrase in my world.

A car pulling up to the drive-through gave me a reason to step away and process for a second. While I warmed up a danish and tossed several coffees into a to-go box, my brain continued to spin through what he said. For as grassroots and quiet as all this started, he seemed to have a better grip on it than I thought.

When I returned, he seemed a little more at ease. Somewhere under all that stress, there was probably a fun guy. If a few drinks loosened him up, I had no doubt we'd have a great time. A karaoke master lurked in him, I could sense the vibes. We'd be a killer Sonny and Cher.

"Here's one email that's interesting." He nudged the computer closer. "A reader wrote in about her husband just dying, and how Jess has helped her have something happy. I always respond to those."

"Do you want me to leave those for you?"

"Yes."

While I watched, he responded to a few emails in that vein. Other emails popped up about reading order or his writing process. A lot of messages from aspiring authors came in, seeking advice. The brief tour of how he responded and what he said was so easy it felt barren. Most of the rote answers were copyable, and I thought of a few ways to make this faster than having to type it all fresh each time. I'd go over that later.

I pointed to an email near the top.

"There are dozens of interview requests here," I said. "Do you just ignore these?"

He shifted. "Kind of."

"Kind of?"

"Well, sometimes I fill them out, but if they want an in-person interview or a podcast or anything like that, I usually just say that I'm only available for written interviews. My readers have gotten used to it."

"Except . . ."

"Except now they want more," he agreed with a begrudging mumble. "Sometimes, readers in the social media groups start speculation threads around who Jess is and where she lives and why she doesn't ever show herself."

"Does Jess comment in the group?"

He shrugged. "Sometimes. The people that start the speculations don't have images or details on Jess. They're not stupid. They know it could be a scam or they could be getting catfished or something."

"Have they ever guessed the truth?"

A moment of levity lightened his gaze. "Yeah, but it's typically shot down by other people, or the idea is just left to die. There's one girl from Canada named Katrina that lives in LA. She's attempting to be a documentary filmmaker, and keeps threatening to make Jess the next topic of interest."

I snorted. The edges of his lips twitched in amusement. "The speculations eventually die down, and I just ignore those messages."

"You should tackle them."

He frowned. "What do you mean?"

"Tackle the topic. Tell them why you want your privacy. They'll stop."

He opened his mouth, then closed it again. "Maybe." He looked away, let out a long breath, and then leaned back. "How does this seem to you? Doable?"

I folded my hands in front of me and shelved the fact that he'd closed off a perfectly normal suggestion. Later.

Meanwhile, my curiosity around Bastian only grew. Not only did I want to brush a lock of hair off his forehead that had tumbled onto it, but I wanted to press a kiss to those lips and see if his response would be as ferocious as I thought.

Yeees! Inner Me sang. *You wanna kiss the boy!*

For once, I didn't silence her.

"One of my superpowers in life has always been an appropriately placed GIF and the ability to mold and adapt to just about anything," I said. "I've got this."

He lifted one eyebrow that made him look like an adorably-concerned little boy. "I won't be here to answer questions."

"I'm aware."

He blinked, then nodded. "Okay. I hope I've thought of everything."

A young girl and her mother stepped inside the shop, so I pushed away from the table, grateful for another moment to think. The hint of a smile on his face contributed an obvious redeeming factor to his hard-to-crack exterior, and now I only wanted more. Was my desire to help born from a hope to satisfy answers . . . or from something else? My fascination couldn't be stopped.

When I returned, a different screen popped up on the computer. It looked like an empty document. He saved it, then navigated away.

"Keep track of your hours and I'll pay you when I get back, if that works for you."

"Sure."

He pulled a piece of paper out of his pocket. "Here's my cell, and I wrote down the access password to the computer beneath it. Text me if you need anything. I probably won't get reception, but if I do, then I'll try to check before I go to bed at night."

"Sure."

"It could be two weeks before you hear from me again."

I shrugged. "No worries."

He hesitated, then pushed the paper and computer to me. He set the backpack he'd been carting around on the table next to it. "You can keep this to work from, since all the passwords are in there."

"Thanks."

I reached for the bag, my fingers just brushing the tops of his. He pulled quickly away, gaze diverted, and acted like it hadn't happened.

Unbeknownst to him, my blood sang. I closed the laptop and tucked it safely inside the bag. I'd conquer the emails later. For now, I wanted to enjoy the low buzz that the warmth of his skin sent through me. The amusement of his reticence sent a smile to my face.

Really, when it came right down to it, this guy was nothing but a shy kid trapped in a man's body. Adorable.

"Is it hard?" I asked, studying the sculpted angles of his face. He glanced up, brow furrowed.

"What?"

I held up the bag. "Giving your computer to someone else? As an author, seems like it would be anxiety-inducing or something. It's sort of your lifeline, right?"

He did smile this time, a quick flash so subtle it shocked me. I longed for more of the way it cut quick hollows across his cheeks and illuminated his entire face.

"Nah. I'm used to being away from it for weeks on end in the summer. I spend all winter in front of the screen, so it's a nice break. Besides, I'm always writing my ideas down when I have them out there."

He drummed his fingers on something in his pocket, and I assumed by the rectangular surface it was a small notebook. The idea of a masculine fire fighter running around a mountain set to flame, but thinking of romantic ideas for his next plot, almost sent a cackle through me. He'd been one surprise after another from the very beginning.

I tilted my head to the side, my hair falling in waves as I regarded him.

"Why are you doing this?" I asked. "Writing in the winter, fire fighting in the summer, and hiding behind a pen name so no one knows who you really are? Is this your dream, or something?"

Any amusement in his features dissipated. He drew in a deep breath, then said, "No, it's not really my dream. I do it because there are people that need me."

Before I could comment, he shoved off the chair and stood up. I had to tilt my head back to take in his whole form. The insane desire to have his strong arms wrapped all the way around me sent a shock through my middle and I caught my breath.

"Priyanka is my agent," he murmured. "She knows I'm going to pay someone to help manage the launch. She should leave you alone, but I can't promise she won't try to snoop in. Chocolate is her weakness, so if she's driving you crazy and emailing in all the time, or something, just ignore her and send her chocolates. Her address is in my contacts. I'll pay you back."

I laughed. "You treat your agent like a puppy? Give her a treat and hope she'll go away?"

To my relief—and delight—another hint of a smile cracked that serious veneer. "If you want to look at it that way, then yes."

"Got it."

I nodded, gratified that I likely wouldn't have to deal with *his people*. Answering emails and responding to written interview requests? Easy. Besides, there was something authentic and beautiful in the way he carefully responded to all the sincere fan emails. Like a butterfly that he didn't want to fly away without thanking it first. It put a gentle edge on such a hard, broad man. The disparity of who he was, against who he appeared to be, struck me yet again.

"I'll start in the morning," I said.

I smiled just to test the waters. As expected, the full effect made him blink, then look away. A hint of a blush lingered on top of his cheeks, and I felt a thrill zip all the way to my spine. Was it possible that this guy had the beginnings of a crush on me? Hope made my head momentarily woozy. Maybe I liked that idea a little bit too much. How many years had passed since I'd been in this position?

Doesn't matter, Inner Me sang. *Just go with it now.*

Apparently, I couldn't help myself.

The draw of my attraction to him was too strong. I metaphorically let go of thoughts of Jakob and positioned myself in front of Bastian. When I did that, Bastian took up all my mental space anyway.

Jakob had never done that, Inner Me whispered.

"Great," Bastian said, drawing me from my thoughts. "I'll be in Jackson City all day tomorrow taking care of a few things. Then, we'll leave early the next morning for an unknown assignment. No rush getting started. Just text as you need to."

With a nod, he headed for the door. I shot to my feet.

"One final question."

He paused, halfway out. When he looked back at me, my breath caught. The raw edge of fire in his eyes startled me. The stress and terror had faded from his body, leaving a tired man in its wake. Tired, but beautiful. There was something alluring about his calmer state. I wanted to wrap my hands around a mug of coffee and talk to him for the rest of the night.

"Why did you trust me so quickly?" I asked. "You don't know me. I could have been a crazy fan that outed you, or something."

"Dunno," he murmured. "Guess I just had a feeling."

With that, he disappeared.

Chapter Eight

BASTIAN

Dad's quiet house met me with silence.

I sat down at the table and exhaled the longest breath I'd ever taken. It trailed out of me until my head swam. I leaned forward, put my head on the flat, cool tabletop, and let my stress unwind.

She's got this, I thought. *This will be fine.*

Dahlia's confidence—one could almost call it arrogance—set me at ease. When she said she had this under control, I believed her. My review of the emails, the social media accounts, and what people said, had been quick. Simple. Maybe not detailed enough, but she had a fast mind and a willing work ethic. I had every reason to believe it would be just fine. My stress over the launch had all but crumbled to the floor.

Now?

Now I couldn't stop thinking about *her.* Dahlia. Romantic subplots and ideas whirred through my mind like a busy interstate. Things I'd described happening for the last twenty books suddenly played out in my own body. A wary

75

uncertainty. An inability to look away. Obsession with how I presented myself because I wanted her to pay attention to me.

Damn, but I liked her.

Writing out a twitterpation and experiencing it myself were two different things all together. I'd just brought her into my world, my novels. As she noted at the end, she could turn my entire life upside down.

Yet . . . I sensed that she wouldn't. Underneath all that glittering brightness and confidence was a woman that, I suspected, was also a little bit broken. The wariness to take the job, her constant study of me. She'd mentioned a bad relationship in the recent past. Her ex burned her for men, perhaps?

No. The smoke that filled me when we accidentally touched wasn't contrived. She felt it too, I could tell.

I closed my eyes, grateful to turn thoughts of Dahlia with a different guy away. I had no claim on her. No right to bristle at the thought, yet I definitely didn't want to think about another guy with his hands on her. I wanted that for myself. A touch on the spot where her neck turned to the gentle slope of her collarbone. The edge of her cheek. Graceful curve of her ear. I shook away thoughts of trailing my hand from her shoulder to her lips with a shudder.

Torturing myself.

Giving away my computer and explaining the process felt like gaining back my soul. Let Dahlia have it. I didn't want the weight on my shoulders right now. Not with Dad and Inessa hovering there, too.

After tomorrow, I could focus on the fire and let the rest fade into the background for the next two weeks.

Really, I could center my attention on myself while I did what I wanted to do, when I wanted to do it. A very competent woman was just about to take over the generalities and could save my family in the process. I'd forget all that stress and Dahlia while I focused on staying alive in the forest. The launch would take care of itself with Dahlia's help.

Goal achieved.

At least, that's what I told myself.

Chapter Nine

DAHLIA

The air conditioner in my RV purred with a gentle hum as I sat down two days later, Bastian's laptop in front of me.

It had been unusually busy at the Frolicking Moose yesterday—with three catering events, one of them almost dangerously overbooked—and late hours. Thanks to Bastian's laissez-faire attitude, I put off diving into his emails for today, my day off, when I could focus. He would be leaving for his next fire assignment this morning, anyway.

When I didn't work, I usually prowled around Alpine or stalked job listings on the internet with a question that circled me like cawing birds.

Who do you want to be without Jakob?

Today, it felt good to have a new purpose that didn't rotate around massive life decisions and the analysis of my personality.

Not far away, bright green letters taunted me with the time. 11:37. The third Jess novel, *Sex is a Guilty Mess*, lay splayed open on the floor. I'd abandoned it in a fit of righteous indignation—and utter love—late last night.

I really needed more sleep.

After rolling out of bed, I grabbed a breakfast burrito, flung it into the microwave, and found Bastian's backpack.

The rickety table where I ate had to be stabilized with folded cardboard, a prayer, and some duct tape, but I held onto hope it wouldn't pitch his computer off.

A text message waited for me while his computer connected to the Wi-Fi.

Bastian: We were assigned to the fire north of Pineville.

I stared at the screen, startled and thrilled to hear from him after a brief exchange of messages last night. Still only half awake, I rubbed the heel of my hand over my eyes and struggled to make my vision work. The blurry words on the phone cleared enough for me to make sense of what he said on the second read-through. Likely, he texted me the update because it might come in handy later.

Somehow.

Did this have relevance to my job? Yes. At least enough that the text was justified. It meant that he'd be closer than not, but probably didn't change the fact that he'd be largely unavailable.

Still, I was on the prowl for further signs of interest from him. Hungry for them, even, although I didn't know why.

Would I do anything with interest from him?

No.

Yes, Inner Me whispered.

I rolled my eyes.

I just wanted the interest to be there to prove that it could be again. My five-year relationship with Jakob left a big gap between the last time I'd ventured into this dating world.

Had I fallen so far away from the dating world there was no retrieval for me? No. At least, I hoped not. Bastian having a return crush on me could confirm that. It was like . . . the security of a bookend. Pretty to look at, functional in its purpose, but not really *necessary*.

In other words, I wanted Bastian to like me but not necessarily do anything with it. Except kiss me. Maybe play with my hair. Tell me things he'd never tell anyone else.

The usual.

So ridiculous, Inner me muttered. *No wonder women have a bad reputation.*

I groaned.

"I like him so much," I replied. Inner Me didn't respond —she smugly felt no need to point out that she was correct. With concerted effort, I turned back to my phone.

Dahlia: Is that a good thing to be close to Pineville?

Bastian: I hope so.

Dahlia: Will you have service?

Bastian: Hard to tell. I'll let you know.

Dahlia: I'll be here.

Just to punctuate the point, I sent three appropriately placed GIFs of firefighters, mountain landscapes, and a woman typing on her computer. A minute later, my phone buzzed against my leg again. I glanced down to see another text message.

Bastian: Sorry, last thing. If you need them, the passwords are saved in a document on the computer.

Dahlia: Got it. Thanks!

I waited another minute, but nothing more came.

With only the quiet swish of the wind in the forest outside the RV, I clicked through his computer and brought up the emails.

He hadn't told me a legitimate frame of reference for how many emails to expect per day, but fifty more emails already popped up in the past two days. Some of them were easily spam, so I spun through the inbox and deleted all those, eliminating over a hundred.

Curious about how Bastian interacted with his readers, I navigated to the Sent folder and riffled through a few.

One stopped me in my tracks.

Jess,

You don't know me, but I wanted to thank you for your books.

They were just what I needed today to get away for a minute. My child was hospitalized last week and I've needed a bright spot. Looks like we might be here several weeks, so I'm grateful for twenty books to get me through.

Not sure you'll even get this, but wanted to put it out there anyway.

Keesha

I blinked.

"Goodness," I whispered, then scrolled further down. His response made my heart twitch.

Keesha,

I'm sorry to hear about your child. No mother should ever have to go through that.

I'm wishing both of you the best and I am glad you're enjoying the books.

Would you mind telling me what hospital you're in? I'd love to send you something.

Jess

My heart leapt into my throat. Twice, I read the email. Did he . . . ?

He did.

I scrolled further, startled to see the email chain continued a week later with another email from Keesha.

Jess,

Oh my goodness, I can't believe you sent me all twenty of your books.

I'm . . . I don't really know what to say. I just stopped crying. I haven't had any money lately and I've been re-reading the first one because I borrowed it from the library and it's the only one I had. I'm wild for Rodrigo.

My son has been undergoing some procedures, so I haven't been able to leave to check out more books.

It's more than just the books, though. You took the time to sign and send all twenty of them. I can't believe you'd do that. Thank you for caring when it feels like no one else really does.

Always your biggest fan,

Keesha

"No wonder everyone loves Jess," I exclaimed under my breath, wiping away moisture that gathered under my lashes. "Criminy, Bastian. There's a puppy dog under your iron mantle."

Several moments passed while I fell into thought, wondering what it was like for him to coordinate sending twenty signed novels. He must have done it, because he didn't have anyone that worked for him. Or did he? Did they quit? Did he have piles of romance novels hidden where he lived that he just mailed off to adoring fans? Which, I realized, I didn't know about that, either.

Where *did* he live?

Here, likely. Or was it? Maybe he had an RV too. Maybe he lived in basements and bounced around jobs. Maybe he lived in a tent in the forest and had a huge home thousands of miles away, in Lamu, Kenya.

You're getting carried away, Inner Me sang.

"I know."

I shook my head out of the mental spiral by creating my own signature as Jess's Assistant Manager. Whatever that meant. At this point, I needed to resign myself to the inevitable. There would be *no* end to the Bastian mystery. I'd probably always have questions about him, the walking conundrum.

Sure made life fun, though.

My fingers hovered over the keyboard before I created a folder titled BASTIAN and filed a similar sort of email away for him to respond to in two weeks. I hunted for emails with questions I could answer without being Jess, but only found two.

Once I went to answer them, I stopped.

Hey Jess!

Hope it's okay that I emailed.

Saw this email listed on your website and thought I'd give it a shot. I have no idea if you'll even read it, but I had to send it and say thank you for your books. They've given me something to dive into and be excited about.

Quick question for you: in Rodrigo's books, you mention that he's from Spain, but don't tell an area.

Can you fill me in? I've lived in Spain for the last five years and would love to picture him in the right backdrop.

Esperanza

Well that wasn't an easy thing to answer. I couldn't respond because I didn't know. My fingers drummed on the keys before I moved to the next email.

Dearest Jessica,

I am also a "Jess" but I hate it when people call me that, so I assume you hate that too, and am going to call you Jessica.

Just wanted to let you know that I love your books, but I'm concerned about the direction you're taking book six, Heart is a Superpower.

In book five, Afterglow is a Promise, *you already established a plot line of enemies-to-lovers, but you've set yourself up to repeat the same thing in the next book.*

May I caution you on this path?

You already show signs of repetitive decision making, and I'd like to see more variance in your work. I'm available for help with this if you ever need it. Contact details are below, and I'd be happy to give you 10% off.
Yours,

Jessica

Setting aside the obnoxious fact that Jess had already completed book six—and *certainly* didn't need help with her plot lines—I hadn't read all the books to know what to think about this email.

How in the world would I answer this question?

"Well that's dumb," I whispered, glancing at the next four Jess books that awaited on the counter.

Lizbeth had stocked me up with all twenty novels. I no longer hid my pleasure at the sheer number of pages awaiting me. The oblivion Jess offered was real.

Except, Jess wasn't.

With a grunt, I continued to scroll through the emails. There had to be something I could do besides get rid of spam messages. This wouldn't be as easy as I thought, and would likely necessitate me reading *all* the books before I could be of real use. Or, at the least, organize this disaster.

Minutes passed while I cruised the internet and constructed a reading order list in a notebook that I'd set aside just for this. I'd have to take extensive notes.

Then I pulled together responses Bastian had sent to readers on another page, hoping to collect answers to common questions in his wording. Even that felt like busy work as I tapped out a pitiful response or two to the most minimal questions.

Oh, no.

I'd vastly underestimated the job.

A pit built up in my stomach as more emails swept past me, unanswerable. *What bookstores are you available in? Do you have translations in Dutch? How many more books are you going to write?*

My heart felt fluttery as I continued to scroll by the question of *how many books will be in the series?* and *when is the next launch coming out after this one?* and *are you hiring a line editor? I have opinions on your adverbs and would like to offer my services.*

With a deep breath, I eased the panic away and grabbed my phone. If my luck held, he'd still be in service.

Dahlia: By chance, do you have any idea how many novels will be in the series? Any anticipated launch dates?

I crossed my fingers and waited.

The question seemed easy enough to tackle without making me appear incompetent. Meanwhile, I tried not to feel like an idiot. If I didn't have *those* answers, what was I really going to do for him?

Not much.

He'd put all this work and expectation into my job and I'd be . . . floundering.

No, that wasn't true. I could read all the books now. That would certainly help, at least a little. And I still had the social media accounts I could manage. The thought sent an eager thrill through me, followed by dread. How many days until the launch? Seven days. One week to read seventeen more books.

Challenge accepted.

While I waited for his response, I logged into Jess's social media accounts. The pages populated with an endless number of comments and DM's with no responses.

"Just heart the posts, or whatever," he'd said with a dismissive wave. "That's fine. Then it'll look like I've seen all of them."

"You're kidding," I muttered. "There's. No. End."

As I scrolled, the comments populated from a seemingly endless pit. Who had this kind of popularity anyway?

Jess's profile picture was a vague silhouette of a woman with luscious hair halfway down her back. There weren't many images she'd posted, and the ones he had were pictures of the books that looked like they'd been supplied from a PR team, maybe with his publisher.

A few half-hearted attempts at a "real" photo were awkwardly executed. At the beginning of the summer, a picture of a coffee mug with smudges on the edges and a short update about the next book appeared. It populated over 1,000 comments alone.

It would take me ages to catch up on these posts, not to mention his messages. Besides, what was the point in "hearting" as he said, each comment? Some of these were months old. The commenters had moved on with their lives and probably forgotten.

Or had they?

Panic crept back in, but I pushed it away. If he wanted to pay me $30 an hour to sit around "heart-ing" comments on his social media accounts, I'd do that. Easiest money ever.

But a squeamish part of me felt like I was taking advantage of him. Clearly, Bastian knew next to nothing about this kind of reader interaction. He thought this wasn't as important as email, but that was wrong.

Everything about this was important.

He clearly cared about his readers and his books, or else he wouldn't be trying so hard. He wouldn't have paid me to keep the inbox moving or some appearance of life behind the launch. What other male would do the same for females that thought he was also female?

Not many, I'd wager.

Bottom line: Bastian needed some help and I was still willing to give it.

While I fumbled to find my place in his strange, online world, I couldn't deny that I harbored a secret thrill that a guy like Bastian gave me access to a world like this. I had a feeling his trust wasn't given all that lightly, despite the hasty situation.

My gaze drifted outside, where the smoke column stacked high in the sky. It had vaguely thickened. Wind pushed it farther out, like trailing ribbons in the higher atmosphere. It spread a brown haze in the air. The air didn't smell like burnt wood yet, which I took as a good sign.

"Stay safe out there, hot stuff," I murmured to the billowing smoke, "because I can't finish this series, and womankind won't be able to handle you dropping it without resolution."

With another deep breath for courage, I began again.

* * *

Four hours later, I had over a hundred emails sorted and the fourth book started.

I stood, stretched, and stepped to the door of the trailer. Wind shifted gently outside, then twirled through a rip down the middle of the screen door that I'd repaired with a strip of transparent tape.

The reservoir lay far away, behind the edge of the RV park and down the hill. This RV park was set up on the mountain, north of Pineville, and a fifteen minute drive from the coffee shop.

Sione had helped me find this spot amongst all the others, in the farthest corner away. The reservoir and mountains splayed out in front of me, uninterrupted by other trailers. The quiet bustle of other tenants continued not too far away, but I could ignore them. They helped me still feel connected to the world, but not so suffocated by it.

If the fire were to turn south, it would blaze through here before getting to Pineville. I'd purchased a slot to stay for the summer and possibly the fall. Eventually, they would winterize the RV park, so I'd have to move on.

Forced decisions, if you will.

Sapphire blue water sparkled with tips of sunshine in the distance, and my soul thrilled to the view. A nice swim would feel good today. Heat bore down on the cracked dirt, intense, dry, and hotter than Hades. Hardly an ounce of rain had fallen since I'd arrived two months ago, and the dry air seemed to rattle in my bones.

The silence out here was soul-filling, but sometimes maddening. During the quiet days, I just wanted someone to talk to. Someone to share the day with, or hear what happened to them. Someone to ask questions of.

What was your day like?

What was the best thing?

Worst thing?

What was important to you today?

The type of questions that Jakob and I had forgotten mattered, until they *really* mattered. By then, it was too late. My gaze lingered on the horizon.

Who talked to Bastian?

Probably no one, if he sat around heart-ing every comment that someone left on his account, or writing twenty-one books in just a couple of years.

Did his publisher get frustrated at publishing novels that quickly, or did they like it? How did he manage it? I knew nothing of the publishing world beyond the handful of tidbits I'd gleaned since meeting him.

Technically, I knew more about Jess than I did about him, but I had the feeling he didn't have many close people in his life. Why else would he ask a total stranger at a coffee shop to bail him out of a big problem? He was best friends with Dagny and Hernandez, so why not ask them?

On a whim, I pulled up my phone and accessed the camera. The sight of a bird swooping nearby broke into my concentration, but I forced myself to push through it before I lost all my nerve. I positioned the camera on my face, turned to video, smiled, and hit the record button.

"Hey, Bastian. Just wanted to let you know that I got through about a hundred emails today, but that was cleaning out some spammy stuff and responding to easy ones. I'm speed reading through the books so I can answer the questions, and trying to organize all the rest. Depending on how many come in per day, I think I could have your inbox back to level zero before you finish with this fire."

A silly feeling crawled over me, but I smiled through it. Why was I doing this? Would he think me a total dork? Maybe he didn't want this level of updates.

I ignored those thoughts and pressed on.

"I have a few questions if you have time, like your plan for the series, how many books there will be, where you get your inspiration, when to expect the next launch, and your favorite type of bagel and shmear."

I giggled, still disbelieving.

"Someone really wrote in and asked that. You can't make this stuff up!"

My dialogue wavered for a moment, but I forced myself not to stop and delete it. Instead, I nodded once.

"Anyway, be safe out there. Text me your answers when you get the chance."

The video stopped, and I let out a huff. Before I lost my nerve, I hit *send*. Why I felt compelled to give him a video of me, I had no idea. Just a hunch that Bastian didn't have anyone to talk to him.

With a sigh, I spun on my heels and headed back to work, Jess's fourth book bright on my mind.

Chapter Ten

BASTIAN

My entire body ached when I finally settled back on my sleeping pad that night.

Sounds from fire camp filtered through the trees where I lay on the ground, my inflatable pad beneath me. I'd spent the last five minutes huffing air into it to get a modicum of a barrier between myself and the pine needles. My joints and muscles already protested, and we'd only dug line for ten of sixteen work hours today.

Darkness spread around me in a gentle skirt, broken only by the distant hoot of an owl or call of a nearby bird. It was a quiet sound, and felt like home.

To my right, Nilla, the only girl on our crew, had already fallen asleep on top of her bag. She snored lightly, but she always racked out first. She'd get cold later and cozy in. Beyond her, a couple guys laughed over a nasty joke, and the sound of someone slapping a mosquito followed.

As much as I hated sleeping outside by the end of the summer, right now the cool air and slowly settling night felt good.

Mack, the Supervisor, murmured quietly into his phone

not far away. I glanced at my phone, startled to see two tiny bars of reception. When we were digging line in the forest to block out an advancing spur of the fire, we never had reception. Back at fire camp, though, we sometimes had just enough to squeak by. A rare luxury. One fire in Alaska had us just below the Arctic circle, clearing trees. For fourteen days, we hadn't breathed a soul of civilization. No reception. Nothing.

I sat up and grimaced as I settled my back against a tree, then rubbed out my forearms. Heat spread across my shoulders, tightening the muscles at the base of my neck into knots.

Before I put too much thought into how much line we'd dug through thick forest that probably hadn't been accessed in years, a notification popped up on my phone.

3 new text messages.

My heart raced when I saw that one of them was from Inessa's main nurse, Shayna. No reason to think anything had changed, except Inessa had always been outside the usual for expectations.

I suspected that it wasn't usual for the staff to text family members updates from their personal phones, but she had been kind about my situation from the start.

Shayna: Things are good with Inessa. She had a good painting day yesterday. The doctor is coming in soon to talk with her again. Probably in three days. I had to bump her oxygen up a little higher so she wasn't breathing so hard. She'll probably sleep better.

I frowned. Inessa's reliance on oxygen had been increasing more quickly than usual. The news left a welling dread in the pit of my stomach that had always been there.

Inessa's mortality was always a question mark on my landscape.

Bastian: Thanks Shayna. Can you text me the doctor's update when you receive it? I'm working the Pinegulch fire closer to Pineville, and I should have reception in the evenings. I appreciate the help.

After I sent that, I navigated back to the main screen with Dad on my mind. He rarely had any changes anymore. Just worsening ones. Yesterday, he looked the same as he usually did. I dismissed the thoughts of Dad. Too distracting.

Too agonizing.

Under Shayna's message waited Dahlia's. After reading it, I realized I'd completely forgotten to brief her on what kinds of questions to expect from readers.

My short tour of the inbox had obviously been wanting. If she dove into my sent mail, she'd eventually see a few replies I'd done before. Those might help a little. She'd probably sent that first text hours ago, although I couldn't be sure. I didn't receive it until we came back to reception this evening.

I moved onto her video message.

Her bright smile trapped my attention right away, and I had to watch it three times before I understood everything she said. The way her eyes crinkled and words came quickly to her had me captivated. Maybe I spent too much time in the sooty air already, but it was damn good to hear from her.

From someone.

As much as I tried to tell myself the quiet nights and busy days didn't bother me, it was a lie. What I really wanted more than anything was someone to end the day with. Someone I could talk to, could ask questions of. Someone that wanted to know what happened in my day. Like Hernandez and Dagny.

While I didn't know if I needed a happily-ever-after-marry-you-until-I-die relationship, anything would be better than the silence of my father's house.

That isn't what happened here with Dahlia, though. Not really. In the video, she'd asked a question, then given an update. But I couldn't help but wonder why she sent the video. Maybe she did videos for everybody.

I shook my head and sent a text reply. Videos just weren't my thing.

Bastian: We have reception at the fire camp.

I held my breath as I wracked my brain to think of what to say next. First, I should answer her questions. But should I thank her for the video? It seemed . . . awkward to not mention that she'd gone out of her way—

A reply stole my thought.

Dahlia: GIF

I blinked three times before I burst out laughing.

She'd sent a GIF of a half-naked man wearing a lei, dancing half naked around a big fire. The words PARTY STARTED flashed in bright letters. It was over the top ridiculous and I couldn't imagine anyone else sending it but her. Such a gutsy move deserved an equivalent response.

But *what?*

My teeth worried my bottom lip as I obsessed over what to say next. Dahlia had such a natural ease about her. She struck me as the kind of person that could talk to anybody. How was I supposed to respond and keep up that kind of energy? I just wasn't that guy.

Apparently, I was a classic overthinker.

Finally, I settled on the only response I could think of.

Bastian: My thoughts exactly.

Only moments passed before I had a return message. I straightened up.

Dahlia: How does the fire look up there?

Bastian: Not out of control yet.

Dahlia: I'll translate that to "good" and pretend you didn't say it like it will be out of control later. Or soon. #givemesomethinghere

I blinked. Was she scared of this fire? I hadn't considered that.

Bastian: You're still safe.

Dahlia: Now we're getting somewhere. By the way, I might have answered my own question earlier. I snooped through the sent mail and found old emails you replied to. They helped.

I tutted under my breath. Smart woman.

Bastian: You're quick.

Dahlia: GIF

A road-runner GIF buzzed through my screen, leaving a dirty cloud in its wake. A second reply followed.

Dahlia: #justyouwait

The hint of flirting made my stomach seize. Time to take a different tactic. Not that I didn't *want* to flirt with Dahlia. I did. That alone seemed problematic, but I couldn't define why. It had been months since my last date, and even that had been obligatory. A girl that Dagny set me up with.

The problem? I just . . . I didn't know how to flirt in person. How to be bright and spontaneous and happy with other people. The absurdity of being a romance author struck me yet again. I could so clearly create a flirtatious exchange on paper because of the power of time, thought, and a delete button. Real life?

Not so much.

Trying to figure out how to flirt over text message without sounding like a creep, and also being this bone-tired, would be idiotic. I'd hate myself for saying something really stupid later.

Better to stick with who I was.

Bastian: To answer your questions: 1. I plan to publish thirty books. 2. The next launch is six months from this launch. 3. I get my inspiration from real life. 4. Plain bagel, veggie cream cheese. Sorry about the wait on my response to the questions. Anything else?

Dahlia: Why haven't you been snatched up by someone?

My brain stopped working entirely while my heart stalled in my throat. It nearly puttered to a stop like a dying engine.

Wait, what?

How did she have the ovaries of steel to ask such a question so point blank? Then again, both of us hid behind phones. Maybe it wasn't that revolutionary.

It just *felt* like it.

I blinked. What was I supposed to say? Most conversations with women were difficult, which made dating not something

I prioritized. Also, I hadn't found someone okay with me being in dangerous circumstances for two weeks. Looming above all those excuses was the mother of all reasons.

No woman has ever wanted me before.

I rolled my eyes and dismissed that dramatic thought. Whatever hole in my brain it spawned from, it could return to.

Before I could formulate a not-super-embarrassed response, a new text message came.

Dahlia: You're such a sweet guy. I've been reading your email responses.

My tension relaxed. She meant in general. Okay. Dahlia had just given me one of those overtly female platitudes that didn't really mean anything, like *bless your heart* or *aren't you adorable?*

Easier to deal with than a real question, but still . . . vaguely disappointing. Because damn if I didn't want her to take the spot of someone snatching me up.

With great effort, my brain started again and formulated a mostly coherent response.

Bastian: You'd be surprised.

Dahlia: I don't think so. Do you think you write romances because it feels safer than dating but it makes everything not seem so lonely?

Bastian: Um . . .

Dahlia: Just a guess, but I'll stop embarrassing you. I'm good for now. Check in tomorrow? Just want to make sure you're okay.

A trickle of warmth and surprise worked through my shock. Who *was* this woman? No one had ever asked me such raw questions before. I didn't like the answers they spurned.

Whether or not Dahlia would be a good thing for my life right now remained to be seen, but I couldn't deny it felt nice to have someone that cared.

Bastian: Will do. Sleep well, Dahlia.

Dahlia: GIF

The GIF of a puppy nosing its way under a sheet, curling up in a ball, and then poking a tiny pink nose out showed up.

With a roll of my lips, I suppressed the idiotic smile that I couldn't help and watched her video one last time. Her happy chatter and quick smiles captured me again. I shook my head, turned the phone off, and stuffed it back into my bag.

Then I fell into an utterly dreamless sleep.

Chapter Eleven

DAHLIA

"What's up, cuz?"

The booming voice came a second before a sharp rap on the trailer door.

An hour had passed since my shift at the coffee shop ended and I'd already finished Jess's fifth novel, *Afterglow is a Promise*. It lay on the counter behind me near a pineapple I'd almost hacked to death. Not as good as what we'd get in California, but it would do.

I straightened, startled away from an email written by a middle-aged woman in Turkey that had recently read Jess's book and couldn't find a copy of the next book in the series. Her broken-English email made my heart warm.

I slammed the computer shut and set it aside as I stood. Meaty shoulders darkened my doorstep.

"Come in, Sione."

Sione stepped inside the RV with a bright smile. Sweat beaded on top of his forehead, darkening the neck of his Polo shirt that said *Adventura Summer Camp* on the left breast side. He wore tan cargo shorts and a pair of dusty tennis shoes.

Given the opportunity, he'd much rather his favorite, gaudy Hawaiian t-shirts so bright it made eyes spontaneously bleed, but this worked too.

"Aunt Lalani told me to drop by when I could." He pulled a pair of sunglasses off, his white-tooth grin wide and happy. "I was in town and wanted to stop by."

"Mom has always been overprotective."

"She has reason. You broke up with your should-be-husband, cashed in all your savings for an RV, and started to roam the world without a job."

I grinned, happy to see him.

"I have a job now! And you're here with me. Life is good."

"Life is good."

The sound of a ukulele streamed through my mind whenever Sione stood near, and I wondered if he still played it for the youth at camp before they pulled the flag down. It had become Adventura's favorite tradition.

"Glad you came," I said. "What's up?"

He gazed around. "Just missed you and wanted to see how you'd been. RV life still treating you well without me?"

"Not as fun, of course, but still great. I think there might be an issue with the black water tank, but I'm not sure yet. My stabilizer jack is acting a bit funky, too."

"You call my dad?"

"Of course." I laughed. "He told me not to tell you because you'd break it while you tried to fix it."

He grunted, but thankfully didn't offer to look at it. Sione wanted to be good at tinkering and fixing stuff, like his father, my uncle, but he ended up further breaking everything he attempted to repair.

I grabbed a bottle of water from the fridge and tossed it in his direction. He caught it, then lowered his big body onto a couch, legs sprawled across the area under the table.

Sione had always filled a room. In some ways, he looked like a younger version of my dad, and it gave me a pang of homesickness. I missed my family. When I lived with Jakob, they were just down the road and I saw my Dad daily . Months had passed since I last saw my parents, the longest I'd ever gone without them.

Sione studied me as he cracked the top of the water bottle off.

"You hear anything from home?" he asked.

Another question lay under that one. I shook my head, shoulders lifting with a deep breath.

"No, thankfully. Still quiet on the Jakob front for the most part. We text every now and then, but it's not much."

He grunted and gazed around. The RV made him claustrophobic after awhile. When he traveled with me, he slept outside or with all the windows open in the back.

"How long are you going to stay in Pineville?" he asked.

"Not sure." My thoughts flittered to Bastian, then back again. "I'd like to see how a few things play out before I decide. Regardless, I'll need to figure out somewhere to park this thing. Wintering in the mountains in an RV? Doesn't sound as fun as Texas or something."

Sione shuddered. He hated snow. The "white stuff" as he called it.

"Don't blame you. Get out of here when the cold comes. Hey, any luck on deciding your life path? My mom said you thought about fashion design a while ago."

I rolled my eyes with a groan. "Fashion design would be fun but too much upfront work. Not as interested as I thought. I called a veterinary office to see if I could shadow for a day, but they're only open a few days a week. I'm always working. Not sure I could handle sad animals anyway, so I didn't follow up with them."

His brow wrinkled. "What happened to the auto mechanic idea?"

"Seems fun but . . . too dirty."

"You've never cared about grease and dirt when you helped my Dad restore the old truck. The two of you worked on that thing for years!"

"Yes, but being covered with grease and smelling like cars all the time is different from smelling like grease and cars on the weekend." I shrugged. "Meh. How is Adventura?"

"Good. I love it. I'm so happy there. Seeing the positive change in the teenagers when they come through? It's my dream job."

"Mark still threatening to have it open all winter?"

Sione chuckled. "No. It's a pipe dream. He thinks he'd like to have Adventura functional all year round, but then he'd have people up in his space too much. He and Stella like the quiet, especially with their new baby."

"Huh."

Sione grunted, then chugged the whole water bottle, crushed it with his fist, and tossed it into the sink to put in the recycling later. "I heard from Lofa," he said.

My voice pitched a bit too high when I said, "From home?"

The expression on his face made my stomach sour. Lofa was a notoriously popular guy from our neighborhood. Lofa knew a lot of people, including Jakob.

I lowered onto the couch next to Sione. The air conditioning blew on the back of my neck now, sending a chill all the way down my skin.

Sione and I grew up only a block away from each other in California. His mother and my father, siblings, needed quick access to the ocean to be happy. We'd spent our childhoods in each other's houses and running into the crisp California waves together.

Sione was, in a word, safety. Which is why I slept in an RV on a reservoir in a landlocked mountain chain, far from my family, my ocean, and my people. Right now, he was the only place I felt not so alone, yet still far from old ghosts.

"Yes, Lofa." Sione leaned forward, forearms on his legs. "Said that Jakob asked about you the other day."

"What did he ask?"

Sione shrugged, which meant he didn't want me to know everything. "Just wanted to know how you were and where you went."

I frowned. "He doesn't get to ask that."

"Why not?"

"This whole breakup was his idea." I waved a hand in the air to encompass the RV. "If I'd had my way, I'd be happily married and probably pregnant with his baby. But, no. He's the one that had to get bored."

Sione sighed. "It wasn't right, Dahlia. You know that. The two of you were . . . you just weren't the right fit, no matter how much you tried to force it. You were roomates, not lovers. You were hardly even friends toward the end. Would you really want to marry a guy like that? Believe it or not, marriage binds you together forever." He tapped his heart. "It happens in here. I'm glad you didn't marry him. He wasn't the one."

That was Sione, a giant, utter romantic to the end.

Unable to deny the truth, I leaned back against the wall. Jakob had been an easy escape. Bright and brilliant and sparkling at first, our relationship had eventually faded into something benign and formulaic.

We lived easily with each other, but maybe not happily. It bothered me that I'd been willing to live a mostly *bleh* way of life for so long. The only reason I'd snapped out of it was because Jakob brought it up.

Would I have stayed that way forever?

Unbidden, Bastian came to mind. He shared no similarities with Jakob. Happy, energetic Jakob. Jakob had always been the life of the party. The originator of the excitement. Karaoke. Stage plays. Saturday game nights. People flowed to Jakob. In some ways, Jakob and I had been too similar. Clones of the same personality, just represented in different genders.

Bastian, on the other hand, appeared recalcitrant in comparison. Brooding, sharp, and quiet. He carried responsibility like a superpower instead of a burden. His gaze could set me on fire in a second.

No, there was nothing similar.

My lips tingled at the mere *thought* of Bastian. He hadn't even kissed me yet, but the intimacy of scenes from his book made me feel like he had. If he could describe a kiss in words that made my heart flutter, what would his actual touch do to me? I'd fall apart at the seams.

"You there?"

I blinked out of my thoughts. Sione had smacked my knee with the back of his hand. I shook my head.

"Yeah. Sorry."

"Lofa just said Jakob asked about you, but it didn't sound crazy."

"Okay." I sighed. "It doesn't matter. I don't think about him as much anymore."

Thankfully, very true.

My thoughts felt heavy in the wake of such honesty. I really didn't think of Jakob as much now that Bastian occupied so much of my mind. Besides, blaming Jakob for my broken heart was the easy path, but not necessarily the fair one. It may have been Jakob's idea to part ways, but I'd agreed to it, then retreated to lick my wounds.

Sione reached over, a big paw of a hand on my knee. For such a large man, he was gentleness personified.

"You're in a good place, Dahlia. I've got you. The family has got you. You may have lost your fiancé and your work as a secretary and your path, but sometimes the best things come when everything is turned upside down."

In another moment of blatant honesty I murmured, "I'm tired of being upside down. Of not knowing what's next or what I want. Deciding is hard. There's a lot of pressure to be right this time."

"Then take the pressure off. Let yourself be fixed. Don't sit in it, okay? There's no badges for suffering here."

The words sank all the way into my heart. *Let yourself be fixed.* He was right. I'd started to wear my frustration and grief over what Jakob and I lost like a protective sleeve over my heart.

Time to let it go.

My life was my own now. I didn't work for Jakob's father anymore. Didn't live in Jakob's apartment or wash Jakob's laundry or attend Jakob's parties.

My life was *mine*.

Tears rose to my eyes. I nodded and blinked them back. No more tears. Not for Jakob. I'd already shed plenty over him. Any tears now would be for some other purpose.

"Thank you, Sione."

He nodded once, a quick acknowledgment without the mushiness of emotions, even though Sione had always been warm, affectionate, and touch-driven. He tilted his head to the door.

"There's a little fire out there, you see it?"

I laughed at such an obnoxiously down-played question. "Is there anyone that *hasn't* seen it?" I asked. That 'little fire' had more than doubled overnight, burning acreage so fast that firefighters had been retreating to stay safe. The updates sent my heart into a worried spiral, so I eventually had to turn them off. Easier not to know.

We glanced through the window to the column of smoke outside. It had also doubled in thickness, but for all I knew, that was expected. Still, getting *bigger* didn't seem like a great thing. I'd been too far buried in work and Jess's novels to think much about it today. Except for my obsession with Bastian's safety up there, of course.

Sione scowled, his upper lip curled. "Ugly thing. Mark is tracking it. He said that it's several canyons west of the camp. Obviously, it would have to cross the highway and cross a river to hit Adventura, but still too close for comfort."

"Can a fire do that?"

"Probably? Dunno."

"How far away is it from Adventura?"

Sione shrugged. "A few miles, I think. Mark says the topography isn't in Adventura's favor. He hiked up one of the mountains behind Adventura with Megan and Justin the other day. They could see the smoke clearly from there. Justin thinks that if the fire made a run with the right wind conditions, it could hit the camp."

My eyes widened. "Do you have to close down?"

"Only if they issue an evacuation order. For now, we're watching."

I relaxed a little. "Stay safe, please?"

He waved that off.

"Always. We'd have plenty of time to get out, and Stella checks for notices obsessively. They said the Pineville hotshot crew went up there yesterday. That's good. I'm grateful for intense people that do crazy jobs."

The text messages with Bastian still rang through my head now, setting me off-kilter. *Intense people that do crazy jobs.* Yeah, that made sense. Bastian seemed like the dive-into-danger type of guy.

"Let's hope they don't do anything stupid," I muttered.

Sione sent me a questioning look that I ignored. He was used to my habit of talking to myself.

"Everyone in town is talking about the fire when they come in for coffee." I hoped to intentionally turn the topic enough to avoid further questioning. "Lots of speculation. Some old people said there hasn't been a fire around here in decades."

"That's not good. More to burn."

"Will it be safe here?"

I motioned outside the RV. Mountains butted up to the back of the RV park where I lived. A cascading flow of trees led down the slope of the mountain in front of me, like I'd parked in a river of pines. Fire in the mountains behind it would quickly flow here.

What if it came in the middle of the night? Were there emergency notifications for that kind of thing? I had a California number, not a local one. Would that make a difference? I frowned at the flood of concerns that followed the topic. Maybe I should have asked Bastian these things before he left.

"Think the fire will get much worse?" I asked.

He shrugged. "I don't know. I'm not used to fire, just water. Hope not."

Truth. Our people were water people, not mountain people. But I couldn't deny the novelty, majesty, or safety of a place like Pineville. As if he sensed the shift in my thoughts, Sione nudged me with a foot. He made a hissing sound through his teeth to get my attention, the same one that Dad made when we were growing up.

My gaze lifted to his.

"Yes?"

"You good? You're distracted today."

His words went deeper than general convention, and I immediately nodded.

"Yeah. Good."

He hesitated, then held up both hands in a concession not to ask anymore. Sione had always known when to back down. Dad, not so much. To change the subject, and do a little exploring of my own, I nodded to the laptop.

"Got a temporary job."

"You need more work?" He threw up his hands. "Dahlia. Why didn't you say it? Come work at Adventura! We need counselors. These *palangis* are afraid of the water. You need to show them how a real woman swims."

"Too far. I can't afford the gas and Adventura doesn't have RV hook ups."

"Not yet." Sione held up a finger. "Mark is getting an RV park put in down the road, so next summer it will be ready for you. Gas doesn't matter. I'll figure it out. Family should be together, and since we're the only ones here, we need to stick it out."

"My mom said she'd come for Christmas if I'm still here. Will that count?"

"I'll be gone!"

I laughed. "I probably will be too."

"Tell me about your new job, then."

I flipped the laptop open, pulled up a picture of Jess's books online, and spun it around for him to see. I'd have to be careful. I'd promised Bastian not to reveal his secret but I desperately wanted someone to know my new job. Sione never cared about details. He wouldn't probe too far into it and I was excited to tell him about the emails.

"I'm working for this author! Her name is Jess. She writes romance novels and needs help with a new book launch. Cool, huh?"

He glanced at the cover, then to me with a dubious expression. "Jess? That's it? One name?"

"Yeah." I bristled, vaguely aware that I'd once been

dubious of such a thing. Now, it seemed fitting. I just didn't understand why.

"Why one name?"

"Not sure," I drawled, and mentally added that to the growing list of questions to mention to Bastian on the video tonight. Sione studied the vague silhouette.

"Am I supposed to know her? I can't even see her in that picture."

"No."

"Oh."

I spun the computer back around. "Just helping with emails and PR stuff. I like it. It's kind of fun."

He quirked an eyebrow, and instant suspicion crawled up my spine. He would only be *that* interested if Mom had been fretting to him over my life choices because she didn't want a direct approach to question me. Which she always did.

Mom had more deeply mourned the break with Jakob than I had—at least at first. She'd loved us together, as platonic as our relationship had been over the years. In hindsight, I think she loved the idea of grandbabies on her hip.

"You wanna do this for a career?" Sione asked.

I shrugged. "I'll see what happens. The online job thing is cool though, because I could move back to California and do it there, with the family. I've never tried that before. Receptionists need an office, you know? This offers more freedom."

"After the summer." He put a hand on his chest, as if offended. "Wait for your favorite cousin, speedy!"

Laughing, I said, "Agreed. We'll move back together."

His expression softened. "When you're ready. Of course."

"Of course," I echoed with a smile.

He stood up, jostling the RV with his large body. "Gotta go back and make sure my camp isn't burning to the ground, or that Mark hasn't made another bad investment."

"I thought that was Stella's job."

"It's a two-person thing these days. Talk later, cuz."

He gave me a kiss on the cheek and gracefully disappeared outside, leaving an empty air in his wake. With a little sigh, I checked my phone, saw no message from Bastian, and disappeared back into book six.

If I couldn't hang out with Bastian, his characters were the next best thing.

Chapter Twelve

BASTIAN

Although I had no reason to believe that Dahlia would send a second video, hope still flared within.

The next evening we returned to fire camp, grabbed dinner, and retreated to our pads to crash. I rinsed off with a rag and some water from a bottle, satisfying myself with the quick spit bath while others dropped onto their mats, half asleep.

Twelve hours digging line, with a few breaks for food or weather checks, left me another weary wreck. My hands had almost gone numb after half the day on the chainsaw, then half the day swamping—pulling tree branches and other wreckage away.

Updates on the fire weren't promising, either.

Continued growth pushed the fire to the east, closer to the highway. Winds made it hard to create a fire line. Another hotshot crew had just arrived to dig line and stop the fire from going north. Meanwhile, we stayed south to protect Pineville, anticipating that a flank of fire could race toward town. A few cabins had been evacuated in the close hills, and volunteers set up sprinklers around houses and cut down brush to prepare.

With all that going on, Pineville remained at the forefront of my mind. My thoughts drifted to Dahlia during the day more than I'd actually like to admit. Even if it was just to myself.

Once I finished wolfing down an extra protein bar, I settled on my pad, grateful to stop moving for more than a few minutes. My phone brightened to life. Each muscle in my arm protested while I rubbed them out, but it gave me something to do while I waited.

Less than a minute after the phone booted up, one measly bar of reception appeared. What felt like an eternity later, a notification showed on the screen.

1 new text message.

Relief spread through me as I tapped on Dahlia's message and a video downloaded. Once it finished, I held the phone close so I could hear, then hit the play button.

A grainy picture emerged at first, eventually settling into something clear. Dahlia stood at the reservoir. No wind down there. The breeze had been a steady twenty miles per hour in the hills all day. The lake was a calm blue band behind her. She sat on a camp chair, aviator sunglasses swamping half her face.

As usual, she had a huge smile.

"Hey again! Just wanted to shoot you a quick update. Got bored at the trailer so I came to the lake to put my feet in the water. My mom does it with the ocean, so it feels like home. Anyway, I finished the fifth book just a few minutes ago. Loved it. How do you come up with these ideas?"

She threw a happily exasperated hand in the air.

"I've never been into romance novels, but you've swept me away. I've already started the sixth and activated my local Lizbeth to discuss. Don't worry—I'm acting like an avid fan. I won't tell her I'm working for Jess."

I leaned back and set my spine against a tree. Already the video was halfway done. She pixelated again as the phone tried to catch up. Seconds later, her voice cleared and her usual bright face filled the screen.

"Emails are steady and fine. I'm still not able to answer a ton, but I've been building a notebook of your past answers so I can mimic those. I still sign it off as my name and tell people that I work for you so they don't think it's you responding. I'd hate for anyone to feel lied to. Some people have written back. Your readers are really quite kind."

Awesome.

Better than I could have ever hoped for, at any rate. The emails weren't stacking up in a horrible manner now, which massively decreased pressure.

"Anyway." She sighed. I imagined her gaze trailed out behind the phone. A crinkle appeared at the top of her nose, between her eyes. I wanted to reach over and smooth it away with my thumb. Then kiss those lips she kept worrying with her teeth.

"Any updates on your side of the fire?" she asked. "Good news, I hope? Like you're going to snuff this sucker out and get a long break?"

She cracked up. I smiled in response, unable to help myself.

"Someone came into the coffee shop yesterday and said it was 4% contained. What the heck does that mean and how can it be only 4%?"

She trilled another laugh. I loved it when she made herself laugh.

"Be safe out there. Take care of yourself, Bastian. I've got things under control here."

The video ended with another smile, and my stomach lurched.

To make sure I didn't miss anything, I watched it again. To

build my courage to respond, I watched it a third time. Then, to avoid the inevitable awkwardness of trying to figure out what to say, I watched it a fourth time.

Finally, I swept aside my crippling analysis and forced myself to respond.

Bastian: Great update. Thanks for all the hard work.

The text sent, and I immediately hung my head. *Thanks for all the hard work.* Could I get any more lame?

Unlikely.

My phone chirped with her almost-instant reply.

Dahlia: It's not really that hard. The hardest part is putting the books down to answer the emails.

Bastian: Oh yeah? What's your favorite so far?

A question. That was good. That was engaging her and would keep her responding. When my knuckles turned white from gripping the phone while I waited for her reply, I forced myself to relax.

This wasn't a first date, or anything.

Dahlia: Is 'all of the above' an option?

Bastian: Sure.

Dahlia: Then I choose that one. You're really talented, Bastian. I mean Jess. ;)
GIF

I chuckled at a GIF of a kitten appearing to laugh, then fall off a table. Happiness in the middle of the woods after an exhausting day would only draw questions from the other guys. Questions I didn't care to answer right now.

Jess made it so much easier to dodge the praise of and questions about my work. Not to mention the awkwardness of people that I knew reading the book and then giving me the rundown. I didn't care if they loved the books or not, but most people seemed to feel obligated to bluster through some praise.

Bastian: Thanks.

Dahlia: A few questions that came up today: 1) Are you married and is your romantic life how you find your inspiration? 2) Have you ever eaten cricket protein? 3) Do you write in coffee shops all the time? If so, what flavor of coffee invites your muse?

Were they her questions or reader questions? I shook my head. No, probably not from her. Sometimes readers wrote in with questions I'd never heard of before. A second grin surfaced while I typed out replies starting with the last question first, then slowed with question #1.

Did she really *not* know if I was married?

Then again . . . how would she know?

Sure, there were strong assumptions to be made that I wasn't married based on the few morsels of information I'd given her, but she clearly hadn't made those assumptions. Or maybe she fished now.

For my part, I hope she fished.

Bastian: I am married. With four children, a dog, and a white picket fence.

Dahlia: GIF

GIF

The image of a zombie walking down an aisle alone, eyes wide and fixed, with normal children trying to get his attention, sent a bark of laughter out of me.

I turned it into a cough at the last moment. Following it was another image of a herd of at least forty small dogs racing along a white picket fence while their toothless owner yelled at them from a porch in the background.

Dahlia: That's how I picture you. #livingyourbestlife

Responses failed me. While I wrestled another round of laughter back, I typed out the only response that came to mind.

Bastian: #nailedit

Dahlia sent so many different emojis, all some form of laughter, that they filled half my screen. She rounded it out with a separate message.

Dahlia: Thanks for the laugh. Update incoming tomorrow. And seriously with the cricket thing. The world needed to know, Bastian. #thisisserious

I lowered onto my pad with a sigh, fatigue making my body loose as jello. My phone turned off while I promised myself I'd message her something witty in the morning. Because there would be another update, and that was something worth being excited about.

Bottled sunshine filled my dreams.

Chapter Thirteen

DAHLIA

Bethany sat at a table in the shop the next day and frowned at an array of paperwork.

She'd been working there for almost an hour without a word until she muttered, "I think the Frolicking Moose needs some help."

A calendar, a highlighter, a binder, and several bright pink pens cluttered the table. She leaned her head into her hands, threaded her fingers through dark locks, and groaned. I settled across from her and set a cupcake near her elbow.

"Here. JJ sent them. Said they were deformed and we could give them away. Personally, I don't think you can deform buttercream, but whatevs."

She took one look at it, blanched, and ran for the bathroom in the back hallway. I blinked, startled, as the sounds of retching followed.

"Oooh," I whispered.

Bethany returned ten minutes later, pale but composed. She'd pulled her hair away from her face in a loose bun that already fell apart on her shoulders. When she sat down, hazy-sick eyes regarded me. I'd already moved the cupcake and swapped it for a tepid ginger tea. Without a word, I nudged it to her.

She had a tentative sniff, melted, and sipped. "This is just what I needed."

"I know. It's a gift. How far along are you?" I asked.

She closed her eyes and nursed the tea again. "A few weeks."

When she opened her eyes back up, a modicum of humanity returned. She leaned back, setting the tea back down. Against her pale face, her eyes remained a startling glacier blue. Chilly, if not for the warmth of her constant smile. Nothing like Bastian's liquid sapphire.

"It wasn't this bad with my son," she murmured. "I'm not that far into it and just . . . can't do smells."

"How are you not vomiting from the essence d'coffee of this place?"

She shrugged. "Doesn't bother me. The most random things do. Egg? Gone. Mayo? Gone. Sweets have never been my thing, but now I have a morbid hatred for sugar."

"Sounds like the best diet strategy ever, if you ask me. It's probably a girl this time." My nose wrinkled. "I hear they're drama queens from the moment of conception. Or maybe that was just me."

Bethany smiled weakly, then laughed. "A girl. Can you imagine Maverick with a girl?"

The idea struck both of us as unaccountably funny, and we giggled for several moments before the hilarity passed. Bethany sipped her ginger tea a couple of more times before she straightened up.

"I haven't told Mav yet," she admitted, a bit sheepish. "He was sort of a mess with the first pregnancy. Especially the first trimester, when risk of miscarriage is so high. Some of his sisters have miscarried quite a bit and I don't want to stress him out before I have too. He's very protective."

I snorted.

Understatement of the year.

"Wee bit." I grinned, fingers held barely apart. "As he should be," I tacked on.

The pang of losing Jakob usually followed such a sweet sentiment, but I didn't feel it this time. Jakob hadn't ever been protective. Affectionate, yes. But not . . . overly concerned about much. Instead, Bastian pushed on my thoughts. He seemed like the protective type. I let that thought linger a bit, and it felt good.

Bethany's brow rose a little. "Keep my secret, please?"

Her plea struck my heart. "Of course. As long as you want me too. Run to me anytime you need a place to vomit or get relief. My mom is an OBGYN. I can get you some meds or something, I'm sure."

"Thanks. I have my first appointment next week." She smiled, then lit up. "Enough about me! Any luck on the finding-your-new-path hunt? Lizbeth mentioned you didn't want to be a nurse."

Her genuine curiosity held a bit of fear. As their only employee, I cradled their store in my little hands. If Bethany was sick as a dog while pregnant, she certainly couldn't stay here long. Maverick had his own career and houses he consulted on for construction work. With Ellie on the other side of the country and no other applicants for a job, I had become the symbol of the Frolicking Moose.

Not a bad spot to be in, but not a forever one, either.

"Maybe," I mused, thinking of my work with Bastian. I likely wouldn't settle in as his assistant forever, but I enjoyed the doors this unexpected opportunity opened. "We'll see how things tease out. Nothing concrete yet, anyway, so I'm still here."

Her shoulders sagged. "Wonderful."

"I just wish I hadn't gotten such a useless degree in college.

General studies?" I grimaced. "I should have just dropped out and finished later, when I knew what I wanted. Why don't they push college for later adult years, after you've done all the stupid things and made the stupid mistakes and actually have a brain?"

She sighed. "I agree. I left early, too. Still haven't finished my degree, just shifted right into real estate. Ellie left early, and I was proud of her. Regardless, I'm sure the right path will find you."

Maybe it already did, whispered Inner Me.

"Indeed," I said in answer to both.

I gestured to the sprawled paperwork to shift the topic.

"I would love to help with coordinating the Frolicking Moose, but I'm not sure what you're picturing for the job. Lizbeth mentioned hiring a manager, or something. I don't know how long I'll be here, but I'm happy to do what I can."

Bethany seemed relieved to refocus on the paperwork.

"Yes, we're looking for a manager, I think. Someone to take over supplies, renting the loft, running the HomeBnb listing, placing food and inventory orders, barista management, and also the schedules and catering of the back room. I really want to strengthen the partnership between us and JJ's bakery, but I haven't had time to figure out how to push catering to interested people. The back room would be great for a wedding reception or party." She waved a vague hand toward the back room. "But how?"

Not a single idea populated my mind. It was a complicated question that, as a pregnant woman, she shouldn't have to deal with. A manager position would be a deeper integration into the Frolicking Moose than I wanted to have, and Bethany would need someone she deeply trusted. Someone with guaranteed longevity.

"Lizbeth mentioned a woman named Leslie." I leaned back against the wall. "Is that an option?"

Bethany sighed. "Yes. I've been pushing back on the idea because I just haven't been sure Leslie would want it. She's just finalized a divorce."

I sucked in a sharp breath.

"Ouch."

"Yeah. Divorce is never an easy process, even with amiability and a great attorney like Kinoshi. Anyway, I think she could use the work and I need her commitment to a task. If there's one thing Leslie has, it's boundaries and pragmatism. I'll keep you updated."

Wearily, she gathered up the paperwork while I put the ginger tea in a to-go container. With a smile, and a quick hug, she stepped back into the hot sunshine.

I stepped up to the large window as I brushed a piece of lint off the table, then looked over the hill north of here. The plume continued to chug away back there, tucked up against the mountains like it belonged. I scowled.

Was there another update from fire camp?

The fire had turned into an obsession. Would I be this absorbed if I didn't know someone working up there? I wasn't sure. I'd never looked at the horizon so much in my life, nor cared about analyzing weather reports. The ever-present smoke column gobbled up a lot of my thoughts. Those thoughts slid to a certain wildland firefighter a little *too* much.

Vague news reports mentioned winds potentially pushing the fire east tonight before a gathering storm, which meant right toward Adventura.

Nothing had stirred up so far today. Only heat on a crackling dry afternoon without a lick of moisture. My lips were chapped and miserable, even though I constantly balmed them.

I slipped back behind the counter when a few cars headed for the drive-through. While I sank into the mindless task of pouring espresso and warming croissants, the door rang. A bright young woman with dreadlocks and a belly shirt walked inside with a smile. I called a greeting.

"Be with you in a sec!"

She waved and stood below the board, studying it with her head craned back. A full pack rested at her side, slung along her hips. It had been pieced together from different pieces of cut denim and old zippers. The bohemian look caught my eye. Something about her registered as vaguely familiar, but I couldn't put a finger on it.

Once the final car sped away, I stepped to the cash register with my usual smile.

"What can I get you?"

The woman's fingers fidgeted with the strap of her bag.

"Something cold," she said. "The strawberry frap looks good. And add a cake pop, maybe? A little sweet something to celebrate."

Her grin widened, revealing startlingly straight and white teeth. I turned to the cash register, which beeped as I entered the order.

"Sure. Are you celebrating something special today?"

She spread an arm. "Just being here!"

I almost snorted, but managed to smile instead. What could that possibly mean? Pineville was a known tourist destination in the summer, when the mountains flooded with people who wanted to get away. Tourists always had some level of enthusiasm, but it centered around boating or water skiing. Maybe she needed mountain therapy, or something?

While I grabbed a cup and reached for the frap base, I glanced back at her. Her gaze darted around the shop, then outside. Something here felt off, but I couldn't peg it down. All kinds of people materialized, grabbed a drink, and then left. I had no real reason to suspect her except a back-of-the-neck prickling.

The Frolicking Moose had something of a violent history. I would not be one of the barista's with a gun pulled on her.

Not happening.

"Are you from around here?" I asked.

"No." She pulled the bag off her left shoulder and set it on a nearby table. "Just stopped by because I heard this was a happening place."

"It's fun."

"Are you from here?"

The frap slipped easily into the clear cup after I took it off the blender. I tacked the lid on and set it on the counter for her to grab, a straw already sticking out.

"Not really."

"I hear there are local celebrities that come here pretty often."

"Oh?"

I wracked my brain for who she could mean. Benjamin Mercedy, perhaps, but he'd been staving off press for so long that most people left him alone now. He and Maverick met at the Diner for lunch all the time. Plus, he was easily accessible at his gym, so no one looked for him here.

She reached for the frosted plastic cup. "Yeah, like actors or actresses or famous authors, or something."

The cake pop I slid her way disappeared off the counter with her drink, but she remained. I felt the pressure of her gaze like a dead weight on my chest. The words *famous authors* rang through my ears like alarms.

Yep.

Something was definitely off now.

"I'm not aware of anyone famous myself," I said. "It's a really small mountain town. There are a lot of hidden cabins or RV parks or HomeBnb's to rent, though. It would be easy enough to hide up here. Do you know a celebrity in particular that you're searching for?"

"Not necessarily someone you might know on sight. Do you know the people that come in here pretty well?"

"I'm getting to know the whole town, it seems like. It's not a super big area, but I'm new to it. I've only been here this summer, so there are a lot of tourists."

Light bloomed in her eyes, which probably meant that I'd just achieved the *opposite* of my goal to make her disinterested. I'd hoped to stop the topic by making it seem like I didn't know any one well, but I had the disconcerting thought that *that* was exactly what she wanted to hear.

"So I thought," she murmured. "Lots of people coming in and out might make it easy to hide, particularly if no one knows you by appearance. Do you know the patrons that come by name?"

She stepped back a little, and I wondered if she could sense my growing discomfort. Dad always said that I wore my emotions on my face. The distance between us did make me feel a little bit better.

The cake pop bag crinkled as she had a pull on her frap, like she tried to be casual. Bethany and Maverick had installed a panic button after Dagny had a run-in with a woman and a gun. I nudged closer to it now. It was on the floor, where I could flip the cover with my foot and stand on it.

"I know the customers well enough," I said. "We have some regulars, but most people just order coffee, use the WiFi, and then leave."

"Any authors?"

"Ah . . . not sure."

"There's a book club that meets here, right?"

"Yeah."

"Have they ever had a local author do the meeting with them?"

"Not since I've been here," I drawled.

An itchy feeling crawled through my chest with a looming

sense of doom. She deflated a little. With a wave to her bag, she said, "I came because I heard a really famous author comes in here to write sometimes."

"Oh?"

"Yeah, a romance author."

The feeling crawled down my back. Her eyes dropped to the counter, where Jess's seventh book, *Blame is a Weakness*, was tucked off to the side. Not necessarily splayed out like usual, but certainly not invisible. She grinned as she motioned to it.

"That author, in fact! What a wild coincidence. I see you're reading her too. I shouldn't be surprised." She chuckled. "Everyone reads Jess these days."

"Oh, those books?" I swallowed hard. "Yes, I just discovered them from the leader of the local book club."

"What's her name?"

"Lizbeth?"

A gleam entered her eyes.

"Lizbeth is a website developer," I said quickly, already catching her train of thought. "Not a romance author, although she probably should be. She's read all the books in the library, then supplied them with more."

"Well, Jess is a very famous author that has never revealed herself. There's a lot of speculation about who she is. Really, she could be . . . anyone."

My voice was almost an octave too high when I asked, "No one knows?"

The girl studied me for a moment, and I wondered if she could see the beads of perspiration forming on my skin. Lying had never been my forte. If my life depended on me telling a falsehood, I'd be dead in seconds.

"No." She shook her head. "And she's been tracked here."

"By who?"

She waved that off. "Doesn't matter. I wanted to come see

if the rumors were true. I'd love to sit down and talk with her a little bit about one of her books, that's all."

I swallowed hard, my mind racing. This wasn't supposed to happen. Working for Bastian was supposed to be an easy gig where I moderated social media responses to make sure fights didn't break out, answered a few questions, and sorted email. This whole lying-to-a-stalker thing had not been a desired skill in my supposed resume.

To get away from her scrutinizing gaze, I glanced around.

"You're welcome to stay and wait. A lot of people come in to bum off the WiFi, so I can't guarantee it'll be easy to track an author down. Lots of women come," I added, then cleared my throat. "They don't say much, for the most part."

"So you don't know a local romance author?"

Her dark eyes probed mine again, and suspicion lay deep in their depths.

I swallowed hard.

"Nope. Don't know Jess." I forced a wry chuckle that sounded strangled. "Wish I did, though. Love her books. I didn't know she'd been tracked to here."

That much was sort of true, since Jess didn't *actually* exist and I definitely loved the books. The woman pointed to my current book.

"A fave, for sure. Just wait until you get to twenty. Twenty one releases next week and I'm just dying. My girlfriends and I are having a Jess retreat at a cabin we rented up here. They're all flying in before the launch so we can prepare for it together. The only thing that would make it better is to meet Jess herself."

She squealed.

I almost swore.

Instead, I managed a bright smile. "Girls retreat over a romance novel!" I cried. "Sounds amazing."

"We're all reading it on our phones the moment it arrives

at midnight. We're going to stay up with sugary food and talk about our favorite Jess book. Mine is thirteen, of course, *Change is a Monster.*" Her nose scrunched up. "Really didn't like book four, *Lust is a Darkening Hellscape,* at all. But that seems normal enough! Anyway, can't wait to hear what you think. I'll be around for the next week or more."

I smiled because there was nothing for me to say.

She pointed to the table where she'd set her stuff. "Mind if I sit down for a while? I need to plan some of the party."

"No." I shook my head. "Make yourself comfortable. There is a fire raging in the forest north of here," I added. Maybe that would deter her. "It's going to be out of control soon, a source of mine says. Just so you know in case you need to alter travel plans. I'm sure the hotel would accommodate any changes."

She dug through her purse as she chewed through a bite of cake pop, clearly not caring about the inherent warning as she pulled out her phone.

"Okay, sounds good."

Her attention refocused on her screen.

And all my hopes for an easy job plummeted.

* * *

That night, I paced back and forth outside the RV. A dry wind stirred hair off my shoulders as I spun for the two-hundredth time while waiting for Bastian to text me already.

I'd sent a somewhat frantic video recounting The Situation, as I dubbed it. Then I followed it with a GIF of a monkey darting away from a woman chasing it in high heels. To seal my emotions, a second GIF of a woman low-level losing it came next, followed by a man surrounded by peaceful mountains. The word *namaste* flashed across the bottom.

Perhaps I'd gone overboard.

To the north, the plume had doubled as the day progressed. A mushroom-like cloud billowed above it, marring the northwest sky with a dingy scar. It lingered in the upper atmosphere in bleak promise. A hint of burning wood lingered in the air.

Just in case, I left the news on inside the trailer where I could just overhear the headlines.

Of course, the one night that I needed Bastian to respond quickly, he hadn't.

Frustrated, I shoved my phone back into my shorts pocket and snatched the seventh book off the step. I couldn't stop reading. Even if I wanted to stop, I wouldn't. The books were too drawing, and it made perfect sense to me why he had women attempting to find Jess and out her. Bastian had serious talent for writing lovers that longed for romance but didn't know how to find it.

There were still thirteen books to go, with book twenty being the biggest cliffhanger of all, according to online forums. I'd never read this fast in my life, and it still felt too slow. I couldn't read as quickly as my desire to hear his stories.

Would I feel the same way about Bastian in real life?

A picture ran through my mind. Bastian cuddled up at my side, playing with my hair, unraveling a story out loud. I'd be snuggled in, probably finding the perfect GIF on my phone to punctuate his drama. I blinked the image away, startled that it had appeared at all. This twitterpation was out of hand.

My phone buzzed in my pocket.

I yanked it out.

Sione: Word is out that they're about to issue voluntary evacuations to the north of the Pineville area. That's you, cuz. You HAD to pick the trailer park up in the mountains, not the one on the lake bed.

My stomach clenched.

Dahlia: What does voluntary evacuation mean?

Sione: Means you leave if you want, and danger is coming. But it's not on the doorstep.

Dahlia: Should I take the RV somewhere else if that happens?

Sione: Let's see what they say. You're probably still safe for a while. But we'll need to pay attention.

His answer didn't help me feel any better, however.

Dahlia: What about Adventura?

Sione: Mark wants to wait until we get the official announcement. There's a highway between us and the fire, so we're good.

"Danget."

The word came out of me in a hiss. I was about to shove the phone back in my pocket when it buzzed again. Bastian's name flickered across the screen in a call. My stomach fluttered when I answered, then pressed it to my ear.

"Hello?"

His rolling voice responded with a casual, "Hey," that sent my stomach into flips. The sound of his voice felt like submerging into a steaming bath. For how frantic my video had been, he sounded calm. My response came quick and a bit shaky, but it had nothing to do with The Situation.

Everything to do with his smooth-as-butter *hey*.

"Hey," I choked out and ran a hand through my hair to get it out of my face. "Sorry if my video was a bit panicked. I just . . . ah . . ."

My mind stopped working.

"No, it's fine. Not your fault."

His voice was low, quick, like he didn't want anyone to hear him. I could picture him leaning against a tree, standing away from a crowd of firefighters, head bent in concentration as he spoke.

"You got my message?" I asked.

"Yeah. Just now. I only have a few minutes."

My nostrils flared at a little stretch of quiet on his part. *Now is not the time to get shy, Bastian! I need answers.* Questions clogged my throat. They dove deeper than what he wanted me to do about the stalker woman—whose name I didn't even get, I realized belatedly.

As far as detectives went, I clearly failed.

No, I wanted information on the fire. On his whereabouts. Was he safe? Did he need to leave and come down here? Because I'd gladly house him.

Those thoughts dissipated when he spoke again.

"First, I'm sorry that happened. I never dreamed it would have or I wouldn't have put you in this position."

I licked my dry lips. The sun sank lower in the distant horizon, casting a brilliant gold and orange on the sky above the mountains. Hot pink lined the clouds, highlighted by smoke.

"It's fine," I croaked.

"Are you safe?"

The undertone in his voice flipped my belly again. I'd need medicine to calm these inner-gymnastic.

"Yes, fine."

"You're sure? She's not unstable or something?"

"No, nothing like that. I'm not in danger or anything. Jess's reputation is, I'd wager, but not me."

He let out a long breath, clearly relieved. "Good. Jess will be fine. You did great."

His praise sent a ridiculous little thrill through me. He asked about my safety before Jess. That meant something!

"I'm going to contact Pri and let her know," he continued, "I'll see if she's heard anything. Have you noticed chatter about it in the social media group?"

"No."

"No threads about this?"

My mind ran back over the comments I'd monitored today, but I couldn't recall an instance that would apply here. I hadn't perused very far, though. There were over 40,000 people in the group and thirty new posts a day. Keeping track of any of it was like picking up thrown glitter.

"I can check again tonight, but nothing stood out."

"See if you can find anything. Look into a girl named Katrina."

"The one that lives in LA?"

"Yeah, the documentary filmmaker. This might be her trying to capitalize on publicity and excitement with the new release. She could leverage Jess's popularity to get attention herself."

"Okay. I will."

His tone dropped again. Not quite a whisper, but close. "Do you feel safe if she comes back into the coffee shop? Because I'm willing to bet she will. I can call Hernandez and have him stop by to check, just in case."

"Uh, yeah." The words stuck in my throat. His concern touched me. "I don't think she plans to get out of control. She just wants to look around, I think. No danger to me."

"Okay. Just let me or Hernandez know."

The inane urge to ask him to send me a video rose up, but I shoved that back down. No, that felt like too mortifying of an ask. I just wanted to *see* him again. I almost giggled in a deranged way, picturing him doing a selfie while coated in grime.

He pulled me back to the present.

"Keep me updated, okay?"

"Of course."

"Just . . . steady on. Maybe she'll let it go when she doesn't discover anything here."

"Any idea how she found it?"

"IP tracker, maybe," he murmured. "Not sure. Lizbeth might. She's got a brain for computers and programming."

The thought hadn't occurred to me. For several wordless moments, I had no response to give.

"Do you want me to ask Lizbeth to find out?" I asked. "I'm not sure I can do that without revealing Jess."

"No. The less people that know, the better."

"Okay."

"And . . ." he hesitated. "The wind is supposed to shift and build through the night. It'll come out of the northwest and blow toward Pineville. There's a chance voluntary evacuations could hit."

"Sione just texted me about it. That means the fire would be headed right for us, right?"

"Yeah."

"So the weather report is accurate?"

"As accurate as they ever are."

I chewed on my bottom lip and thought of Sione's text. Maybe I should get the RV prepped, just in case. One of the stablizer jacks had been having an issue retracting. I wouldn't be able to leave with that still down.

"Okay, thanks."

"You'll be safe," he added quickly. "There are emergency alerts that go out to anyone in an area, so keep your phone close and keep it turned up and loud."

"Oh, I didn't know that."

"I have to go back out soon. They're putting us on a different part of the fire tonight to try to get ahead of it.

Hopefully, we can stop it at the highway so it doesn't jump."

Jumping over the highway, if memory served correctly, would put it on the path to Adventura.

"I hope it doesn't," I murmured.

"We'll get it."

He sounded so easily confident and calm about this building conflagration thing. Darkness had started to settle, driving me inside. The comfort of the bright RV interior settled the building uncertainty. Or maybe it was his voice and reassurance.

"Thanks, Bastian."

The sound of a scuffle and calling voices came from the background.

"I'll update as much as I can, but I'm not sure when we'll get back. I need to go, this was a short break. Thanks."

"My pleasure."

"Oh," he added, "thanks for the videos. I . . . I've really enjoyed them. Send more."

The call ended before I could squeak out another word.

Chapter Fourteen

BASTIAN

Mother Nature was a beast.

Sometimes on fires, I'd debate with myself over which element was the most heartless and destructive. Fire. Water. Wind. Earth. All of it captured power. When swept into a rampaging force, true escape from any element became a farce. Infernos. Tidal waves. Tornados. Mud slides.

Fire was the mark I saw all the time. Charred devastation. Darkness. A stark desperation in a previously healthy land that lasted for generations.

Heat, smoke, and the scent of burned wood filled my head as I lay back on my pad at fire camp. Stars speckled the sky overhead, despite the building wind in the tops of the trees. Branches waved back and forth, subject to the caterwauling gusts. In the far distance, clouds built up. They'd drive in on this outflow wind and, with any luck, drop some moisture.

Meanwhile, the very wind that brought the rain also grew the flame.

I didn't look at my watch, because it would only tell me what I already knew. About 3:30 am. My arms ached after sixteen hours of swinging shovels and pickaxes in what would most likely be a futile attempt to dig line and stop the building inferno. We'd be up early to get back at it after breakfast, in which I wouldn't be able to eat enough calories to recompense what I lost today. Didn't matter. It would have to work out somehow. Likely, on sheer grit.

My mind turned to Dahlia. Thoughts of her usually made it easier to relax, but her concerned voice when we spoke tonight set me on edge. After talking I had no new video update. I missed it, even though I still got to hear her voice.

I shook my head to clear those thoughts. They wouldn't serve me tonight.

Although I couldn't explain why, I had a feeling the fire was toying with us. My theory didn't make sense. Hardly anybody but other wildland firefighters would agree with me, but fire had personality.

Sometimes, you'd have a small blaze that petered out and played possum. We'd think it safe, back off, and it would blaze back to life after creeping around in the root systems, sometimes for weeks or months. Like it just wanted to mess with us.

Other fires started and ended hot, blazing, and ticked.

Others provided a gentle burn. Consistent. Steady. Not too troublesome, but enough to be respected.

This fire?

This sucker danced.

It would blaze and burn, then retreat. Retract, grow, stop. Other fires did the same, but this one felt . . . nefarious. Like it had a vendetta come due, and it would get its payback. None of that was true. Fire was fire. Conditions fueled it, and sometimes conditions were a son of a bitch.

Still . . . I had a feeling.

The voluntary evacuations had already gone out, but I doubted many people would leave. Those with animals would probably start moving them to safer ground. Bags would get packed. All that meant Dahlia was fine so far, but I didn't like the thought of that changing rapidly. If fire did anything, it was change rapidly.

I contemplated the picture of her in my mind as I dropped into a restless sleep. Dahlia and I had met twice.

Yet I felt her surround me, kind of like smoke.

* * *

While riding the green wildland fire truck out to our assignment the next morning, I checked my phone. No messages from Inessa or Dad's caregivers, which was a win I'd take. I wished I could call them. Inessa didn't like the phone, but sometimes I could snatch a minute or two of her gabbing. Dad was a lost cause as he wandered around, lost in his own mind all day, every day.

My throat tightened at the thought.

A text message popped up with Dahlia's name attached. Seconds after I tapped on it, a video began to download. So soon? It was barely nine in the morning. I couldn't tell if it was a good sign or a bad sign.

Her immediate smile set me at ease. She wore her hair down around her face, like usual. Her dark eyes had a sleepy look in them, as if she'd just gotten up. The background of the coffee shop was visible behind her strong shoulders.

I tapped the play button.

"Hey! Just wanted to send you a quick update. I checked the social media group last night and couldn't find any trace of Katrina posting recently. Her last post that I can find was a few months ago, but it was in response to a question about book twelve. Doesn't mean she's not posting about Jess elsewhere, but I can't see it from your profile if she is. I also finished book eight at like four in the morning."

She sent me a stern look, and I laughed.

"I need more sleep, thank you very much. Anyway, I'll keep an eye on things here and update you. If presumed-Katrina pulls anything crazy, I got yo' back."

She giggled, then her face softened ever-so-slightly.

"Please be safe. Don't do anything stupid out there. The voluntary evacuation arrived late last night via an alert, like you said. I'm not going to leave this place yet, but I probably will prep after work, just in case. Thanks again."

The video ended.

After it, she'd sent another message.

Dahlia: Let me know if text messages are easier when you're out.
GIF

A short clip of a woman chewing her fingernails and looking uncertain followed. I had to stop myself from writing a too-emphatic NODONTEVERSTOP response.

I typed out a quick:

Bastian: Videos are great. Thank you for keeping an eye out.

It felt too impersonal and a bit standoffish, but whatever. Just as I clicked the phone off to save battery, a call came through. My neighbor, Mrs. Cortez. I answered it, ducking my head as the truck pulled onto the highway.

"Hello?"

"Bastian? Oh, thank heavens. Listen, I'm so sorry but I broke my hip when I fell in the shower last night. I can't watch your cat, I'm in the hospital up in Jackson City."

Her voice cracked, like she was about to cry.

Awkward.

"Oh. No problem. Hope you're okay."

"I left the key on the nail like always, and I called around to find someone else to help but no one is answering. There's enough food for a few days. I—"

Her teary voice started to cut out. We still had over a week left out here, so I couldn't leave Psycho to herself that long.

"Don't worry about it, Mrs. Cortez," I said. "I've got someone that can cover it. I hope you feel better soon."

Mrs. Cortez started to break up as the buggy sped away.

"You . . . sure? I . . . find . . ."

"Thank you Mrs. Cortez. I appreciate you letting me—"

The call cut out as we sped toward the dark plume in the distance. I typed out a quick message to Dahlia, even though I wasn't sure she'd get it.

Bastian: Care to save my ass again? My neighbor busted her hip and can't take care of my cat, Psycho. Just need someone to check the food, water, and litter box. Key hangs on the doorframe.

After that, I sent my address. My teeth worried my bottom lip as the circle below the messages spun around for a while. Finally, in a vaguely-more-open spot on a forest road, it sent. I let out a long breath. Ten seconds later, all reception cut out.

Hopefully, she got it.

I plugged my phone into the port to charge while we drove, rested it on my pack in the seat next to me, and looked out the window.

Two days left until the book launch, and I'd officially found my first real-life stalker.

Weird.

No doubt my hotshot crew would be turned right back onto the same fire after our 48 hours of rotation out. Who knew if this inferno was going to turn on us and roar with sparky rage?

If Jess could just push through another launch or two

without being revealed, then everything could fall apart without impacting Inessa and Dad.

That's all I needed.

Chapter Fifteen

DAHLIA

Despite myself, I couldn't wipe the stupid grin off my face.

Bastian had asked me to take care of his cat and that felt like a win. Not only because he turned to me when trouble came up, but now I'd get to see inside his house. For a closed-off man like him, this could be a game changer.

"No," I said out loud. "This is just him asking for a favor. This doesn't mean he returns my somewhat speedy and concerning interest in him. That's not what this is! I will approach cautiously."

This is not the same as Jakob, Inner Me said. *You were young and lonely and twenty-two when you met Jakob. You knew there were problems, but you proceeded into the relationship anyway. You never really felt much around him. Nothing like Bastian.*

"So physical butterflies are an indicator of a powerful relationship?" I cried, hands thrown in the air. "That's insane! You sound like Lizbeth. I have a tendency to find someone else that gives me attention and I latch on without asking myself what *I* want."

One person isn't a tendency.

"It's close enough!"

Do you want Bastian?

"I want to stop feeling like I'm mentally unstable because I'm having a conversation with myself," I replied. "In short, I don't know the answer to your question yet." I swallowed hard. "I'm . . . giving it time."

Oooookay.

I scowled. Down the road Inner Me pointed out way more self-analysis than I wanted. No, I didn't want to think about just how much I liked Bastian and what it meant. Right now, I'd enjoy the fact that Bastian trusted me with his cat, but that was it.

Nothing further.

Setting aside the giddy rush from Bastian's request and the surge of curiosity that followed, I turned my thoughts back to work.

The Frolicking Moose had been quiet and steady through the drive-through, as usual. In Jess's world, the launch of the historic twenty-first book in the series was only two days away, and the social media group vibrated with energy.

The typical thirty posts a day had exploded into sixty. Sub groups formed as people re-read the series in anticipation of the launch. They held video meet ups to talk about the characters and what they thought would happen next.

Emails poured in from book bloggers, reviews, and influencers. My notebook had extensive details on the influencers that had posted about Jess the most, what they preferred about each character, and our last correspondence. They seemed to like the attention, even if it wasn't Jess, which only fed the inferno.

Meanwhile, another conflagration continued to burn, this one far more real.

The voluntary evacuation hovered over Pineville like smoke from the Pinegulch fire. RV's sped away, half-emptying the lot. Locals eyed the plume as they walked around. Radio stations chattered updates. Tourism had started to slow because of restrictions on the National Forest, so Maverick grumped around the shop, mumbling about *bottom lines* and *in the red*.

Outside, a constant, sooty pillar decorated the horizon and loomed in every conversation and thought.

Meanwhile, I fretted over my phone and turned Jess pages like a dying woman whose pain could only be sated by these words. In my haste to read the books as quickly as possible, I made it all the way to book twelve, *Engagement is a Fantasy*.

Which is exactly where I found myself an hour later when the door opened to the Frolicking Moose.

Startled by the early customer—normally our morning rush went through the drive-through on their way up the canyon—my heart instantly fell into my stomach.

Presumed-Katrina, which Inner Me called her until I confirmed her identity, strolled inside. Days had passed since I'd last seen her. My constant perusal of the groups showed no sign of her yet.

She'd pulled her dreadlocks away from her face in a big bun and a bright smile crossed her lips. A short skirt, long boots, and silky top adorned her today. Several moments passed before I realized what she'd done.

Words burst out of me.

"You're Lolo."

The woman beamed. "You noticed!"

My mouth dropped open, startled by the similarities. Lolo was a character out of Jess's fourth novel, *Lust is a Darkening Hellscape*. Lolo was a quirky, fun girl that meets the love of her life on top of a mountain right before she goes bungee jumping. Heartbreak, near-death drama, and hijinks ensue. Everything about this girl looked like Lolo, as if Bastian had met presumed-Katrina in real life and slapped her on the page.

But . . . wasn't book four the book that presumed-Katrina hated? Confusion swamped me. What was going on here?

"Yes," I managed to stutter out. "Yes, I . . . finished a few days ago. It's . . . this is uncanny. Did you do it on purpose?"

"No!" she cried, laughing. "Isn't it weird? I read the book and thought Jess had written me into it *intentionally*."

Her face tightened a bit, making the smile seem a bit contrived. Was there something lurking behind that statement? I couldn't help but feel a dark vibe. It quickly disappeared as she rushed happily into her order.

"Can we replay what I bought last time? I'd love another strawberry frap with a cake pop, please."

"Of course."

Frap and a cake pop at six in the morning? Definitely the sort of sugary, spontaneous kind of thing that Lolo would do. Had done, now that I thought about it. The frap and the cake pop were *in the book*.

"I'm just going to park myself in the corner for a while, if that's okay," she continued, glancing around. The empty shop soon lost her interest. "I just finished my fourth read-through of book twenty in anticipation of the launch! My friends are flying in today to prep for our party. I'm excited to see other people after days of just filming by myself."

My blood turned cold.

Um, what?

"Filming?" My voice lifted in question. "What are you filming?"

"Oh, just a few things." She waved an errant hand. "You know, the mountain views and some documentary-like stuff."

Inner Me squeaked, *confirmed! This woman must be Katrina!*

I silenced her with a short, *that could be a coincidence. We must confirm it first.* I forced a bright smile. "Documentaries? Sounds so fun."

"Hope so," she chirped.

"Well, help yourself to the shop. WiFi password is on the board. Should be a quiet day. What name should I put on the order?"

"Kat is fine."

"With a K?" I managed to ask without choking.

"Perfect."

My mind tumbled over all she'd just revealed. Kat was close enough to Katrina that I dropped the *presumed* and mentally thought of her as Katrina. If that hadn't been enough, *filmmaking* and *documentary* all but confirmed it. Katrina settled into a chair near the wall that gave her a sweeping view of the entire shop as well as outside.

By sheer willpower, I managed to avoid looking at her every other second, but it wasn't easy. *Park myself in the corner for now* turned into an hour.

Then two.

Then three.

By ten o'clock she hadn't budged from her spot. I couldn't even snoop on her computer screen because of the angle of where she sat. Every now and then, I thought I saw a glimpse of a familiar social media site in the reflection of the window, but I couldn't be sure. She spent most of her time staring outside, deep lines between her eyebrows.

Whenever I could, I snuck a glance at my phone to check Jess's social media group. Of no great surprise was the fact that Katrina had activated and posted several times in the main Jess group. Mostly excitement for the launch, nothing that would give her away as being here, unfortunately.

Also nothing of concern.

I doubted she wanted to sniff out the Jess mystery alone, anyway, with all her girlfriends coming tonight. She didn't seem all that rushed, either. Instead, I pegged her as . . . watchful. Maybe hopeful. Nothing rabid, at least.

Somehow, I had to figure this out. The mystery of it would slay me if nothing else. But there was no way to really suss out the truth unless I cut her a super straightforward question.

Are you stalking Jess?

That seemed even more awkward. Plus, too high-risk. It might make it seem like I knew Jess. Questions and attention would follow. I had to either be more subtle, or not engage at all.

The implications of this woman being Katrina spread out. How long would she stay? Why was it worth it to her to figure out Jess in real life? There had to be some other motive behind it aside from sheer curiosity.

There could be a lot more people in on this, too. What if she had a separate conversation with other people that I couldn't see? She could be planning said documentary right now. She'd mentioned filming. Had she been haunting different neighborhoods or talking to other people to try to find Jess? I pictured her walking down the street, camera in hand, using a creepy voice to narrate her thoughts out loud.

Now you *are getting creepy,* Inner Me said.

True, I agreed, and shook out of the deepening thoughts.

The morning remained slow for in-person visits, but the drive-through continued with its usual pace until the lunchtime rush around noon.

Katrina actively scoured each person that walked in but never spoke to them. Thankfully, no one stayed for long. The lulls passed while I puttered through the daily checklist. With Katrina there, it felt weird to read Jess, despite my hunger to find out what happened next. How Bastian had hooked me so thoroughly, I had no idea.

Around one, I finished the latest round of tasks, audits, and answered questions when Bethany called in about another cancelled event related to the fire. After talking through the changes, Katrina stood up. I glanced up, startled by the movement. She slung her bag over her shoulder and smiled.

"Gotta go pick up my friends and get a few more shots. See you soon? Happy launch day in two days!"

With a wiggle of her fingers, she disappeared outside.

That, Inner Me murmured, *is not good news. What was she doing sitting here so long? And why will she see us soon?*

"I have no idea," I whispered, "but it's probably not good for Bastian."

* * *

That evening, I double checked the address on Bastian's text with the house I stared at now.

Correct.

With a grimace, I glanced back to the waiting home. Waist-high fence. Dark windows. Abandoned feeling. Creaky garage door. Faded white paint above a half-wall of red brick that had once probably been bright and happy.

Ooookay.

Definitely should have had Sione come. I glanced to the left, where Mrs. Cortez presumably lived. I had always appropriately pegged her as a hot chocolate-over-coffee kind of woman. I made a mental note to check on her tomorrow. For now, I had to go into this creeptastic house.

With a deep breath for courage, I shut my car door and started up the path. I kept my keys in between my fingers so I could slash out if I needed to, and approached. A rock scraped along the ground when I stepped onto the cement porch. I ignored it and felt along the edge of the door for the key. The tips of my fingers found it at the exact spot where I assumed a spider nest waited, so I quickly yanked it off and shoved it in the door knob. It twisted easily and the door swung open.

"Hello?"

Nobody responded, so I used my fingertips to press the door open wider. It groaned as it swung back, admitting blunted light into a mostly dark room. Despite an aged exterior, the inside had a warm, updated feel. Mostly-new carpet led down a short hallway. A bathroom to the left. Bedroom to the right, framed by a coat closet. I flipped on a light and shut the door, lest the kitty-in-question escape.

"Hello?"

I advanced a few steps, probably imagining a rustle in the back of the house. The kitchen and a living room opened up at the end of the hallway. The entire place smelled a bit like fire and burned wood.

Like Bastian.

I set my car keys on an oblong oak table ringed by matching chairs. A tower of wet cat food cans stood on a nearby counter with paper plates and plastic spoons. On the ground lay a small water dish, half full. Shiny cat toys littered the ground here and there.

Driven mostly by curiosity, I moved farther into the living room. A sectional filled up a portion of the space, facing a wide fireplace and a window that overlooked the reservoir. No television, which struck me as odd.

Pictures populated the mantle of the fireplace. I grinned at a dorky photo of what must have been high-school Bastian. He had his arm flung around the shoulders of a younger version of Hernandez. Bastian's skin was deeply tanned, almost burned. They stood in bright sunshine, grinning. I couldn't stop my giggle. They looked like they were twelve.

Other photos lived there, snapshots in time. A towering Black man, a lot like Bastian, had his arm around Bastian at high school graduation. Next to them, a girl with Down's syndrome and a bright, toothy smile stood at his other side, tiny and pale next to their broad frames.

My heart caught.

There are people that need me, he'd said.

Was this what he meant?

I spun around. More photos littered the walls. The coffee table. A desk tucked into the corner. Post-it notes littered the wall in front of it, a variety of colors and sizes. Chicken-scratch writing filled them, nearly illegible. As if someone here didn't want to forget something. Or *had* forgotten and required reminders.

The aging house clearly wasn't Bastian's. His father's, maybe. So where was he? Had Bastian's father passed away? I presumed the Black man was his father, because he filled most pictures. Was Bastian adopted?

A few older pictures of a woman with auburn hair and bright green eyes were displayed here and there, but not many. Bastian's mother, maybe? The resemblance wasn't strong to her, if so. What happened to her?

To any of them?

My curiosity only grew, expanding with more and more questions. I thought about texting Dagny to ask, but stopped myself. No, that felt like too much of an invasion. If I wanted Bastian's story, I needed to get it from Bastian. Really, I should just feed the cat and go.

But I couldn't help myself.

Grateful to have a second away from the strangely close rooms, I stepped outside to get the mail. The lawn was a short, rectangular box of land behind a wooden fence. My car waited just beyond it. I returned to the curb, reached into a mailbox made out of old license plates, and reached for the mail. Although I didn't *intentionally* look, when I returned inside to set the envelopes next to the rest of them on the counter, my eyes snagged the corner of one.

Memory Care Services.

Geez.

Was his father sick?

Something soft and silky touched my ankle. I jumped with a gasp and glanced down to see a calico cat threading itself around my legs. The purr melted me. I reached a hand down. The cat sniffed it, studied it, then butted its head against my palm.

"You are lovely," I murmured, then crouched next to it.

The silence of the house settled around me as I petted her. Eventually, I put a hand around her and lifted her up.

"Psycho, huh?" I murmured.

She purred against my jaw, boneless in my hands. Oh, this was a cat I could bond with. None of that holier-than-thou stuff.

"Yeah, you're not a tough nut to crack like your owner."

Unless Bastian's father was the owner. In which case, this puzzle continued to complicate.

Why had Bastian sent *me* here to take care of the cat? Surely Dagny would have happily taken over. Had it been a spur-of-the-moment decision? Hernandez and Bastian had clearly been friends for much longer than the hot minute that we had known each other.

Why not ask them?

I had my suspicions, but I also had my own emotions over this whole situation. Emotions I didn't really trust yet. As I had resolved before, I needed to move slowly. I laughed into the quiet house.

This was so beyond that now.

"The road this attraction leads down is a road that I've taken before," I said to twelve-year-old Bastian in a picture. "I want to like you, Bastian. And I'm reluctant to admit that I do. But I've done this before. Liked someone quickly. The road it took me down ended with heartbreak. Is it worth it?"

Time-frozen Bastian just smiled at me with a warmth and delight I'd only caught hints of now.

Also growth, Inner Me said. *The road with Jakob provided lessons, love, and good times. Those things too.*

"True."

So was it worth it?

With a roll of my eyes, I muttered, "Yes."

Will you ever move on if you're intentionally keeping yourself in the past? Inner Me asked. An echo of sorrow lived in the question.

"No, but what do I have if I move onto something else?"

Everything.

"Yes," I murmured. "I suppose you're right."

I set the silent back-and-forth into the depths of my mind to stew on.

"C'mon, kitty," I murmured as I scratched behind her ear. "Let's get you some fresh food and water, then send Bastian a video. I think he'd probably like to see you."

Chapter Sixteen

BASTIAN

Psycho purred through my phone, her head butting up against the camera.

Dahlia laughed and tumbled backward, nearly dropping her phone in the process. She sat on the kitchen floor. The layer of cat hair on top of her pants meant she'd likely been petting Psycho for a while.

"Sorry," she cried in the video sent not long ago. "Your cat is strong."

The corner of my mouth twitched up as she laughed again. Psycho attempted to climb on her lap. I could only tell by the way the video angled at her outstretched legs. Legs I'd like to have wrapped around me while I kissed her breathless.

"Anyway," she continued in the video, "not sure when you'll get this, but I got in the house and all is well. I was going to stop by and check on Mrs. Cortez, too, but I think she's still in the hospital. All the lights are off at her house. Oh, your mail is on the counter."

Finally, she flipped the video around and her bright face filled the screen. She blew a raspberry and wiped her lips off with the back of an arm.

"Sorry." She did it again. "Cat hair."

I laughed. The sound echoed off the nearby tree and drew a few interested gazes. Two guys were sitting on a log nearby, staring into the forest. They glanced my way, but I ignored them.

"Anyway, things are good to go for the launch in two days. Well, one-point-five days, technically. The social media groups are bursting at the seams. I actually requested to join all of them from my personal account so I can snoop around a bit more. Weird what goes on in some of those places. One of them is a writers group. They analyze your sentence structure. Enlightening. Do you really choose your adverbs carefully, with the intention of foreshadowing or creating a certain energy? Or does it just flow?"

A little ridge formed in her brow as she spoke. My brain mulled over her ingenious idea to join as a reader from her personal account. Why I hadn't thought of making a dummy account and watching that way, I had no idea.

She certainly went above and beyond what I asked of her. I liked the trust that built. If I had thought of that idea myself, I may not have asked her to snoop with her own name. Seemed like too much to ask. Now, however, she could really check what was being said.

I made a mental note to give her a bonus.

She sighed and leaned back against a chair. Psycho continued her obnoxious purring from where she stood on top of Dahlia's thigh, kneading. I felt jealous of that cat, because I'd like to get my hands on those thighs.

I shook the thought free. Dahlia ran a gentle hand along Psycho's back, not seeming to mind Psycho's relentless attention.

"Nothing concerning in any of the groups that I could get into," she continued thoughtfully. "One, out of Portland, required a certain 'password,'" she did air quotes "to enter it. I mean, come on ladies! What is there to hide? Well, maybe something. That is why I want in."

She held the camera closer to her eye.

"And I'm gonna get in."

I chortled. No, it didn't surprise me that people had branched off in their own groups. Rarely did I delve into the depths of what women said about Jess and her books on social media. Too overwhelming. I tried once and it locked me up for a week.

Priyanka did that kind of sleuthing for me, and said she thought the marketing team at my publisher tracked them also.

Platinum status, Pri had once said of Jess. *No publisher is going to dedicate that kind of marketing to an author unless they really sell.*

Which only made the pressure to stay hidden—and relevant—feel that much stronger. My attention flipped back to Dahlia. Psycho finally settled on her lap like she owned Dahlia now.

A very lucky cat.

"Emails are going much better now that I've read so many of the books." Dahlia leaned back against the table, hair on her shoulders. "I'm halfway through thirteen and closing in fast. Obviously, I won't get all of them read by the launch, but I'm close enough. I've mostly figured out what happens anyway. Sorry." She grimaced. "This video is probably too long. Send me any questions. Byyyyyye."

It clicked off too soon.

When I glanced at the time on it, it had run for over two minutes. Her first videos were about thirty seconds. Either she'd been growing into this, or I had. Or both. Either way, it wasn't long enough. I rubbed my hand over my eyes. Another week and I'd be home.

In less than two days, the book launched.

With a muttered hope for reception to hold, I navigated to my email, just to check. The gods of the internet let me in, and I stared at it in surprise.

The 1,456 emails I'd left her had whittled down to 245. Of those, only ten were fresh in the last few hours. The rest were scattered, old emails that I hadn't known what to do with, so I left there.

New labels populated down the side of the screen, and my mind caught on one titled BASTIAN. I left that page to deal with later, navigating to a new browser to log into my publisher.

With time zones, *Wanderlust is a Battle* would launch in Australia first. Preorder e-book sales would hit on the hourly sales report page starting before midnight tomorrow. Before that, however, the pre-launch marketing would likely show an uptick in sales on the other books in preparation for book twenty-one.

The page finally loaded. Sure enough, a spike in the sales graph clawed higher than usual. Jess often sold upwards of thousands of books a day, but the launch would push her into the tens of thousands. I shook my head and navigated away.

The launch hadn't even begun and madness already started.

For several minutes, my thoughts roamed to Dahlia's bright energy, her in the social media groups, and finally to the fire that awaited me again in the morning.

While I dug through the soil and broke my body with hard labor, she'd be launching my novel into the world. Dahlia created safety for my family now. So what was I doing here? Maybe I should finally pull the plug on wildland firefighting.

That would throw me into the writing business full time. I'd eventually have to let my friends know the truth, and embrace the obvious and most successful path.

Even as I thought it, the building darkness in my body prevented me from believing it.

No. Writing was an escape and I often loved it. But it wasn't my sole path. Would never be my sole path. I didn't like the idea of ever settling into one sole path, like my friend Grady.

Grady married, found his career, and thrived in his new happily-ever-after. Me?

I wanted more change than that.

Besides, writing wasn't real. None of it. Jess's stories? They were all . . . constructs. Maybe even buried hopes of being the man that one of those women wanted me to be. Or the life I *wished* Inessa could have lived or the life I would have given Dad after Mom died.

Whatever my motivation for weaving such complex romances, it wasn't something I wanted to survive on for the rest of my life.

At least, I didn't think so.

But maybe.

Sounds from fire camp filtered back through my mind. The steady day had given a gentle reprieve from the previous fire push, but the monster was drawing it's breath. In a few days when the wind kicked back up, it'd throw fire like a dragon. Thinking about fire is when I felt the answer all the way down to my bones.

This is why I fight fires, came the thought. *Because it's real.*

Chapter Seventeen

DAHLIA

Launch day dawned with a glittering pink sunrise and gentle wind out of the west. I closed my eyes, breathed in the smell of the forest, and sighed.

Inner Me crooned gently in the back of my mind. *This,* she said. *We want more of this and we want it with Bastian.*

I didn't correct her. Instead, I sat with the thought for a moment and didn't hate it.

"We can try," I said.

Then I scrambled off the bed with a happy little shout and headed to the counter, where my phone charged. "It's launch day!" I cried to no one in particular.

No messages from Bastian yet.

Dahlia: Thanks for taking my shift today. Let me know if things crash and burn.

Mav: No problem. I needed to audit some processes anyway. It's been awhile since I had to work here. Now I can update the binder.

Dahlia: GIF

A GIF of a little girl with bouncing ringlets blowing a kiss showed up on the screen. With Maverick covering my shift, I didn't have to worry about the launch happening without me. Asking him had felt a bit desperate, but now I was glad I did. I wanted my whole attention on the launch.

With the fire, tourism in Pineville had almost halted entirely. Hardly anyone wandered in for coffee yesterday, and Katrina didn't show herself again. I thought I saw her down the street from Bastian's house when I fed his cat. The person disappeared before I could be certain.

As his assistant, I felt like an extension of Bastian. He'd hired me to help things roll smoothly, and I couldn't do that while tamping beans and carting around gallons of milk. I wanted to be here for him.

Not that he'd even notice, but whatever.

Outside, growing light crept in from the edge of the horizon, which left the forest steeped in black. I shivered at the creepy effect and pulled my blanket closer around my shoulders. Never had I ever and never *would* I ever venture into the dark forest all by myself.

Bears. Moose. No thank you.

Another drink of coffee sent a bolstering shock through my system, pulling me a little further out of my sleep haze. I'd turned on every light in the RV to make sure I didn't fall back asleep. This perpetual lack of rest was going to add up.

Still so worth it, Inner Me sang, luxuriating in the deliciousness of book fourteen's heart-stopping kiss at the end.

"All right." I opened the laptop. "Time to get this party started."

Before I came into his life, Bastian had only posted occasional updates on social media. The haphazard moments when Jess appeared sent fans into wild tizzies.

He'd once posted about a RaiseMoney campaign collecting money for a company that supported special needs Olympics back in April. So many people donated to it with Jess's subtle nudge that the fundraiser finalized within twelve hours. They even wrote an article on it, thanking her for what she did.

Fortunately, my undeniable talent for the perfect GIF had spruced up his social media accounts in the last week. Not much, or it wouldn't feel sincere. I'd posted once every other day, responding here and there with appropriate emojis. Try as he might, he couldn't deny that emojis had as much response power as words, particularly as tiny little visuals.

The posts themselves were easy. I'd haunted emails he sent to Priyanka—apparently she demanded weekly updates—copied some of these words and tweaked them to make sense, then put them up. The fans had gone bonkers. One post garnered 1,000 comments and made me wish I had access to see if sales jumped.

Maybe Bastian didn't need a constant flow of books. Maybe he just needed to talk to his readers.

When I opened his email, there wasn't much to see. A few messages from across the ocean written by readers that had already started reading. A store requesting a book signing on his next tour. Notifications from Tweetastic—wait, Jess had a Tweetastic account?—and some vague emails from his publisher that I filed into his label. The social media accounts were a different result entirely.

I scrolled through the growing, burgeoning posts. Some of them were intentional spoiler threads already filling out. Selfies with various versions of the book populated. One woman posted a picture while driving, then talked about the narrator of the audiobook making her cry because she'd waited so long for this novel.

I grabbed my phone to text him.

Dahlia: Your life is bananas.

Not expecting a response, I set the phone aside. Moments later, it buzzed with a notification. I blinked, stared at it, then checked. My heart galloped for a moment when his name appeared.

He responded so soon!

Bastian: The launch is going that good?

Dahlia: You can text this early in the morning?

Bastian: We had to pull off the road to wait for lightning to pass. I have one bar of service.

Dahlia: Then let me update you.
GIF

I sent a GIF of a child rubbing their hands together in a maniacal, menacing way, then typed all my observations in quick-time fashion.

Dahlia: Social media is raging, although the influencers haven't posted yet. The e-book is spoken about more than the audiobook. Paperbacks have been sent, but no paperback-specific influencer has received them yet, from what I can tell. Emails are sparse. Did you know there's a Tweetastic account?

Bastian: Oops, forgot. Sorry

Dahlia: You had so many people talking about you there, the page wouldn't load.

Bastian: GIF

I burst out laughing at the GIF of a blushing little boy that whispered *sorry* and crept out of the frame. If Bastian hadn't had my heart before, his perfect GIF did it now.

Dahlia: Fortunately, I've got all day.

Bastian: Don't you have to work at the Frolicking Moose today?

Dahlia: Mav is covering for me.

Bastian: Because of the launch?

Dahlia: Of course! How could I show up for you while making cappuccinos? I got your back!

Several minutes passed before his next reply followed.

Bastian: Thanks.

I suppressed an eye roll. For being an author, he didn't have a lot to say in real life. Maybe he used up all his words in his books.

With a sigh, I turned back to the computer. Before too long, another text came.

Bastian: Any sign of Katrina?

I chewed on my bottom lip. *That* was the real question. I'd hesitated to back out of my shift because I wanted to see if Katrina showed up. Ultimately, I decided that it wouldn't matter if she did. Mav would have no idea what Katrina was talking about if she asked about Jess, and Katrina had girl-friends with her anyway.

Besides, I hadn't mentioned Katrina's appearance as the Lolo character to Bastian. It seemed too . . . weird . . . to say over a text. He returned in just a few days, which would be an easier time to let it spill.

Dahlia: No sign of Katrina problems yet.

Bastian: Good

The utter lack of hearing from his agent made me nervous, but I had no idea why. Surely, she emailed him to a personal account that he'd vaguely mentioned. Texted too, I would imagine. If I really wanted to snoop, I could probably get into his personal email, but I wouldn't do that.

From what little he'd said about Priyanka, she seemed like the involved type. His computational disarray and lack of connection to social media probably meant that he needed her to be the involved type.

Dahlia: Have you heard from Priyanka?

Bastian: Nah. She'll call when I tell her I'm back. She normally leaves me alone when I'm on fires.

For some reason, that didn't alleviate my concern.

Dahlia: Any updates on the fire?

Bastian: It died down a bit last night, but still creeping along. Nothing massively concerning right now except there's no rain. Humidity is up though.

I took that to mean higher humidity was a good thing, which

made sense. My head spun with all the weather talk running around the mountain. The voluntary evacuation had been issued, but people still hung around and waited. I'd never known what a pyrocumulous cloud was before this, and now I couldn't imagine what anyone here would talk about once this was over.

If Pineville survived.

Bastian: Looks like we're going to leave in five. I'll lose reception soon.

Dahlia: I'll send text message updates throughout the day.

Bastian: Can you make it video?

A huge smile slipped across my face. I sent him a selfie of me winking and pointing at him, followed by a GIF with an old man in board shorts saying, "You got it, dude."

Bastian: #bestassistantever

I set the phone aside and tried not to fall in love.

* * *

By the time the sun fully rose and morning slipped into place, a small thundercloud moved away from Pineville.

It didn't drop any rain that I could see, but the air had cooled. Only open sky lay behind the lone storm, and I felt stupid for investing any hope in actual moisture. Today would roll out as blistering hot as all the days before it. Time to get the air conditioning on before it was too late.

After making breakfast, changing into a pair of shorts and a tank, and coordinating a time to join Sione, Mark, and Stella at Adventura for dinner next weekend, I sat back down at the computer and my makeshift desk again.

Five emails cluttered the top of the inbox. All of them had the same subject line.

Priyanka Patel: To Bastian's Assistant: open this email.
Priyanka Patel: To Bastian's Assistant: open this email.
Priyanka Patel: To Bastian's Assistant: open this email.
Priyanka Patel: To Bastian's Assistant: open this email.
Priyanka Patel: To Bastian's Assistant: open this email.

With a heavy swallow, I obeyed. What could this development possibly mean? A quick note waited inside each email, reading the same thing each time.

To Bastian's New Assistant,

At 9:30 your time, I will be initiating a video call to this email account. Please answer it, as the purpose is to speak with you.

Sincerely,

Priyanka

My gaze darted to the clock in the corner of the desktop. Three minutes away.

Almost the moment the clock changed to the half hour, a screen popped up on the computer to announce Priyanka's call. I flattened my hair, shoved it out of my face, and hit the green answer button.

Seconds later, a middle-aged woman with short, subdued hair and a steady expression filled the screen. I forced a smile. She blinked twice, regarded me for the space of a breath, and spoke in a succinct voice.

"What's your name?"

"Dahlia."

"Dahlia, I'm Priyanka. You may call me Pri."

"Good morning, Pri."

She lifted one curious eyebrow. A moment stretched between us while we studied each other. Her gaze encompassed me faster than I could for her because I was stuck on the fact that she was Bastian's agent. This was the only other person that shared our secret. Her lovely expression and dark eyes made me, if I was honest, a tad jealous. He hadn't mentioned how attractive she was.

I shook myself out of it.

What are you thinking? Inner Me cried. *Don't be a jealous freak.*

I know! I cried. *I'm sorry.*

The truth sent a thousand nervous knives into my stomach. I only felt threatened because of the growing depth of my crush on him. I forced myself to focus back on Pri.

"You are the one he texted me about, I assume?" Priyanka asked. "The one coordinating with influencers and the social media around the launch."

"I'm responding to questions that come in the emails, particularly with influencers and readers, yes. *Coordinating* would be a generous term for it."

"And you're posting for Jess on social media. With GIFs and smiley faces."

"Yes."

"How has it been?"

I struggled to find the right word. Unlike Bastian, I had no skill in that world. "It's been fine. Enlightening, I suppose you could say?"

"That seems for the best."

The absolute neutrality of her tone stymied me. Obviously, she'd been checking on things. What did she think of it?

Her expression didn't give me a single clue. I deeply wanted her to like it.

"Yes." I cleared my throat. "He . . . let's just say he needed some help. I believe he cares about his readers but doesn't know what to do with them."

She blinked three times before her entire manner softened a bit.

"Yes," she said with finality. "He does. You have done well. I wanted to meet you and see if you needed anything while he's out on the fire. It can't be easy trying to figure out what must surely be a mess while he's constantly throwing himself into danger."

A hint of a blush rose to my cheeks. While figuring out his business hadn't been simple, it hadn't been arduous. Bastian had been more accessible than expected. Priyanka must still be under the belief that Bastian and I hadn't had any communication. *I* wasn't going to tell her otherwise.

"It's been fine," I said. "A few details to sort out while I read through the series, but it's manageable."

Her voice piqued. "You hadn't read the series?"

"No."

"Then how did he meet you?"

"I work at the coffee shop in Pineville. He met me there when he got off his last fire."

The sharp look that filled her eyes told me everything I needed to know. She knew *exactly* how sketchy my hiring had been. I didn't blame her for her concern.

"Are you qualified for this work?" she asked.

I laughed. "Not at all."

"Hmmm."

My amusement died in the face of her lacking response.

"Well, a little," I quickly said. "I did secretarial work before this job, then promoted to manager of a store, and I love social media. But do I do this specific thing for a living? Not before Bastian."

She looked off the screen to something—or someone—then nodded and turned back to me. Assessment had returned to her gaze. I forced myself to hold it because, deep down, I could admit that I wanted Priyanka to like me. Why it mattered, I couldn't fathom.

At the least, I appreciated that she must be one of the only people he consistently spoke to. Business relationship or not, she had insight into Bastian and he respected her.

For a guy like him, that meant something.

"Are you answering emails for him?" she asked. This time, I blinked several times. What had the defensive note in her voice meant?

"Well, yes, but . . . I'm not pretending to be Jess, if that's what you mean. I sign the emails as her assistant."

She hesitated. "Oh?"

I shrugged. "I'm just responding to the emails that I can help, like people that ask for PR opportunities or questions about the books or availability or translations. That sort of thing. The people who reach out to Jess personally are left for Bastian to respond to."

"And are you doing interviews for Jess?"

"Written ones that he's sort of pre-filled out. If I don't know the answer, I try my best guess. Sometimes he can text, so I send him the weird questions that no one on planet earth knows the answer to."

"No podcasts?"

I shook my head, incredulous. "No! Of course not. I . . . I'm not Jess. I refused. I couldn't take that on."

"I see."

"Do you?" The question came out of me before I could stop it. My gaze tapered. Although she'd given me no direct condescension, I felt it all the way through her tone. "Because I'm not sure you do."

Priyanka's nostrils flared as she drew in a deep breath. "You're right. When Bastian presented the idea to me, he wanted to pay someone to become Jess. I thought it was a bad idea. He never told me he had done otherwise, just sent a text that said it was taken care of. I wanted to . . . check in on it."

"Oh."

The implications rushed through my mind. No wonder she'd been a little testy. She thought I was trying to *become* Jess. To act like her at a time when Bastian would be unable to direct what I said and did. It was the prime opportunity for someone to really take over Jess's brand and financially benefit. An ideal chance to put Bastian on a hook and drag him where I wanted.

Pri was just looking out for him.

That thought sent a noodle-like feeling all the way through my body, and I sank lower in my chair.

"Ooooh," I drawled. "I see. No, no. Absolutely not. He sort of presented the idea of me acting like Jess initially, but it sounded like the very worst possible plan. I shut it down and told him no."

Her lips twitched with the second sign of humanity I'd seen. "Did you talk him out of it?" she asked.

"He'd mostly talked himself out of it by the time he and I spoke," I said with a rueful smile, "but I helped it along. I could tell he didn't really want to go that route, but wasn't sure what else to do."

Her teeth shone white when she grinned, and all tension left her body. "I'm happy to hear it. You've done a lovely job with the posts. I recognize some of what's said, which means you've found his emails to me."

"Guilty."

"Smart."

"That doesn't feel like I violated your privacy or something?"

She shrugged. "Nah. It's fine. These are strange circumstances. Besides, using his words keeps it close to him, but helps the readers understand the books better. They've certainly been more active than usual, and they were already quite active. You should work for a marketing team in New York publishing."

I snorted. "They couldn't afford me."

She tilted her head back and laughed, her glossy back hair sliding around her ears as she did so. A diamond pendant sparkled at her throat. When she stopped laughing, I relaxed completely.

"Jess is safe," I said. "So is Bastian, for that matter. I'm just making sure emails get answered and opportunities aren't missed. There's a fan that, I think, might have tracked him to here somehow, but I haven't been able to confirm."

"That would be troubling," she murmured.

"Let's hope not."

"I believe Jess will make the push for bestseller," Pri said. She glanced to the side, as if looking at another screen on her computer. "Sometimes the retail websites are slow to update their bestseller positions, but we'll know more by the end of the day. I can't remember the exact number, but if she sells at least 15,000 copies today, we would be safe to secure the slot."

"What if she doesn't?" I asked.

Pri shrugged. "Then she doesn't. It's a nice distinction and title to hold, but ultimately only means that a lot of readers bought her book." She gave a quick wink. "I believe Jess will easily achieve it this time."

I smiled. "Good. She deserves the distinction."

"Agreed. Keep me updated," she said. "Bastian is quiet, and I tell him he holds the honor of being my most difficult client, but he's also my favorite. Don't tell him that. Not that he'd let it go to his head, or anything. He's actually quite humble."

"I understand."

"And if I can do anything from my side, I will."

"Thanks, Pri. It was good to meet you."

"You as well."

The screen closed before I could issue an official *goodbye,* but that seemed less awkward anyway. For some reason, meeting Priyanka and finding approval made me feel a step closer to Bastian.

To . . . something that loomed ahead.

The sound of the silence that followed crackled slightly, like fire burning every bridge to the unknown, vague future that I still hadn't built yet.

Chapter Eighteen

BASTIAN

The launch of my twenty-first novel passed in a smoky blur.

After texting Dahlia, I had to mentally set aside all the implications that her supportive text message built inside of me. The words looped through my head for minutes before I could dismiss them.

Of course! How could I show up for you while making cappuccinos? I got your back!

She did, in fact, have my back.

Maybe something more.

With that thought, I put a mental wall up and dove into fire work. I couldn't be at the Frolicking Moose, so I had to be wholly here. Divided attention would only endanger me and my team, so I stuck to the chainsaw and cleared line like a machine. Trying to forget what I couldn't control gave me ample fuel.

Smoke stung my eyes and filled my lungs most of the day. We worked ahead of the fire, but the air remained thick as custard anyway. Char drifted around the mountains and cast a haze over everything. It became part of me. By the time we left, I almost didn't know myself from the smoke.

Showers were rare for this job. Some wildland firefighters wore their grime like a badge of honor. After ten-something days without scrubbing off under streaming water, my skin had started to itch. By this part of the summer, I'd usually gotten used to it. The heat of the sun and the dryness had increased tenfold this year, though, and everything felt worse. Some days, salt dried on my skin in a white, powder-like grit that I'd rub off and replace within hours of more back breaking work.

As I settled back onto my pad that night, I still hadn't let myself think about the launch. About *Wanderlust is a Battle* or even about Dahlia.

There was too much angst to let my thoughts stay there for too long. When I finally did think about it, everything settled like a weight.

Before I turned to my phone, which I had ignored while it charged in the truck, I sat in the fear of what would come next. Launches inevitably meant more attention. Had Katrina figured out my secret and outed me? Had the hopeful push for the bestselling slot failed? Did the influencers come through? Was there a flood of issues and nothing happened?

The anxiety sat on my chest like a constricting weight until I finally muttered a curse word and flipped my phone over.

Two video messages from Dahlia waited and a plethora of text messages.

Dahlia: Your sales ranking finally topped #5 around noon. And . . .
GIF

Her GIF of blowing trumpets made me raise an eyebrow.

Almost a full minute later, a picture finally downloaded. I zoomed in, startled to see a picture of the computer screen.

After a beat, I finally comprehended what the array of numbers meant.

Damn. Jess had hit number one on her launch.

I mean, I did.

My thoughts bumped over themselves for several moments. I sat in them, unsure of what I felt. Should there be more excitement about the number one slot? Of course, I was proud of Jess. Relieved for the income that it would provide to Inessa and Dad, but . . .

But what?

I clicked the first video with an unsettled feeling. Dahlia's usual smile calmed my queasiness.

"Hey! Just grabbing some lunch. Everything is looking good here. Social media is steady. Initial reports show that everyone loves the book. Emails have been simple. Talked to Pri and I love her. There are some trolls mucking up that one review site, but otherwise nothing to report."

The video clicked off almost as quickly as it started. I blinked.

Wait, what?

I navigated to the next video. She stood outside this time, the gleam of the RV filling the background. She'd pulled her hair up and wore it in a high ponytail, revealing the graceful curve of her neck. I swallowed. Her teeth shone a lustrous white when she smiled through a pair of aviators that reflected the image of her phone.

"Hey again! Nothing big and new. Just been keeping on top of emails most of the day. The groups are exploding. There's been like 100 posts today. Some of the closed groups have even let me in, like they have open enrollment now or something."

Behind her glasses, I imagined her eyes rolled so dramatically, I chuckled.

"No sign of Katrina anywhere, and I'm just about to finish book fifteen. You're number one on most fiction lists that I can see. Priyanka sent me a few other places to track. I don't have access to the reports, but it's safe to say you hit number one for not just one bestseller list, but *all* of them, I think."

Thankfully, she didn't cut the video off at the end of her report, but rambled about a few more things. I watched it two more times, just to cement the fact that one of my books had launched and I didn't have to expend all my emotional effort over it. The whole thing made my brow furrow.

Did I overdramatize things?

How was this so much easier for her?

Launches normally left me emotionally wrung out. On the rare occasion that one of my books released while I was on a fire, I tried not to think about it and jeopardize my safety or anyone else's. An almost impossible task.

During the winter and spring when I launched new books, I spent the whole day just trying to understand what to do, how to talk to these women, and how to display compassion or empathy or excitement. Those things came far more naturally to Dahlia.

Which, in hindsight, felt pretty obvious.

I let out a long breath, grateful that the day was almost over though I'd had almost zero part of it. I'd check the sales later. They didn't matter as much as what Dahlia had done for me today.

Bastian: Thanks for the updates. And for everything you did. Sounds like it was a good launch.

I stared at the screen and wondered if I should say more. Compared to her natural brightness, my responses felt bland. Her reply arrived moments later. I lingered so deep in my mind I almost dropped the phone when it vibrated in my hands.

With a shake of my head, I cleared the cobwebs.

Dahlia: Stop it. It was a GREAT launch! At least, I think it was. I've never done this before.

Bastian: You're right. It was awesome.

Dahlia: Awesome? It's way better than that! When you get back in three days, I'm going to take you out to dinner.

Bastian: I'll take that offer.

I sent the reply before I could overthink it—because overthink it I would. Thankfully, she didn't make me wait.

Dahlia: It's a date.
GIF

The GIF that followed showed two pretentious people lowering themselves at a finely lit dinner, clearly high-end. At the last second, the GIF exploded into a party. They jumped into the middle of a mosh pit, hair and clothes unwound. I snorted.

A jumble of things that I wanted to say to Dahlia ran through my head, but I didn't know how to thread them into sentences.

My fingers itched. If I had a blank page in front of me, I'd know what to do. I'd know *exactly* what to say. If I were Rodrigo or Adrick or any of the other males I usually wrote, this wouldn't be so hard. Life was so much easier to experience through them.

Instead, I tucked my phone underneath my pillow, stacked

my hands behind my head, and tried not to think about how much I wanted to go back to Pineville. The number one slot, the launch, even Inessa and Dad . . . none of those occupied my mind. Not even thoughts of a hot shower or the feeling of being clean.

Only Dahlia.

Chapter Nineteen

DAHLIA

Three days later, Lizbeth blinked as she stared at me through wide eyes.

"Shut. Up."

She'd wound her silky red hair into a braid, then a bun on top of her head. A few tendrils dropped down around her ears, creating a fuzzy, halo-like appearance. Freckles smattered the bridge of her nose. She reminded me of a fairy.

An adorably-pregnant one.

"All of them." I gestured toward the stack of nineteen romance books in front of her. "I couldn't stop. I've been reading like a maniac the last two weeks because of the launch."

She blinked. "The launch?"

Too late, I realized my blunder. With a smile meant to smooth over a bolt of fear, I said, "Yes! The new Jess book? I wanted to be in on the action."

"Oh, right!" She squealed, her petite hands clapping. "The new book. So good. Totally worth it. I read it in four hours in between coding new prebuilt components before I worked on issues with JavaScript plugins. Hello? Not surprising. Love me some bootstrap, right?"

My brain scrambled every time she slipped her website programming into our talks. Seeing my expression, she brightened.

"In other words—I knew it! Romance is changing your life. You went from a hater to a believer. I'm the shiiiiiz."

My mouth remained open, torn. What could I say? While mostly right, she wasn't entirely wrong. I never hated romance. I . . . danced around it. I inwardly sighed. Holding Bastian's secret wasn't easy. Let her have her moment. The woman was pregnant. She needed every win.

"You were right, Lizbeth. These books are incredible."

Admitting it caused me no pain, although I would have expected it to kill me just a few weeks ago. It had been just under twenty days since Lizbeth first introduced me to Jess, and I was already done with all twenty one novels. My high school English teacher would have fainted with pride.

Lizbeth sobered, leaning one arm against the counter.

"I know. The books really are that good. The launch a few days ago? It was a *big* deal. People plan vacations around these launches. Fandoms everywhere let out a collective squeal the moment the books arrive on our e-readers. I also hosted a party in the bakery for my local Jess fan club. Twenty women showed up as strangers and left best friends. Romance at work."

By sheer willpower, I managed to keep a straight face.

"So I've heard."

My phone buzzed in my pocket with a text. Could it be Bastian? The thought sent a thrill through me. He would return home today at some point and every single minute dragged by. Excitement sent frissons of giddiness into me at odd intervals, and I ended up making a quiet giggle-squeal every seven minutes.

Lizbeth's left arm held the twenty-first Jess novel anchored firmly against her ribcage. A ratted napkin—her bookmark, I presumed—frayed out the end of the book. A contemplative expression had come over her.

"Jess did an interview, you know?"

Real interest piqued my voice higher. "Oh?"

Lizbeth waved a hand. "Written, of course. She does those every now and then. There was a secret, quiet hope amongst a bunch of her fans that this launch would be when she revealed more about herself. There was more social media noise, as expected, but nothing concrete." She rolled her eyes. "Not counting that stupid post from that Kat girl."

My heart almost stopped. All my considerable willpower barely kept my restraint in place. I cleared my throat.

"What post are you talking about?" I asked.

Lizbeth tilted her head back and groaned. "This one girl claims she found Jess, but she has yet to provide any real evidence."

"You said her name is Kat?"

"Katrina?" Her perky nose wrinkled. "Something like that? Dunno. I've seen her before in some of the groups, but not often. I thought I saw a comment about her being a filmmaker or something? Anyway, these kinds of things surface now and then, but nothing comes of it. Everyone wants to figure out who Jess is. Sometimes, I think I'd rather Jess stay hidden. The mystery of it is kind of *novel*."

She released an adorable laugh. I loved it when she cracked herself up. My hands snuck into my apron pocket for my phone, but I closed my fingers into a fist to stop them.

Wait until Lizbeth is gone to look, I thought, filled with the urgency to find that post right now. *Don't jump the gun and act all weird now!*

Lizbeth let out a long breath, then winced. She held a hand against her lower back.

"You okay?" I asked.

She huffed a smile. "Fine. I'm just ready to ditch this pregnancy and get her in my arms already. I'm tired of having her on my hips."

"Soon the many eternities of the third trimester will be over."

A weary smile came next.

"I'm barely starting the third trimester, so it certainly feels like an eternity. Any news on the fire?"

She hooked a thumb to the north. The trailing, indomitable cloud filled half the sky today. It still made me shudder.

"Should be a calm night," I said. "No wind, but very dry."

"Good for no winds, at least." She scowled. "JJ and I have been watching the reports out of the fire camp every night. Bleak, aren't they?"

Last night, I'd been riveted to the computer to get the update. The sheer number of people such a fire required struck me as amazing.

"Last night wasn't so bad," I said. "It's the wind that really wreaks havoc, isn't it?"

"The fire is moving toward Adventura." She chewed on her bottom lip. "Mark and Stella packed up computers and valuables and brought them to our place in Jackson City, just in case."

"Sione texted me about it."

"Think it'll be okay?"

"Of course! That fire has a highway, a river, and a hotshot crew it has to get through first." I waved a hand. "Adventura will be *fine*."

The last thing this pregnant lady needed was something else to stress about. Or maybe, on the flip side, it would help her out. If she stressed about the weather, maybe she wouldn't think about being pregnant.

Either way, big things awaited.

The door jangled, admitting JJ, her tall drink of water husband. His shoulder-length hair was pulled into a man bun that made lesser women swoon, especially with a jaw cut like a diamond. I smiled at him and he smiled back. JJ had a special warmth and a gentleness I couldn't help but be jealous over.

In seconds, he was at Lizbeth's side with a concerned brow.

"You okay?"

She smiled dotingly at him. His hand found the small of her back. "Fine." She waved a hand and yawned. "Just celebrating Dahlia's foray into romance. She reads so fast it puts me to shame."

JJ smiled. "Lizbeth is spreading her romantic fairy dust again, I presume?"

"You presume correctly. But it's not unwelcome," I quickly added.

He chuckled, curling her close into him. She leaned on him, and I wondered if she actually let him take some of her physical weight. They were so sickeningly cute together, I couldn't look away. My brain kept wandering over to Bastian, and I needed it to stop. Because where my brain wanted to go with thoughts of Bastian and romance and grossly adorable interactions, I didn't.

Yes, you do, Inner Me sang.

Okay, I couldn't deny that was true. Bastian had given me breadcrumbs that led me to believe he was interested in me, but until I knew for sure, all was supposition. *Then* I'd swim in thoughts of Bastian, romance, and adorable interactions.

Not a moment before.

Time. We just needed time. On the flip side, I wanted *less* time. I just wanted to see him again, already! A car pulled up outside, parking in the far slots. In my pocket, my phone vibrated with a text at the same time.

Lizbeth straightened with another yawn. "We should go," she murmured, and I noticed the pull on her energy then. She did look tired. JJ studied her in concern as he veered her toward the doors. I couldn't stop watching them together. His long, graceful form against her adorable baby belly.

They captured my attention so long I barely noticed the customer that slunk into the coffee shop after they left. All I saw was a pair of brown, muscled arms that gave way to a familiar tank top, and a head of dark black hair. My heart plummeted all the way into my stomach as I straightened up.

"Jakob?" I whispered.

He grinned.

I swore.

* * *

Jakob standing in the Frolicking Moose was a dichotomy my brain couldn't process.

For several long moments, I stared at him, lost in memories. Some of them were good memories. Laughing on the beach. Long dinners with my family. Dancing under the stars on our back porch. Some of them were not-so-good memories. Spans of silence that lasted for days. Clenched teeth. Frustration. Angled expressions, hard as nails.

For that brief spell of time when he stood before me again, wordless himself, all I could do was think.

He broke my trance with a voice I remembered all the way to my bones.

"It's good to see you, Dahlia."

His words trembled a little bit. He'd tucked his hands into his pockets, but I wondered if they shook like mine. It had only taken a few seconds of us staring at each other to produce a physical reaction in my body.

Six months.

I hadn't seen him or heard his voice in six months.

Our breakup had been amicable. Or, at least, not angry. Not desperate. Not woven with deceit and treachery and unfaithfulness. The relationship had been slowly dying. A general letting go. Drifting apart. The most agonizing death of love: disinterest.

When we broke up, I dissolved all ties to our former life together. My job, my apartment, my life outside LA. I packed, sold, pawned, and got rid of everything until all I had was cash-in-hand and the urge to leave.

Which led me right to my RV.

For months, I'd wondered if I'd made a mistake. Could love be resurrected? After five years together, did we not care enough to work hard and save each other? If so . . . why not? Why couldn't five years of our combined lives be enough of a base for us to *fight* for each other?

Those questions plagued me again.

He stepped forward once. The counter stood between us, but I shifted back out of instinct. That made me feel more confused. Jakob posed no danger to me, yet I didn't want him near.

Why?

He stopped, clearly troubled.

I licked my lips and asked, "What are you doing here?"

Disbelief, even defensiveness, colored my tone. Jakob rubbed a hand across the back of his neck. He studied me, but didn't make eye contact. Like he wanted to drink me in, but couldn't face me.

"I came to talk to you," he said.

"All the way from LA?"

He hesitated. Did I imagine that he seemed to silently ask himself the same doubt-filled questions? Why did I feel like a wary cat?

"Yes, from LA." He nodded with a half shrug. "You've . . .

you haven't been around very much and I wanted to see you. Six months is a long time. Your parents said you've been driving the RV around this whole time."

"Oh," I whispered. "Yes. I have."

You don't want to talk to him, Inner Me pointed out, sounding a bit gleeful. *You once thought you'd give anything for him to stand in front of you again, just like this. But now that he's here, do you feel the relief you expected? The elation?*

No, I thought.

The truth shocked me.

"I can see that this may not have been the best idea," he said quietly. His fingers drummed a beat on his pants. "You don't seem like you want to talk."

"I mean . . . I guess I do?" I rubbed a hand over my forehead. "I'm sorry, Jakob. You've just . . . you've taken me by surprise. I'm not really sure what to think."

His mien came across calmer than I would have expected. This casual Jakob looked a lot like the man I originally fell in love with. The gentle touches. Quiet words. Jakob had always been easygoing . . . until he became bored and routine and disinterested.

The return to the Jakob I loved should have brought a complicated jumble of emotions. Instead, I didn't feel as much as I expected. Affection rooted in shared history, sure. Maybe some regret and lingering sadness. The rush of attraction, though, didn't follow. I stepped back again until I felt the other counter at my hip. He didn't venture closer.

"How'd you know I was here?" I asked.

"You posted about it on social media."

My nostrils flared. Yep. Definitely did that. A bit creepy that he'd followed through on it, though, without contacting me. A flicker of movement in the parking lot caught my eye. A group of four girls moved toward the shop.

Sweet baby pineapple, as Lizbeth would say.

A reprieve.

"I can't talk right now. I'm at work and some customers are just about to come in."

"I'll wait."

My nostrils flared. Could I kick him out? No. Yes, I could. Did I want to? A little bit, yet not all that much either. Could I make *less* sense? My thoughts were half-complete gibberish now.

Part of me saw this very unexpected opportunity as a gift. I longed to talk to him. Sit down, hear what he'd been doing, and why he came. How were things different without me? How were they the same?

We could talk about the good times that mattered. Laugh over old jokes and our favorite old whodunnit mystery movies. The other part wanted him to go so I could think through this.

The girl leading the pack opened the door and stepped inside. Katrina. Or was it Lolo? I still couldn't wrap my head around the strangely perfect in-person representation to one of Jess's characters. Three days had passed since the launch, and I hadn't seen any sign of her. This must be the group of women that came to do a Jess retreat with her.

Instinct kicked in, saving me from myself.

"Give me a few minutes to help them," I said quietly to Jakob, meeting his inquiring gaze. "I'd like to speak with you."

Lips pressed, he nodded.

"Welcome to the Frolicking Moose," I called as the women assembled in front of the counter. "What can I get you?"

Jakob faded to a table not far away, distant enough he didn't crowd customers but close enough he wouldn't be forgotten.

Katrina popped up to the counter first, a grin on her face. Despite the heat, she wore a pair of black leggings beneath ratted jean shorts. A flowered tank top and bright sunglasses adorned her from waist up. The exact outfit Lolo wore when Adrick confessed he loved her and her quirky self, if I remembered correctly. In the novel, Adrick yanked her close, put his hand in her back pocket, and scolded her for looking so perfect.

Then he kissed her until she couldn't breathe and slid a ring on her finger in the meantime.

I swallowed when Bastian interposed over Adrick and my brain unravelled.

"My usual!" Katrina cried. "I'll pay for the rest of these ladies. We're just finishing up their Jess retreat. They're heading home later today."

"Are you staying with us a bit longer?" I asked with a falsely eager smile while I reached for her cake pop.

"A few days." She gave a vague wave. "Just wrapping a few things up. Mind if we sit at my usual spot?"

"Of course not."

Jakob's unexpected appearance robbed my energy for my favorite game, so I let them order their drinks without guessing. The work gave my thoughts a chance to stop paddling upstream and go with the current.

While the ladies jabbered quietly amongst each other, words like *Jess* and *next book* and *can't wait* flew around several times. I couldn't hear any deeper than that.

I poured Jakob a coffee with half cream and too much sugar and set it on the table next to him without making eye contact. He murmured a thank you, but I had already returned to the counter.

Out of the corner of my eye, I studied him. He stared at the table, outside, the other girls. Every now and then, a musing expression would cross his face. One of them asked him for the time. He leaned forward, replied, and they spoke for a few minutes.

My heart didn't flip-flop.

My stomach didn't flutter.

The visceral reactions toward Jakob had long since stopped. Until this moment, I hadn't truly accepted it. Now, I had to.

I stared down the face of our failed relationship . . . with gratitude. We really *hadn't* been great together. Fine, yes. Steady, of course. But we lacked luster. Confidence. Change. Our life could have been platonic and safe, but how much life would we have missed out on?

For the first time in six months, I was grateful toward Jakob. He'd done the hard thing that I didn't.

He'd stopped what didn't really make us happy.

I couldn't forget he existed, even though that seemed like an easy path. All that time. All the layers of connection we'd forged. It couldn't and shouldn't be erased. Neither, however, should it be continued.

For the first time in months, Inner Me remained utterly silent. Maybe because I'd finally landed on the branch I'd been fluttering around for months.

Fifteen minutes later, all four ladies popped back to their feet. Katrina folded her computer and shoved it into her bag. They gathered up all the Jess books they'd laid out and headed toward the door in a flood of estrogen.

"See you later!" Katrina called, waving.

"Travel safe!"

As they disappeared, I turned and squared my shoulders to Jakob. My mind fluttered to Bastian and—No.

I yanked it back with a firm reprimand. *He is not mine to think about that way,* I sternly told myself.

For the first time in six months, I was ready for this conversation with Jakob. Seeming to sense my stare, he glanced over. Then he leaned forward, arms on his legs. He had smooth lips that turned into a charming smile when he wanted them too.

"I won't stay long, Dahlia. I just wanted to see you. I guess

. . . I guess I felt I needed some closure. The whole thing happened faster than I thought it would. I don't think I was ready to never see you again."

His expression morphed into a maze of serious lines. He was as familiar to me as childhood. Jakob and Sione had been good friends for years. Guilt over mudding up their friendship after we broke up plagued me again. They were cordial, but they hadn't returned to what they'd had before.

"I know you don't want me here," Jakob said softly.

"It's not that."

He lifted a dark brow. "Oh?"

"I just didn't expect you." I grabbed my drink, circled around the counter, and sat across from him, startled by how easy it felt to be casual. "I'm glad you came. You're right. I think I needed some closure too. It's been six months but . . . after five years, that doesn't seem like all that long."

He nodded.

My gaze narrowed. "How are you? What's going on back at home? How's work?"

He hesitated, then leaned back against the seat. His strong legs sprawled in front of him—rugby legs. Sione and Jakob used to play with the other neighborhood kids. Sione had size, but Jakob was faster.

"It's good."

A brief summary of our shared life followed. Same routine at work. Same people. Same places. He still had the same apartment. In fact, everything sounded the same.

While I wallowed in the uncertainty of the future, he wallowed in the miasma of the unchanging present. With a bit of a jolt, I realized I'd chosen the better path.

The path of my new self.

Although not perfect, I preferred the uncertainty of what lay ahead of me to the unending sameness at home. There had been safety in that for awhile, and I'd probably have more of it in my future. For now, however, I looked forward to what lay ahead.

I schooled back a giddy laugh.

A lock of hair fell onto Jakob's forehead, but he shoved it away.

"Are you trying to grow your hair out?" I asked with a tilt of my head toward him. Ever since we'd been together, he'd always worn it short. A hint of color dusted the top of his cheeks as he played with a lock.

"Yes."

I laughed. "Lofa got to you after all! How did he finally convince you to grow it out?"

"I used to have long hair," he said, half-defensively. "It's time to try it again. Do something different." He eyed me. "And what about you? Do you like having an RV and driving around?"

"Being lost?" I quipped.

"No." He smiled. "Maybe now you're found."

My teasing expression faded. "Yeah," I murmured, then dropped my gaze to fiddle with my cup of black coffee. "Maybe. I do enjoy the RV. I haven't been many places, honestly. Visited some aunts and uncles and my grandparents."

"Tour of your family?"

I grinned. "You know it. Now I'm here with Sione."

"Looks like a great place."

The answer hummed all the way to my bones. "It's a wonderful place."

"No ocean."

I sighed. "No ocean. The mountains almost make up for it. When they aren't on fire, anyway. I still miss the surf."

We fell into small talk, discussing the career paths I considered, his plans to see his grandparents in Tonga at Christmas, and updates on his family in California.

When the chatter dissolved, so did the conversation. Though I wracked my brain for something else to say, it didn't come.

Hadn't it always been that way, though? We never had much to say to each other. We enjoyed each other, but beyond our love of people and our culture, we didn't have much else in common.

"I'm happy," I finally said. He met my gaze. "I'm grateful, too. If you hadn't broken things off, I wouldn't have. We'd still be in something that didn't really serve either of us. So thank you."

An expression I couldn't read flitted through his eyes. His shoulders lifted with a breath, swelling high on his neck, then dropped all at one. He swallowed and said, "I thought you hated me."

I laughed. "At first, I think I did. Now? I see it."

He closed his eyes. "Thank you. That's . . . that's what I needed to hear. I worried I'd made a mistake or . . . I don't know."

His eyes opened again, a rich velvet that I'd always consider a friend.

"Thank you, Dahlia. I miss you but I know we made the right decision. I just needed to be sure."

He stood up, arms held out. Willingly, I stepped into a warm, familiar embrace. A rush of affection welled up inside me, but it was soft. Present, but not overpowering. Nothing like what I felt when I thought of Bastian.

I stepped out of Jakob's embrace, but I held onto his arms. He smelled like home. "Flying or driving?" I asked.

"Flying," he said. "Going to stop, see Sione, and fly out tonight."

"Be safe doing all of that. And thank you. That's . . . a big trip to make for a single conversation. Give my mother a hug for me?"

He smiled. "Of course. The trip was long but worth it."

The door opened and the smell of smoke entered the shop on a breeze. My head snapped to the right to find a familiar figure silhouetted by the sun. Bastian stood there, halfway inside, his body crowding the doorway. I sucked in a breath.

Good heavens, but Bastian could enter a room.

Bastian's gaze darted from me to Jakob and back again. Suddenly self-conscious, I stepped all the way out of Jakob's arms and kept my attention centered on Jakob or else I'd never get through this moment. I'd throw myself into Bastian's arms or kiss him or something equally desirable and crazy.

"Have a good trip," I said to Jakob. "Sione is up the canyon, really easy to find. Follow the signs to Adventura. Park in the lot there, and go inside the main building. Mark or Stella will find him for you. He'll be excited to see you."

Clearly seeing a change in me, Jakob studied my face, then Bastian. He opened his mouth, then closed it again. His expression became a silent question, but I shook it off. *It's good*, I mouthed.

Jakob reluctantly nodded, then sent an assessing look to Bastian, who stood tall at the door.

By sheer willpower, I didn't look at Bastian. My heart galloped in my chest as Jakob gathered keys to a rental car and headed for the door. When he stepped outside, he sent one last wave, a long look, and turned his back.

Moments later, I stared right into Bastian's ocean-sapphire eyes again.

Chapter Twenty

BASTIAN

Getting released from the fire, shucking my stuff at the house, and hopping into a shower felt like heaven.

Psycho remained fed, happy, and purring. I threw some food into my stomach, dirty clothes into the laundry, and hauled back out of Dad's house to head into Pineville, all within sixty minutes of arriving back home.

Then all the excitement I felt at seeing Dahlia broke the moment I walked into the Frolicking Moose.

Didn't take a genius to sense tension in the room once I arrived. Whether it was good or bad tension, I couldn't be sure.

Nor was it hard to figure out that the other guy didn't love me being there. Whoever he was, he didn't appear to be a stranger. Family, maybe?

Whoever he was, somehow, I'd shown up at the exact wrong time. Should I leave?

Nah.

I'd never roll over like that.

Besides, if Dahlia didn't want me here, which I sincerely hoped wasn't the case, she'd tell me.

A thousand questions ran through my mind when the guy stepped up to the door and gave me a quick nod. Once he left, I looked right at her.

Dahlia stared at me with her heart in her eyes. Terror, elation, shock. I read every single emotion there. All my willpower kept me from gathering her up in my arms and kissing those full lips. The fact that we hardly knew each other struck me again, rendering my excitement to see her as completely insane.

Sometimes, insanity felt so good.

Her voice pulled me from the edge of my thoughts.

She swallowed and softly said, "Hey."

The top half of her wavy black hair was pulled into a ponytail, the rest lay on her shoulders. A tank top with a dahlia flower on it led to tight black shorts that made me want to die. She stood three seconds—two long strides—away. That's all it would take for me to pick her up, slam her back against the wall, and—

"Hey," I croaked.

She let out a long, pent up breath. "I wasn't sure when to expect you. I . . . I hoped you'd come by."

"Why wouldn't I?"

A tentative smile appeared on her face, banishing the uncertainty that had originally shown up. I tucked my fingers into my palm to keep from reaching out for her. No, it was too soon. Although I craved her touch and dreamed of how soft her skin would feel, I couldn't break that barrier yet.

Then Dahlia launched herself into my arms.

I caught her out of shock. My arms went around her, but bright, blaring alarms rang through my mind. What did I do now? What was appropriate? If I had my way this second, we'd be in the empty loft, tearing—

She gave a little sigh. Seconds later she extricated herself out of my arms. Once she stepped back, her missing warmth felt like a lost limb. I wanted to claw it back.

"Glad you're safe," she said.

Her beaming smile rendered me further speechless. No sign of sheepishness appeared in her grin. I went with it, eager for any sign that she could be as interested in me as I was in her. Because I was.

No denying that now.

"You're back and you're safe." She put her hands on her hips. "That's a great starting point. You look like you've showered. Did you get back earlier today?"

I nodded and followed her farther into the shop. She returned behind the counter and reached for a coffee pot. I sat at the closest table, not far away. This was the girl I'd been mooning over through video and dreams. Part of me expected to be a little bit disappointed at real life Dahlia. How could any girl, even Dahlia, measure up to the version that I'd built in my head while in the mountains?

She did.

"Around noon." I cleared my throat, managing an awkward smile. "You definitely didn't want to smell me then."

She grinned. "I'm glad you came over. I'm closing in an hour and I'm starving. I bet you are too?"

"Always."

"Great! We can go to dinner then. Will that work?"

"Sure."

I stuck my hands in my pockets, suddenly awkward. I had no computer to hide behind, and didn't have any apps on my phone. What was I supposed to do while she worked? Retreating back to my place until she left made the most sense, but that wasn't what I wanted.

Not at all.

"You can stay." She gazed around. "With the forest and the

reservoir closed now, hardly anyone is up here. I've spent most days reading."

I grinned. "Oh yeah? The books are good?"

I made myself ask it before I found a reason to back out. The delighted smile that illuminated her face made it totally worth it.

"Fantastic."

She drummed her fingers together, then gestured to a stack of books on the floor behind the counter, out of sight from any customers. I stood up and peered over the top. Jess's books.

My books.

Her grin spread as she grabbed a book off the top and slammed it on the counter between us.

"Now that you're stuck here with me, I have you all to myself."

The sound came out like a threat, but I wanted it as a promise. If I had Dahlia all to myself, the things I wanted to do to her—

She continued, breaking apart my escalating thoughts.

"Because I just . . . I have so many questions. Let's start with book one."

* * *

"What?" I cried forty-five minutes later. "No. Just . . . no."

Dahlia's jaw dropped. "You have to be kidding me? You've totally set it up for them to be together."

"How?"

"Stacey and Amina are beautiful together. They'll be such a cute couple, and I've already figured out their relationship name! Stamina! Like stah-mee-nah, right? Besides, Stacey is pregnant and she's going to need some support." Dahlia waved a dismissive hand. "Amina loves her. The two of them will be the cutest mamas ever."

I sat on a chair near the cash register, sprawled back. A coffee mug that had been regularly refilled waited half full next to me. My body buzzed with the extra caffeine, or maybe just the onslaught of Dahlia.

Dahlia stood behind the counter after finishing with a drive-through order, a glass of iced orange juice at her fingertips. Ten of Jess's books lay open on the counter, butterflied open to her favorite spots. She'd been grilling me on the stories behind the stories for almost an hour now. I'd never had so much fun with my books.

"I concede your point," I said, palms spread. "I just hadn't thought of it."

She laughed. "I mean, you need more ideas, right? There it is."

"Not for long."

Her eyes bugged out of her head. "What?" she cried. "Why wouldn't you need more ideas? You're not stopping soon, are you?"

My response stalled, tripping over itself. How did I explain this to her without explaining *everything* to her? Inessa, Dad, the burden of their care that loomed over me like a living thing. The sheer cost of taking care of both of them would have boggled anyone's mind. Never would I jeopardize my ability to provide for them, but . . . I wasn't sure I could keep all of this to myself anymore either.

She straightened, clearly concerned by my silence.

"Not yet," I said with a conciliatory hand in the air. "Jess is not my forever. Romance novels are fun and pay the bills but . . . I'm not in love with this career path. I can do it for now, but I don't want it to be my whole life. Honestly, I'm not sure I want any single career to be my whole life. Why choose just one?"

Dahlia shrugged. "That makes sense."

"Really?"

"Sure."

All the tension I'd bottle up over that reply deflated. I stared at her, at a loss for words. How could such a loyal fan be so blasé? I'd kept quiet about my real feelings for this career because I'd always worried what anyone would say.

"You just . . . accept it like that?" I asked.

"I wouldn't want to be a barista forever. I might love it, but it wouldn't feel like it challenged me long term. If that's the case for you, you should do what you really love. Which is . . ." she drawled and motioned toward me with a hand.

"I don't have any idea."

Admitting it cost me something. Pride, maybe. Ego, certainly. Normally, I didn't care about the fact that I had a lot of careers and never planned to settle in one. Most people didn't think that hard about my life. With Dahlia, however, it mattered.

A startled expression came to her face, then she grinned, orange juice raised in salute.

"Same."

Eager for any opportunity to change the topic away from me, I said, "Oh?"

"Not sure yet what I want to be next either." She had a sip of juice, then tilted her head to the side. "Maybe something like what I've been doing for you. I've dabbled with college and a few other things, but . . ."

She trailed away, then shook her head.

"Those were derailed and I haven't picked back up where I want because, frankly, I don't know what I want. Seemed easier to coast for a while. Eventually, I'll figure it out. I think I'd like to have a family one day. Not now, but . . . some day."

The thought of squalling babies and a mortgage sent a shudder through me. So far, married life had worked out great for my friends Grady and Hernandez, but that didn't sound like my cup of tea. There were enough people on my plate, thank you very much.

Waking up every day next to someone like Dahlia, however, I could wrap my brain around.

"Fair," I said.

"Is it? I feel like by my late twenties I should have this figured out."

"I'm thirty and I haven't."

"But you have *something* figured out."

"I have a lot of somethings figured out." I shrugged. "Doesn't mean anything about me."

She raised her juice. "Then here's to us again."

I silently toasted her. Before she could say another word, the door opened with a jangle. Lizbeth strolled inside with a pale Bethany in tow.

"We came to take over!" Lizbeth cried. "Give me that apron. I'm going to close out tonight while Bethany sits down and figures out her plan for Leslie's job. JJ is occupied with cinnamon rolls and Maverick is renovating a shed into a book sanctuary for me."

The quick burst of life and words didn't seem to startle Dahlia. She ripped her apron off and tossed it over.

With a grin directed at me she cried, "Great! I have a dinner date and I'm not waiting any longer. Lizbeth, I finished all your books, but please don't take them away yet! I need to re-read them one more time."

* * *

If I'd doubted whether I could fall harder for Dahlia than I already had, I received an answer an hour later.

Instead of shoving me into a restaurant surrounded by

chattering people and too much noise, we bought Chinese to go and drove to her RV.

She pulled two folding chairs out and set them up a few steps away from each other. We settled in, overlooking the distant reservoir while I dove into fried rice and double broccoli beef.

"This is perfect," I mumbled around my third potsticker.

She grinned. "I know."

The calm silence filled me with a little more courage. For all she had to say on video, she didn't put pressure on me now. Or maybe she had her own thoughts to battle. I certainly hadn't forgotten the man she'd been halfway embracing. It gave me all the more reason to speak.

"Tomorrow and the next day will be my 48 hours off," I said.

"Will you return to the same fire afterward?"

She had a sip of a sugary strawberry drink, while I drank a root beer. Something in the classic flavor always drew me back to happy times with Inessa and Dad.

"Probably. We won't know for sure until we go active when the 48 hours is over."

"Huh."

"Do you have to work tomorrow?"

"Not at the coffee shop, but I have this other boss that's super sensitive about my work hours and makes me slave over his computer. I also have to take care of his cat, so he's pretty needy these days."

She sent me a sidelong glance that I pretended to ignore while I edged a piece of broccoli around my plate.

"You should refuse to work for him and play hooky with me all day."

If possible, she brightened further. She already sat over there like a star. I couldn't fathom what made her so happy.

Her hands planted on the arm rests and she pushed herself up a little.

"Really?"

Until I'd extended the invitation, I hadn't realized how much I meant it. How much I *needed* it. Despite the piles of smoky laundry that awaited me at home, I had nothing to go back there for.

Why face it all alone again? Although it would go fast, the 48 hours of quiet in that house would feel interminable now that Dahlia wandered out in the world.

I swallowed hard, feeling as if this decision counted for more than just a day together. Whatever subtext it meant, I'd take on. It meant more Dahlia, so it would be worth it.

"Really."

Her smile grew, lopsided at first, until it wreathed her whole face. It lit something inside me like fire.

"You got it." She leaned back in her chair again, still smiling. "I'll just tell him that I'm on my period or something. That scares all males."

I sprayed root beer in front of me, unable to help myself. She dissolved into laughter.

It felt so very, very good.

Chapter Twenty-One

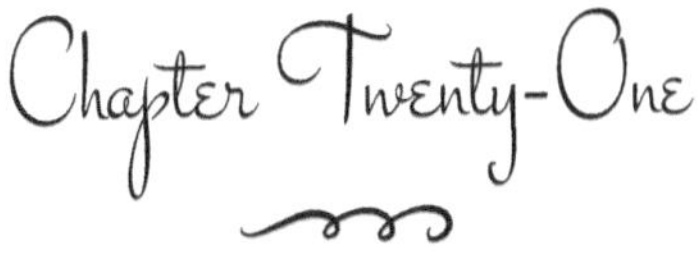

DAHLIA

My eyes fluttered open early the next morning.

I groaned, but rolled out of bed and forced myself away from the groggy cocoon of blankets.

Heat already radiated up from the baked ground outside and wavered into the RV. It would be hot, hot, hot today. For more reasons than just smoke and fire.

Images from yesterday still whipped through my mind. Jakob. Katrina. Bastian. Pictures from my warm life in LA with old familiar friends and my favorite taquería just down the street.

The way Bastian swept into the Frolicking Moose and took all the air out of the room.

Today, I focused on Bastian.

Jakob's final holds over me had dissolved yesterday, and the relief that rolled through me as a result felt buoyant. Inner Me gave a little sigh of relief at the thought.

Panic shot through me when I caught sight of the clock.

8:57.

"No!" I squeaked, hopping into a pair of shorts. Of

course, I was already late. No makeup, my hair in utter just-woke-up-disarray, and Bastian would be here any second now.

I grabbed one flip flop off the ground while rushing into the front to find the other one. Somewhere in a mess of clothes I'd dumped on the bed was a shirt I could wear, I just couldn't find it.

There!

The sound of tires on the gravel outside followed.

With another cry, I lunged for the shirt. An emerald green color with light, silhouetted coconut trees against it. I yanked it on when the sound of feet approached the trailer. Of course, Bastian would be on time to the very minute he said he'd arrive. Meanwhile, I'd slept until three minutes before said time.

So much for my plan to wake up early, get ready, and present my best front.

Rapping came on the door.

"Just a sec!" I called in a failed attempt to sound calm. How could I stall long enough for a quick mascara job? Tell him to wait outside? No. Lame. Make an excuse about . . . *something*?

A quick check in the mirror confirmed my medusa-style hair. I paused, stared at my still-sleepy reflection. Mascara smudged the skin below my eyes. What did it matter? This was unfiltered Dahlia.

I drew in a deep breath and muttered, "The hell with it."

Seconds later, I yanked open the door with my usual bright smile.

"Come in. Forgive the mess. Just woke up."

He paused outside, one foot halfway up a stair. After a moment of indecision, he stepped inside. Like Sione, his tall frame seemed to take up most of the space, but he didn't appear uncomfortable. He gazed around, arms at his side. The smell of smoke drifted in with him.

No incriminating glance at my clothes.

No side comments on my hair.

Just a simple, sincere, "Nice place."

"Thanks." I stepped back and swept an arm around. "It's home. I did a tour of the US to see family members before settling here. Sione came with me the last leg of it. It was a blast."

"Sione works at Adventura with Mark Bailey, right?"

"Yeah. Sione's a pretty cool guy."

He nodded, eyes still taking the place in. "I don't know him well, but have heard good things. This is a nice camper. My Dad used to take us into the mountains in an old one that didn't have much more than walls."

"Yeah?" I murmured, searching for my sunglasses, then added a flippant, "You know how to fix a stabilizer jack?"

"Yes."

I paused. "Really?"

"Do you need it fixed?"

"Yes, actually." I bent over to grab a ponytail holder that had fallen to the ground. My hair threaded through my fingers as I pulled the top half back, away from my face. "The stabilizer is stuck on the ground near the front left. It won't retract, so I can't leave. With this fire building . . ."

When I straightened up, he was already gone.

I let the words trail off, then grabbed my wallet-phone combination, shoved it in my back pocket, found my sunglasses near my keys, and slipped down the stairs. No mascara today, apparently.

Bastian already stood near the front left, where the jack stuck. Yesterday, I'd spent time packing up the various things that would prevent me from a quick escape, if needed. The stabilizer jack was on back order in the nearest place in Jackson City.

He studied it with a concentrated air. "Easy fix. The leg is a bit bent. I think we can replace just this leg, not all four on the whole unit."

"That would be great. The place in Jackson City said it'd take a few weeks to order in."

He nodded. "Yeah. I think Dagny knows some people with RV parts through her work. I'll text her about it. She might be able to get them sooner."

"Wow. Thanks. I can do that if you don't want to bother."

"No bother."

He straightened up, brushing his hands off on a pair of jeans that fit a little *too* well. I slipped my sunglasses on to better hide my obvious perusal.

"Besides," he murmured, "I want to make sure you can get out of here safely if you need to."

"I'd appreciate that."

We turned and started toward his truck.

"So," I drawled, feeling a bit giddy at the thought of an entire day stretching before me with nothing but Bastian inside it. "What are we doing today?"

"Visiting a few people." He peered ahead. "Running some errands in Jackson City, if you want to go. I need to check out new sole inserts for my boots, get some back up laces, and find a weather proofer for my boots." He hesitated, then said, "It's not really that exciting, now that I think about it. If you—"

"I'd love it. I'm up for anything. Normal life stuff is important. If you can't do everyday things with a friend, what can you do?"

He smiled. Subtle, and quiet, just like him. When we arrived at his truck, he opened the passenger door in a sweet, unexpected gesture.

"Thanks," I said.

He closed it with a nod, and I gave into the girly squeal that bubbled up inside me as he walked around the truck.

I was *so* ready for this day.

* * *

An hour of steady chat later, we pulled to a stop outside a brick building near the outskirts of Jackson City.

The forty-five minute drive up the canyon had been undeniably easy, not to mention gorgeous, in late summer. Glimpses of the white, frothing river below sent little bursts of excitement through me. Not the ocean, but at least it was water. I'd take what I could get.

The brick building in front of us was nondescript. A small parking lot, ringed with well-manicured trees and thick green shrubs gave it a cozy feel. A sign on the far wall quietly stated, *Adult Care Services.*

My curiosity soared.

Bastian stared straight ahead, unblinking. Sensing a need for silence, I kept my lips together. My mind spun with possibilities. His Dad, perhaps? There were so many pictures of him in the frames. No, there had been a young woman there, too.

Finally, Bastian drew in a deep breath and looked at me. "Sorry, just . . . mentally prepping myself for what I'll find in there."

"Take your time."

"My sister, Inessa, lives here."

His gaze returned to the brick wall. Tension returned to his entire body, but it was hard to read. Was he afraid? Nervous? Didn't want to be here? A summation of all three, maybe? I couldn't tell.

"My parents adopted both of us. Inessa first when she was a few months old. She was born with Down's syndrome. Her birth mother left her at a fire station because she couldn't handle a special needs kid. Not only was Inessa born into tough circumstances, but she also had heart problems, amongst other things. She's ten years older than me."

My eyes widened.

"Wow."

"Years later, they adopted me when I was a baby. My birth father walked away from my birth mom, leaving her alone to raise me. She was only seventeen, so she gave me up for adoption."

"Do you know her?"

He nodded vaguely. "We meet up at Christmas sometimes. She calls, writes, and sends me a birthday present every year. We're friends."

"That's pretty cool."

"Yeah. My adopted parents, whom I think of as my real parents, struggled with infertility for years. Then Inessa came along, and then me. A year after they brought me into the family, my adopted Mom was diagnosed with cancer. She died six months later."

"Oh."

The startled word flew out of me. Bastian didn't seem to hear it, and I was grateful that he kept going. My quick math meant he would have been just under two years old when he lost his mother. Probably didn't even remember her.

"Dad took care of me and Inessa. When I was old enough, I helped. Inessa's medical conditions have always been significant. She's almost forty now, and we were told she may not make it that far. Her heart is weak. She was born with a ventricular defect that was fixed around three months old, but she's always struggled ever since with her lungs, her blood sugar, and her thyroid." He shook his head. "She's been getting worse recently and it's so hard to watch."

A beat of quiet followed his revelation. I attempted to soak up all he'd revealed, startled. Inessa was the girl in the pictures that I'd seen at his house, then. It had been obvious he had some people in his life, but I hadn't known where they were.

"I see."

"My father—we'll see him next—declined in health the past couple of years. Right before last fire season, Dad had to live somewhere else. I couldn't take care of him anymore. Inessa and I did fine together until her health became worse. When fire season started last year, I had to bring her here."

His words thickened a little, and he swallowed. Something burdened his voice now, and it sounded like guilt.

"This is where she lives?" I asked.

"Yes. We tried everything before we went to a full time place like this. Respite care. Other facilities. Daytime programs. But I couldn't make it work with my fire job and have it be safe for her. She's just too sick. She's been living here since the beginning of last summer."

He glanced at the building again.

"It's a wonderful place. They take excellent care of her. They provide her with activities and help me to speak with her as much as I can. It's home for her now. Her home. Her place. Her people. She loves that. She's thrived amidst her medical challenges. I had planned for her to stay here only during fire season, but she asked to stay full time last fall. I couldn't tell her no."

"That's a tough situation, Bastian."

I reached over and put a hand on his arm. He didn't flinch, but I couldn't tell whether he welcomed the touch or not. He still hadn't looked at me. By sheer willpower, I didn't move my hand away.

"Yes, it is hard," he said. "This sort of facility costs a lot of money, which is why I stayed in wildland fire. With high-fire years, I could rake in overtime, make money, and live out of Dad's house. His mortgage isn't that high and I've almost paid it off. The problem is that Dad's care facility is just as expensive as Inessa's."

The puzzle pieces shunted together.

"They are the reason you need Jess?" I asked.

"Jess," he murmured with a slight nod. "Years ago, Dad struggled under some of Inessa's medical debt. To help out, I threw a book together to see if I could sell something that didn't cost money to make. Dad had to retire early because of his . . . challenges . . . and there wasn't a lot of money coming in. I'd always loved to write, so I wrote a cheesy romance novel and sent it to a bunch of people."

"Pri?"

He laughed. "No. Pri heard about it from another agent that had just rejected it. She saw promise, so she reached out, suggested a few things, and I did them. She decided to take a chance, because she knew an editor at a mid-sized press that wanted something like it. It worked out, so I kept writing up through book ten. The publisher handled my frequent releases pretty consistently. I was able to build up a big base of books fast, although my readership wasn't super strong at that point."

A group of people strolled by, arm in arm, then disappeared into the building. I watched them go as his story unfolded. Bastian revealed more about himself in this conversation than I had ever thought possible. Facets began to piece together. The pictures at his Dad's house. His quiet manner. The deep desire for a veil between him and his readers.

He sighed, drawing my attention back. "Then Dad's diagnosis came."

A pause lingered behind. "Do you want to talk about it?" I asked, with a little squeeze on his arm.

"Early-onset dementia."

He said the words with a voice like steel. That diagnosis must have felt like drowning. With his mother dead at a young age, he was likely close with his father. Probably very close as they cared for Inessa together.

Did he see his father's sickness as a betrayal? It would explain the anger I sensed in him.

"Dad regressed slowly, then all at once. He began to struggle at work with his engineering job. Then he had to quit. It worsened from there. Once he lost his routine, he lost himself. I had to put him into a memory care place a year and a half ago. His body is mostly healthy. His mind is . . . not."

My issues of lost love and thwarted plans seemed to pale in comparison to what Bastian faced every day. Caregiver for two medically needy people. Financial supporter for them as well. No maternal influence. Now, no paternal influence either.

Who guided Bastian?

Who showed up for him?

No wonder his text messages had been so awkward when he found out that I'd taken the day off to help with the launch.

"Your father's dementia must be hard to watch," I whispered.

He snorted. The sound was half derisive scoff, half vulnerable child.

"Torture," he said. "My strong, indomitable father became a shell of a man. He wanders around all day looking for his wallet. His hands shake. Mumbles are almost all I can hear from him, when he speaks at all. He doesn't know me anymore, and when I stare into his eyes, it's like he sees all the way through me."

His impassioned response sounded pressured, like he'd been waiting for it to come out for years but hadn't had the opportunity. Had no one asked him this?

Had he *let* anyone ask?

"I couldn't just let Dad and Inessa live anywhere. I wouldn't let either of them be neglected, or in a place that I couldn't trust. Which meant I had to be able to pay a lot of money every month."

"Were the books making enough?"

He shrugged. "With wildland fire work, I squeaked by.

The big numbers hadn't hit at that point. Jess continued to grow steadily, but it was last summer that the influencers came in and Jess's name grew."

"And now," I murmured when he stopped, "you're trying to save for the future?"

With what he must be making on royalties, I had little doubt that what debt had once existed was likely caught up. I'd wager that he could meet the financial demands of both places for now.

But a middle aged man with dementia might live far longer than an older one. When the mind aged, but the body didn't, what kind of longevity did that mean? Bastian might have to pay for full-time care for years, or maybe not. No one would have a crystal ball for that kind of situation.

And Inessa?

Both stories explained why Bastian strove to keep Jess's financial system alive and well.

"I don't know why I keep returning to fire work when Jess clearly makes so much money now." He spoke more to himself than to me, but I listened intently all the same. "I think . . . I'm worried that Jess's fame will just dry up one day. Or it'll start to die away and I could be left stranded. Fire is something I can do that guarantees money every summer. Money and . . . escape, I guess."

Sensing that he needed a shift of attention after revealing so many heart-driven things, I let my hand fall away. My gaze returned to the building in front of me.

"In the meantime," I drew in a deep breath. "Shall we go check on your sister?"

The haunted expression returned to his face. He nodded. "Yes, I always love to see Inessa, but I'm nervous. Nessa's nurse texted me just before I returned. She said that Inessa's getting worse. They've started hospice."

"What does that mean?"

He shrugged. "I don't know, but she doesn't have much longer left. With Inessa, it's hard to tell."

I reached over and squeezed his hand.

"All the more reason to see her now."

* * *

Bastian led me past a reception counter, signed a clipboard, said hello to a few people, and then guided me through a maze of hallways.

We didn't touch, but I wanted to take his hand. Tension crackled off him like a force field, so I stayed back. Revealing so much about himself had been hard. The signs were there.

Eventually he slowed, then knocked on a door marked with Inessa's name. After a call that I barely heard, he twisted the handle and stepped inside.

A woman lay on top of a bed, an oxygen tube strapped to her face. Her eyes fluttered open as we stepped inside, then brightened. A wide smile spread across her face. Dark, black hair laced with gray lay in a braid on her left shoulder, silky strands sliding out of it. Her slanted eyes crinkled from the width of her smile. Bastian illuminated like a candle bouncing to life.

"Hey!" he said softly. "There's my favorite sister."

She beamed.

"Hi Bastian." She lifted a hand and waved him over. The word *Bashtyun* slurred a little, but came out happy and bright.

He leaned down, wrapped his arms around her, and held her in a long, long hug. When he pulled away, she grinned and adjusted a pair of glasses on her face. I hovered back, content to watch.

A cough racked her body, wet and difficult. Bastian grabbed her a tissue and handed it over. She lay back after she coughed into it.

"I missed you," she murmured. "You're safe from the . . . from the fire?"

"I'm safe." He nodded and sat down at the side of her bed. "I have two days off and wanted to see you. I'm sorry I only made it for a short time on my last break. They said you're feeling a little weak."

She nodded, the first signs of trouble clouding her brilliant expression. She licked her lips, biting her bottom lip. She patted her chest. "I'm sick like Daddy." Her hand reached up to her head. "But not sick up here like Daddy."

He nodded. "Yeah, your lungs and heart are sick."

She laughed a little. "They're sick a lot."

He nodded.

"Dad's head is sick. Yeah. Does he remember me?"

"Not yet. Maybe soon?"

She worried her lip with her teeth. Her gaze darted to me, then back to him. She cracked another smile and motioned to me with a hand. "You brought a friend?"

"Yes! Nessa, this is Dahlia."

Inessa waved.

"Good to meet you, Inessa." I waved back.

"Your name is a flower. I like dahlias."

I smiled. "Me too."

I leaned against the wall while they turned their discussions to the rows of paintings that cluttered the far wall, clearly created by Inessa herself. The angst Bastian carried into this room had completely dissolved away now, and he chattered with Inessa like a fat, happy squirrel.

The canvases at the end of her bed were expertly filled with lakes and mountains and trees. The use of bright colors amidst the earth tones wasn't accidental. They enhanced the majesty of the peaks with high tones that weren't natural to nature, but somehow *looked* natural in that setting.

Bright pink moss. Orange streaks on rocks mixed with

various shades of mossy green. Her fingers had flecks of paint on the end of their stubby lengths.

Did Inessa channel a lot of her energy and day into her paintings? Or did they come easily to her? Clearly, she had a fair amount of experience to have them so well-crafted.

One of the smaller ones deviated from the natural theme to a representation of the kitchen at their Dad's house. Another painting showed Psycho with electric blue streaks highlighting the whiskers. Somehow, she'd trapped Psycho's affection for life in the painting.

As if she read my mind, Inessa asked Bastian, "How is Psycho? I miss her. I want to pet her."

Bastian looked back to me. He motioned with an outstretched hand. I straightened and walked over, self-conscious in front of someone that meant so much to him. Inessa's smile grew. He stood at my side, a hand on the small of my back.

"Dahlia has been taking care of Psycho while I was fighting the fires. She can tell you more about her."

"Is Psycho okay?"

Concern layered her thickened tone. I nodded to put her to ease. "Doing great. She plays with me every day and eats all her food by the time I've returned."

"Does she have the metal balls?" Inessa made a circle with her thumb and index finger. "She likes the pink one."

"She does. I've seen her play with them. She seems very happy."

Her face dropped a little. "I miss Psycho."

"I think she misses you. I try to pet her and hold her as much as I can, but it never seems to be enough. Do you want to see some videos of her?"

Inessa immediately brightened when I dug out my phone and pulled up my photo album. Bastian remained next to me, although the warmth of his hand faded away. Inessa giggled over Psycho's antics until the videos I'd sent Bastian were gone.

"Have a seat." Bastian motioned me into a chair next to the bed. "Inessa can tell you about her paintings."

For the next hour, Inessa gave me a tour of her work. She explained each picture, many of them associated with memories of her father and brother. Bastian displayed old ones that sat on the floor, filed and lined up by subject. Inessa explained her love of nature and mountains and the hikes that Bastian took her on when her lungs were better.

There had to be 100 paintings stored in various spots through her wide, spacious room. Whatever Bastian paid to keep her in such a place and stocked with so many comfortable clothes and things to do, it must be very expensive.

But oh, how happy she seemed.

My heart flip-flopped over this side of his life, filled with a new sense of determination. If I had to volunteer to work for Jess to make Inessa's life comfortable, I would do it forever. Bastian could have all my money. I wanted Inessa to have *this* for as long as possible.

Given Inessa's productive cough and reliance on oxygen, not to mention a generally pale pallor, that might not be long.

My heart clenched at the thought of Bastian dealing with losing his sister alone.

A tentative knock on the door, and a light voice calling out, drew my gaze. Inessa sat up in bed, her legs crossed, as she explained a few more ideas to her brother. She pushed her glasses higher on her nose and tucked a piece of hair behind her ear. Hearing aids looped the shell of both ears.

A nurse with spiraling, black hair cut short and velvety eyes walked into the room with a warm smile.

"Good morning Inessa! Good to see you again Bastian."

"Hi Shayna," Inessa said quietly. "This is my new friend, Dahlia."

A shot of warmth slipped through me. My heart couldn't take the quick affection in her voice. I gave a wave and Shayna nodded to me. Inessa coughed, taking the tissue Bastian offered. It came away tinged pink. Was that blood? Her breathing had become more labored as she spoke about the paintings, but she didn't seem to want to stop.

Bastian put a hand on her shoulder while she caught her breath. Shayna turned to him with a welcoming smile.

"Good to see you safe, as always, Bastian. Are you fighting the fire down the canyon?"

"Yes. Just returned for a few days. It's likely we'll head back."

"Any updates?"

"Nothing exciting."

"It's only 10% contained, correct?"

He nodded a bit reluctantly. Shayna smiled at Inessa and said, "If anyone can put out that fire, it's your brother. Don't you think?"

Inessa nodded dotingly. Bastian grinned.

"I brought your lunch and some medicine," Shayna continued. "Are you hungry?"

I startled. Had we been here that long? My gaze traveled to a clock filled with cats. Indeed. Noon sharp.

Inessa nodded. "I'm hungry."

"Probably tired, too."

Bastian chucked her softly on the jaw, earning another smile. She whacked him back, hitting him on the hip. Bastian leaned over, wrapped his sister in another lingering hug, and straightened. She smiled, adjusting her glasses again.

"Love you, Nessa," he murmured. "I'll try to see you tomorrow morning again, okay?"

"Love you, Bash."

Taking it as a cue, I stood up. On a whim, I stepped forward and gave Inessa a hug that she returned, holding me tight. When I straightened, I felt sad to go. Shayna stepped back to let us through, then touched Bastian on the shoulder.

"I'll speak to you outside."

He nodded, gave one last farewell to his sister, and we stepped into the hall. Shayna followed us out, closing the door behind her. When she turned to Bastian, something like fear lived in his gaze.

"She's doing great," Shayna said in a soothing voice. She put a hand on his shoulder. "For what her body can do, she's hanging in there. But she's growing more uncomfortable as the days pass. Her lung and heart function are declining, and so is her energy. The doctor will be here tomorrow morning at his usual time if you want to speak with him, but the decision to call hospice is really one to make sure she remains comfortable."

"Has Nessa spoken with you about it?" he asked. "Does she understand what hospice means?"

"Not really, but she's starting to understand that she won't get better. Sometimes she asks me what happens when we die, but not often."

Bastian nodded. "Of course I want to speak with the doctor. I'll be here tomorrow. And I'll have new oil paints and canvases for her."

Shayna nodded with a warm smile. "She'd love that. Have you had any update on your Dad?"

He shook his head. The hard wall in his gaze slammed back into place that had lifted around Inessa. Shayna patted his shoulder, and her eyes fell to me.

"I'm sorry," she said with a smile, "I didn't introduce myself. I'm Shayna, the nurse here most of the time."

"This is Dahlia," Bastian said, before I could speak. He set a hand on my shoulder. "My friend."

A breath of relief almost escaped me. For half a moment, I

thought he'd say *assistant* or something awkward like that. Friend I would take, and gratefully.

Shayna smiled. "I'm happy to see someone with you. Call me with any questions, and we'll see you tomorrow."

Bastian and I exited the bright facility without saying a word. Shayna's voice reverberated in my head.

I'm happy to see someone with you.

We fell into our separate thoughts as we returned to the car. Once there, he opened my door again, brow knitted as he shut it after I had stepped in.

Did he work on autopilot? Did he realize the sweet, small things he did? While he walked around the car, I closed my eyes and drew in a deep breath, letting it out seconds before he opened the door. The air had grown heavy, but not in a bad way.

His truck rumbled to life, and I realized then that it was kind of old. Functional, certainly, and well taken care of, with a tool box in the bed and new-ish looking tires. The floors were vacuumed, no dust lingered anywhere, but the carpet and seats had worn thin. Did Bastian live so simply and quietly so Inessa could have this?

And what about his father?

The quiet air broke when I said, "Would you like to go visit your father now?"

"I need to."

He put the truck into reverse, but didn't say where we were going. Nor did I miss that he said *need* instead of *want* in his response. Did he dread seeing his father? He certainly showed no excitement.

I clicked my seat belt on and watched the mountain world fly by. The hills had been scorched by the sun, turning once-green hillsides into crispy brown. Bikers, tourists, and hikers ducked under shade where they could find it, wearing wide-brim hats and sunglasses to shield themselves from the hot glare.

In between mountain peaks, glimpses of the building smoke plume were apparent. Not as close here, but still alive.

Several minutes later, we pulled into a parking lot. The moment the truck sputtered to a stop, Bastian slipped outside.

My gaze stopped on the sign ahead of us.

Memory Care Services.

Chapter Twenty-Two

BASTIAN

If I didn't get out of the truck, I'd never go inside.

It's why I banked on the inertia of the moving vehicle to propel me out of the driver's seat almost the same second we stopped.

The moment I thought about what I had to do next would be the moment I chickened out. Dahlia asked no questions. She joined me outside almost as quickly as I'd moved. With her there, I found my courage.

But was this fair?

I'd never brought someone with me to see Dad before. Not Grady. Not Hernandez. Not even Vik. The Merry Idiots knew about Dad's situation, but I'd drawn a silent line and they didn't cross it. They asked, they didn't follow. That suited me just fine.

With Dahlia, it was different.

I didn't know why.

We moved inside without a word. I said the right things, spoke to the right people. Without needing an escort, I walked the same path I'd trod countless times before. Daily, when the fires didn't sweep me away.

What felt like mere moments later, we stood outside a set of locked double doors. I peered through the windows to see a calm scene inside.

That spot is where my momentum stopped.

Dahlia waited to my right, a step behind me. My heart crashed like drums in the quiet of this place. Not many people came here, which is why we stood in the middle of locked, swinging doors without fear of getting hit should they open.

I waited.

Every now and then, someone would shuffle by. A nurse going into a room. Another patient making their shaky way across the tiled hall. Somewhere in the distance came a shout, and then silence. I swallowed hard, waiting.

Dahlia must wonder what I was doing. Did she think I'd lost my mind? She had to know I didn't want to be here. Didn't want to see him like this again. Surely, I owed her some sort of explanation.

I swallowed, my throat bobbing. "He gets agitated when he sees me."

Dahlia's regular breath paused.

"Your Dad?"

I hesitated, then kept going with a nod.

"He doesn't remember me. At least, not that we can discern. For the last six months, whenever he would talk to me, there has been no recognition. Eventually, I stopped trying. I'd act like a stranger instead. A guy that just came around to visit and saw him there. He'd tell me stories . . ."

Emotion lumped in my throat, sitting like a rock. Normally, I could swallow around it. This time, I couldn't.

Dad moved into sight right then, a nurse at his side. They stepped out of his room and headed toward us. Tremors shook his dark hands. His once thick hair had faded slightly. The tall frame, lean and too thin now, stooped at the shoulders. Still, there was a handsome, familiar man under the layers of confusion in his gaze.

A warm hand linked through mine.

Dahlia tucked herself against my side, her body pressed close. She felt warm, and soft, and a gentle hint of coffee rose up from her hair. I wrapped my arm around her, pulling her closer. She held me up when I wanted to fall.

In a broken voice I said, "That's him."

Dad shuffled slowly with the nurse, his head bent toward her as if they were talking. I could just make out his wrinkled expression.

"He's probably telling her that he can't find his wallet," I continued. "That's mostly what he thinks about now. When I come, the receptionist calls the nursing station here and lets them know. They have him walk down here so I can see him, but I don't go in anymore. He agitates and tires himself out. It's too hard for him."

"And for you?" she asked quietly.

I nodded.

Dad approached with the nurse at his side, chattering warmly to him. His hair had thinned out on top. They didn't always shave him on the days when he was more upset, so white curls stuck out against his skin. He didn't look up to see me at first. The nurse glanced at me through the glass, smiled, and I recognized her as Bernice, a woman that had been caring for him since he arrived.

"He seems like a good man," Dahlia said as she studied him.

I nodded.

Despite a difference in our race, I'd always seen myself as an echo of my adopted father. A strong, virile, healthy one. The version of Dad without all the additives of family and kids to care for. The version that he'd always wanted to live—or so

I'd assumed. Carefree. Unrestrained by grief or children with medical issues or needs.

Dad had never implied any burden to me, but I'd seen the wear that Inessa and I had on him over the years. Women he dated had disappeared, seemingly without explanation. One had been upfront enough to say she didn't want kids with special needs.

No one wanted to sign up for *us*. Except him.

He'd always stayed when everyone else left. Now *he* was gone. Where he went, I could never go.

Bernice said something to Dad in a quiet tone. He didn't respond. She held onto his left arm while his right hand patted his pants pocket. Searching for his keys, probably. Dad looked up right then and his gaze slammed into mine. I sucked in a sharp breath. Dahlia tightened her hold on me.

Dad blinked. For half a breath, I thought I saw something there. Then his unseeing gaze dropped to Dahlia. He regarded her curiously through the window, then smiled at her. The toothy grin gave him a comical expression before he muttered something and turned around. He tried to shuffle off on his own but stumbled, unable to stand in his own power. Bernice caught him, put an arm around his back, and turned him toward his room.

I watched him retreat until he was gone. An empty feeling riddled my chest. My soul, a restless chasm with a father-sized hole punched through it. My breath left all at once and I tilted like I'd been on a tilt-o-whirl. Dahlia tightened her hold on me.

"That," I murmured darkly, "is usually as far as we get."

"This is hard, Bastian."

I turned away. "Come on. Let's go do something less soul-sucking. I'm starving and food always make me happy. I know a great Armenian place."

She said nothing to my quick retreat. This time, I didn't

hang around to wait for an update from Bernice. I had to get out of there.

Two minutes later, I cranked the truck back to life. It roared awake, then purred. I blinked, attempting to banish the cobwebs of thought and focus on what came next.

What did I need to do?

What came next?

Try as I might, my thoughts wouldn't shuttle back together. Instead, they hovered around Inessa and Dad and fires and control and Jess and money and maintaining everything for everyone and the pressure it left on my chest tightened, tightened, tightened until . . .

A warm body slid next to mine.

Dahlia sat right next to me in the truck, her arm looped through mine. She rested her head on my shoulder.

"I'm here," she said. "You're not alone this time."

She'd shocked me right out of the anxiety dive. Her grip on my arm tightened in a friendly squeeze. Not sure of what to do—or where to touch—I lowered my hand to the most natural spot. It stopped on her thigh.

For a long time we sat there. She looked ahead. I stared at the steering wheel. Eventually, she broke the quiet.

"Now that you've let me meet your family, can I share something with you?"

I nodded, desperate to get out of the spotlight. A rush of gratitude followed. Let her take the metaphorical wheel and decide what needed to be said next, because I had no idea.

"That guy at the Frolicking Moose yesterday was Jakob, my ex-boyfriend."

A hundred thoughts swirled through my mind like little tornadoes, eating up the anxiety centered around Nessa and Dad. Dahlia's voice settled them down.

"Six months ago, we broke up," she continued. "Mutual, for the most part. He started talking about it, and I realized he was right. We really weren't doing much. Sort of roommates, living our lives together but not . . . not really in love anymore."

Her voice had become unmistakably soft, filled with a gentle pain. The distant kind. The sort of pain that you look at from the power of perspective.

"When we broke up, I gave up everything. My job as store manager at his company—a hardware supply chain he inherited from his father—outside of LA. Our shared apartment, which was ten minutes away from my family. My friends, my life. Everything. I just . . . I'd lost myself somewhere in the routine. When our love sort of died, I felt awful. Betrayed, relieved, confused."

Her shoulders dropped with a long, long breath. She relaxed further against me, her cheek resting on the side of my arm. I didn't hate anything about this scenario, except her tone of regret and pain.

"After I'd graduated with my associates degree in general studies at college—which is where Jakob and I met—I started to work for him. Everything in my life after college began and ended with him. Everything. So when we broke up, I didn't really know what I wanted to do. So I . . . did the only thing that felt good."

"What was that?"

"I sold everything I owned except a suitcase full of clothes. I kept my truck, which was *barely* big enough to tow an RV, cashed out my savings, and bought my own place. Then I traveled the US for four months visiting family. Sione came with me. In April, he went to Adventura. In May, I started to work at the Frolicking Moose. I've been trying to figure out what I want to do with my life next in the meantime. Then, Jakob showed up yesterday."

She tucked herself under my arm when I lifted it up and settled it around her shoulders. Something about her warmth at my side felt like a drug. I absorbed the feeling until it could have controlled me if I let it and curled her closer to me.

The caveman inside my chest wanted to immediately reject the idea of Jakob anywhere near her. Dahlia wasn't mine. No matter how much I wanted it to be different—and how much sense did that make?—we didn't know each other well enough for that.

Instead, I let the quiet ride until I couldn't anymore. "What did Jakob want yesterday?" I asked.

"Closure," she murmured. "He left. He's back in California now."

"Oh."

"I tell you all that," she continued after a pause where my thoughts became a weird mess, "because you revealed yourself today in a big way. I appreciate the vulnerable position it must have been for you and I wanted you to know my heart, too. Fair's fair. I think we're all a bit of a mess inside."

She'd offered a gift. Transparency for transparency. On impulse, I leaned down, pressed a kiss into her hair, and whispered, "Thank you."

She stayed at my side as I lifted my arm back over her shoulders and reached for the gear shift. We pulled away from Dad's, homeward bound.

This time, not alone.

* * *

Later that night, I stared at the laundry twirling in the dryer, my own thoughts a jumbled mess.

The latest briefing on the fire played in the background, complete with a weather report. Outside Dad's house, wind brushed against the windows with angry bursts of attitude.

My brain registered the words of the incident commander as he appeared on the screen, but not what they meant. Didn't matter. Tomorrow was my last day of our break before I had to head back out there. My fingers flexed against my palm, less eager than they'd ever been to get back to the fire.

Dahlia's hand in them, however . . .

I slammed that thought closed.

No, I didn't know what to think about Dahlia. Although the day had been fun, the opening of wounds had come at a cost.

By the time we finished eating harissa at an Armenian restaurant, we both seemed ready for a break. I'd felt a twinge of regret letting her go back to her RV, but shucked it off to focus on all the things I had to get done. Laundry. Bills. Errands. Nessa needed more oil paints and canvases. Dad probably needed some more clothes and his favorite shaving cream.

Grungy yellow shirts and dark green pants whirled around each other in the dryer as I stood there and thought about Dahlia. A whole new aspect of her had cracked open and spilled fresh light. It only gave me more to tumble over.

The ring of my phone startled me out of my thoughts. I accepted the call without checking the name.

"Hello?"

"B-bash?"

I stepped away from the wall where I'd been standing for ten minutes.

"Hey Dagny."

"C-calling to check on you. I saw the t-truck in front of the fire station today and wanted to s-s-see how you're d-doing."

"I'm . . ."

Good died in my throat. *Fine* wouldn't even make it to my lips. None of those applied on any level. There weren't a whole lot of people that I could really open up to, but there was something about Dagny I trusted. If I'd ever needed a woman's insight before, it was right now.

"Hernandez working tonight?"

"Yeah. Swing sh-sh-shift today for a b-buddy. Should be home at m-m-midnight."

"Can I come over?"

"S-sure."

Twenty minutes later, Dagny cracked open her door, saw me standing there, and threw it open. Her warm smile and tight hug felt like coming home. She motioned inside. "C-come on. I l-left out some d-dinner if you want."

My stomach rumbled, never satisfied. "That would be great."

She shut the door, locked it, and headed to the kitchen. "Let's t-talk in here. I c-can't wait to hear. Rumor m-mill says that you were with D-dahlia today. C-c-considering she showed up here unexp-p-pectedly the other day, I can't wait to hear th-the updates."

Over a bowl of chili and corn chips, I let the whole story spill. I started with the moment I met Dahlia at the coffee shop and had the wild idea.

My retelling laid it all open. I didn't hold back the truth about Jess, because how could I? I couldn't explain Dahlia working for me, my obsession with her video updates, or my confusing anxiety over how to speak to her without explaining why we came together.

Finally telling the truth required so much time my voice went hoarse. These were things I hadn't released ever, so I let them spill and spill and spill and spill without realizing how deep the need to be totally open had been.

Dagny listened, eyes wide. Once I finished speaking, she leaned back in her chair.

"J-jess," she murmured. "Wow."

What should I say to that? Her disbelief was well founded.

"You know," she murmured, "I n-never thought you were a writer. J-jayson and I always d-d-debated what you did on the c-computer." Her eyes sparkled. "I said d-day trader. He said online c-c-counselor for kids that d-didn't know what they wanted to d-do for their life and thought ab-bout being f-f-firefighters."

I tilted my head back and laughed. Hernandez, the idiot. I'd never been to college and had no active plans to start now. Certainly wouldn't be paid to guide other people in their lives. I didn't even know how to manage my own. Dagny was closer, but still way off.

Her amusement calmed. She reached across the table, nudging aside my empty chili bowl, and put a hand on mine. I looked right in her eyes.

"I'll k-k-keep your secret, B-bastian. I won't tell Jayson ab-bout Jess . . . but I still think that y-y-you should."

"I know. I will. It's not fair of me to ask you to keep secrets from your husband. Just . . . give me a little time?"

Her hand withdrew. "Of course. J-Just let me know how else I can help. All the M-m-merry Idiots love you, whether they'll say it or n-not. They all w-w-want the b-best for you, too. W-whatever that is, l-l-let us know, okay? B-besides," she added with a sour sigh, "n-no matter how crazy your life s-s-seems, you're doing better than V-vik."

The comment wasn't misplaced either. Vikram had become a hot mess. After taking off to the Arctic to go dog-sledding last year for our first annual Merry Idiots adventure together, he'd injured his knee and already suffered through two surgeries. His attitude hadn't improved since he took leave from his job as a train driver and wallowed in an apartment in Jackson City, feeling sorry for himself. All my attempts to speak with him had only yielded text messages and stalemates. After this fire, I'd go shake him up a bit, remind him not to be an idiot.

"B-but let's talk about D-dahlia," she said with a brighter tone. "Th-that's the real m-meat of this c-conversation."

I lifted an eyebrow. "Do I want to hear what you're going to say?"

"D-d-depends on how much you l-like her."

"What's that mean?"

She smiled with warmth. "I think she's w-wonderful. I think you like her and you're scared out of your m-m-mind about it. You've always t-t-tried to d-do things all on your own. D-don't push her away."

"I like her."

"I can tell."

I spread my hands. "What do I do? I don't know how to approach this. I get all up in my head." I threw my hands in the air, then leaned back and closed my eyes. "My life is too crazy to bring someone else into it. I'm taking care of too many people. I'm . . ."

"D-desperate for help but unwilling to t-take it?"

"Maybe," I mumbled.

"Lonely and sad b-but don't trust any w-woman with your heart?"

I sighed. "Yes."

The quick admission pained me, but her honesty finally hit a truth that needed to be thumped a bit. Dad had always been proud of my self-sufficiency, but maybe I'd taken it a bit too far.

She smiled warmly at me. "Time for ch-change, Bash."

"Thanks, Dagny."

She reached across the table again, and squeezed my hand. "You'll f-f-figure this out, B-bash. We're always here f-for you when you need us."

"Thanks."

A clanking sound followed a muttered curse. Hernandez appeared through the back door a minute later with a foul expression that almost made me laugh. His gaze dropped to Dagny's hand on mine.

"You cutting in on my girl, amigo?" he drawled.

I leaned back. "If you're not home, might as well."

He laughed, smacked a fat kiss on Dagny's lips. I stretched, shocked to find we'd been talking for hours. I felt bleary-eyed tired. My body needed more sleep than this on my day off, but I couldn't bring myself to feel too upset about it.

"Thanks again for dinner, Dagny." I stacked my bowl, spoon, and cup in the sink after rinsing them. "Delicious, as always."

I could feel Hernandez studying me. Through the reflection in the window over the sink, I saw him give Dagny a questioning look. She shook it off.

"*Ab-b-buela* has been t-teaching me her ways." She winked at Hernandez. "One day, I'll get that t-t-tamale recipe."

* * *

The next day passed in a blur.

I visited Inessa, her doctor, and the hospice team that would start to check in on her. Her skin appeared a bit more gray and she seemed tired after a restless night's sleep. She laid with her head on her pillow, a favorite fairytale movie playing in the background. The sight gave me a throwback to my childhood, when she'd calm with the cartoons that we'd watch together for hours while eating popcorn.

"Could be months," the hospice nurse said with kindness and warmth. He was a middle-aged man named Gregor with a salt-and-pepper goatee and a slightly slavic accent in his voice. "Her body will decide when to go. We'll keep watching. She'll be comfortable when she passes, whenever that is."

The uncertainty didn't sit well with me, but Inessa had always kept me guessing. I'd had years to grapple with her shortened lifespan, but as it approached, I felt even more at a loss for what to do with it.

What sort of world would I have without Inessa in it?

A bleak one.

One with no one.

Dahlia rose to my mind then, but I pushed her back. No, I didn't have that claim on her. My world was so . . . sad. Dagny's conversation hovered in my mind for half the day while I battled myself.

Let Dahlia in?

Spare her the pain and keep her out?

I had to banish those questions to visit Dad again, which only set me on edge further.

This time, he wandered the halls with a walker. His head bounced a little as he walked, gazing around. I stood outside the doors, hands in my pockets. His doctor came by, shook my hand, and proceeded with an equally morose update.

"His body remains mostly healthy, but his mind continues to deteriorate. His weight loss hasn't slowed much from the shakes we've been giving him. He also hasn't been all that interested in food, but we'll keep trying. We'll see more and more of this as the disease progresses. His body has started to follow his mind, which is normal."

Dr. Ferdinand watched him through the doors with me, her gray hair pulled away from her face with a clip.

"How long could this be?"

"It's hard to say," she murmured. "Months. A year?" She reached out, a hand on my arm. "I'm sorry, Bastian. I don't have any certainty to offer you, especially at a time when you're also dealing with your sister's medical problems. You stand to lose a great deal in the next span of time, and you carry a lot on your shoulders. Is there anyone that can support you?"

"Yes, I have help."

She studied me, then seemed to accept my bland response, despite all evidence to the contrary.

"We'll continue to do our best to take care of your father, and if there's anything else I can do, please let me know."

I nodded.

"Thanks."

A quick stop at Vikram's ended in failure. He didn't answer the door. I had to suppress the urge to pick his lock and break inside to shake some sense into him, which we'd done before.

The thought of getting back to Dahlia propelled me away from his place with a few threats to return as soon as I could.

Before leaving Jackson City, I texted Dahlia.

Bastian: Can I stop by and see you?

Dahlia: Of course! I just got off work and am watching online videos about replacing my stabilizer jack. Dagny's guy should have parts a week earlier than the other place. You know, the usual.

Bastian: Leaving Jackson City now.

The clock crept past three by the time I made it halfway through the canyon. There was still laundry to fold and a list of things to buy. We'd abandoned my to-do list yesterday after the Armenian restaurant. Now, after laying everything out to Dagny, my mind churned around with new mental space to think.

I didn't know where things lay between me and Dahlia after the intensity of yesterday. It wouldn't be a stretch to call us *friends*, yet I'd plunged her face first into the drama of my life. She took care of my cat and my company. Those pushed us a step beyond friends.

Was I desperate?

Was this fair to her?

I wasn't an idiot, even if women and relationships and pressure gave me anxiety. Dahlia had some interest in me or else she wouldn't have been so kind yesterday. Or maybe she would have. Some people felt obligatory kindness.

Maybe she'd turn me away today. Tell me *sorry, I'm not interested in this because I want Jakob back* or far more likely, *sorry, I'm not interested in the details of your life.*

Hadn't that been happening forever? Women weren't interested in what I had to offer. They wouldn't be interested in Jess's books if they knew a male wildland firefighter wrote them. Dad had plenty of women he'd tried to date over the years that had eventually left, unwilling to invest in children with special needs. My birth parents hadn't been interested in me either.

At least, not at the time.

Which is exactly the moment I chickened out.

Despite my discussion with Dagny last night, I knew then that I couldn't invest more time in Dahlia. Yes, I wanted more help in my world. No, I didn't trust more help. Because people left.

I didn't want to endure Dahlia leaving, not when Inessa and Dad had so little life left.

What would happen to me when Dahlia left too?

Disaster.

Difficult or not, things flowed more easily in my world when I took care of them myself. It had always been that way. Dahlia had already taken on too many pieces of my life, I had to stop the process before I gave up too much.

Instead of steering the truck to Dahlia's once I rumbled into Pineville, I navigated through the old neighborhood and sat in Dad's driveway with a sinking feeling.

Coward. Major, major coward. Unable to help myself, I

grabbed my phone and sent her a text before I could stop the momentum.

Bastian: Sorry, forgot a few things I need to grab before tomorrow, and still have some laundry to do. Maybe we can meet up when I get back? I leave early.

Her response took several minutes to come.

Dahlia: Totally fine. Need any help?

Bastian: I've got it, thanks.

Dahlia: Everything okay with your sister and dad? Did you like the hospital people?

A wary smile stole over me, but quickly died. Surely, she meant hospice. Another sign that she didn't live in the same world as me. Frankly, I wasn't sure I wanted to bring her into it.

Wouldn't be fair or simple or safe or any of those things.

Bastian: Went fine, thanks.

Dahlia: This sudden change of plans doesn't have anything to do with how much vulnerability you showed yesterday, does it?

Her question turned my chest to ice. Well. There was a point-blank question if I'd ever seen one.

At first, I had no idea how to respond. My thumb hesitated over the phone. The truth or a lie were my only options, and I respected her too much to lie.

I settled for somewhere in the middle.

Bastian: Probably.

Dahlia: I'm on your side, Bastian. You don't have to do it all alone, you know? You shouldn't. I'd love to help. And I'd love to see you again.

Her moxie deserved respect. She fearlessly put the truth out there. I swallowed past the lump in my throat and leaned my head back against the headrest. Nope. Didn't want to deal with this right now.

Five minutes passed before I found the words in my spinning mind and typed a reply.

Bastian: Thanks. Give me time.

The dark feeling of being an utter jerk crawled over me as I climbed out of Dad's truck. I'd just shut her and her kindness down in a cold way.

First, I changed plans. Second, I messaged her instead of calling. Forming words and articulating them in person was too much to ask right now. Third, I did the over-the-phone equivalent of turning my back and walking away without explanation.

Now, I walked into Dad's house and fought off the panic. Sirens blared in my head, screeching around like strobe lights. There was no way to think through anxiety. I just had to put some space between me and this situation so I could massage it with time.

In the distance, the smoke plume doubled. Reports spoke of high winds overnight, and I had the creeping feeling that my reckoning with fire had just about come due.

Chapter Twenty-Three

DAHLIA

4:00 the next morning came far too early.

Bleary from lack of sleep, though not from a book this time, but from Jess him/herself, I shuffled around the Frolicking Moose with a coffee in hand, one-handedly attempting to do my job.

The constant flow of caffeine took awhile to chug my brain back to life. My phone vibrated with alerts from social media, but I ignored it for now. Those could wait for later. Residual release posts, probably.

When the caffeine revived my brain, I almost wished it hadn't.

Questions lay there.

Yesterday had been a vague blur. A weird conundrum. Bastian and I had parted at the end of our previous day with some strangeness between us. Both of us seemed to feel it, like the end of an intense time when we both needed space to think.

That didn't bother me much. I'd wanted some time to process through everything I'd witnessed, and lunch with him had been easy going despite the day.

His ditched attempt to see me yesterday *did* bother me, however. Clearly, he'd gotten into his own head.

But *why*?

What did it mean?

Did I push him too hard? I'd come at him with pure, observant truth. Maybe he hadn't been ready for it. Pele told me all the time I came on too strong when I felt like I was right. Maybe my cousin had wisdom I didn't.

Bastian remained an utter puzzle to me. Reading the latest Jess release didn't help matters. Knowing him better now, though I didn't know the details of his non-fire-affected life super well, I saw him laid out in the words.

Love interests with lingering maladies. Grouchy and imperfect, often broody males. The quiet way he spoke, normally saying so little, put him at odds with his chattering protagonists that bubbled full of life.

Katrina lay amidst the maze of problems. Was she still around? She'd indicated a likelihood that she'd be here for a few more days, but doing what? It was entirely possible she'd stationed herself at the shop yesterday while Lizbeth ran the place. Katrina could have staked out looking for Jess all day . . . but I doubted it.

Something else brewed there.

Regardless, I resolved to have patience with Bastian. He'd requested as much, anyway, which all but affirmed my suspicion that he felt he'd been a little *too* open with me. Freaked him out, I bet.

The weight of what he bore for his family meant he needed a friend. I would willingly be that friend for him, although I couldn't deny that I felt something for Bastian. Meeting his family and seeing his burning, compassionate core had dropped me hard into new feelings.

My raging, school-girl-age twitterpation developed into

something that looked a lot more raw and real. Admiration and shock and amazement.

The undeniable urge to be part of his world couldn't be denied.

The jingling bells on the door yanked my thoughts back to the store. I turned around mid-yawn, then stopped completely. Katrina stood there, looking oddly *not* like Lolo. Instead of wild outfits, she had a calm pair of jeans, black shirt, and backpack slung over one shoulder. Her dreadlocks were pulled away from her face, which had no eccentric makeup today.

"Hey," I said.

She smiled. "Hey."

Sensing something different about her, I carefully asked, "Usual today?"

"Nah." She set her computer bag on the table nearest the counter, then leaned back against it. She studied me, her gaze thoughtful. The acrid scent of forest fire swirled into the shop with her. It dried out my throat and made my already nervous heart beat a little harder.

"Everything all right?" I asked. My gaze darted to the clock. 6:05. I'd been puttering around, lost in my own thoughts, for hours.

"Would you mind if I asked you a few questions?" she asked.

I shrugged, even though alarm bells pealed through my mind.

"Sure."

On the counter next to me, my phone buzzed again. I ignored it, even though two rapid-succession vibrations followed. She glanced at it, then to me. Her expression narrowed further.

"You know Jess, don't you?"

Accusation hardened her tone. I lifted one eyebrow.

"What?"

"Jess. I know she's here and I think you know her."

Shock rendered me totally speechless. "But . . . I . . . why do you think that?"

Katrina held herself calmly, but her chin angled up.

"Why wouldn't you? This coffee shop is known as the center of town. I've been here long enough to see that it's true. You're the only barista here that I've seen so far except for a redhead yesterday. If anyone would know Jess, it's you. Jess has been here." Katrina leaned forward. "I *know* she's used the internet here."

I blinked, attempting to pull my thoughts together.

"Um . . . this is awkward," I whispered. "I . . . listen, I know you really enjoy her books but she clearly doesn't want to be found. Why would you push that? You can't force anyone to reveal themselves."

A flicker of pain crossed her eyes. She shook her head. "No, I don't buy that. I suspect you know who she is and don't want to give her away."

"If that's true, this isn't going to make me want to do it even more."

She rolled her eyes. "I guess I can respect that if you're friends or something, but . . . I just came here to . . . to meet her." Her eyes closed. "To *finally* meet her. It's been years and years and . . . I deserve that much."

No guile entered her tone at just how *weird* that seemed. Did she think that sort of stalking was okay? A few puzzle pieces were clearly missing here.

"Why would you expect a famous author to reveal herself to you when you stalked her here?"

"I didn't stalk her. It's . . . it's not that hard to trace an IP address. And she's not just a famous author to me."

"IP address tracing is hard for the average human!"

Katrina rolled her eyes. "Whatever. I'm convinced she's

here. It's the perfect place to hide in plain sight. The perfect place to write books for a living. What can I do for you that would convince you to tell me more? Or to tell her that I'm here, if you haven't already."

Something in her body language clued me in. This was more than just a mystery. Pain lurked beneath Katrina's obsession.

"Why are you so determined to speak to her?" I asked.

Her nostrils flared. Katrina drew in a deep breath, then let it out. "Because I think she knows me," she finally said. She chewed on her bottom lip. "I think she wrote me into her book as Lolo."

"Why would she do that?"

She spoke the words so softly I almost didn't hear her. "Because she loves me."

"I'm sorry," I murmured, utterly confused, "what?"

Frustrated now, Katrina straightened up.

"I just want to talk to her. See her. I want . . . I want to see if my supposition is correct. The person that I am and show up as everyday was frighteningly represented in that book. That can't just be coincidental. She must be Brooke!"

"Brooke? Who is Brooke?"

Katrina pushed on. "There was this girl I dated once online. Brooke. We spoke all the time for years. Years! Together, we had a true, soul-level connection. She . . . anyway, I loved her. A lot. She broke up with me before we could meet in person, and it's possible she catfished me. But I haven't been able to find her ever since and I look for her all the time. She was an avid writer and she loved romance novels. Her greatest dream was to publish her books. When we last spoke, she had some interests from a small publishing company, but she hadn't said who."

Katrina's voice trailed away into a mournful tone. I stared

at her, at a loss for words. How could this situation get any weirder?

Any sadder?

"About a year after Brooke disappeared, I stumbled onto Jess," Katrina whispered. "She was a growing name in the romance book world and her writing seemed . . . familiar. She reminded me of Brooke. Then I read *Lust is a Darkening Hellscape* with Lolo in it. Me in it, essentially. And . . . ever since I read the book, I've had to know. Is Jess really Brooke? So I emailed Jess. Told her how much I loved the book. How much it meant to me. I coded it in a way that Brooke would know it was me. I . . ."

My stomach felt a little tremor of fear when she couldn't finish her sentence. Had Katrina's emails been one of those that were buried in Bastian's life? Had he deleted it without responding—maybe even on accident—and now she felt ignored and slighted and bitter?

"And?" I asked.

Tears filled her eyes. She tried to blink them away, jaw tight, but they glimmered there anyway.

"And Jess sent me a signed copy of *Lust is a Darkening Hellscape.* At the bottom it said, *Love, Jess* and had a heart thing drawn underneath it. The same way that Brooke had signed her hand-written notes to me. Except with her name, not Jess. It was a sign. It . . . I was certain of it. Jess *is* Brooke. I've been determined to find her."

With a flood of understanding, my entire body melted. Katrina was a heartbroken, seeking soul attempting to find her new place in a world she hadn't asked for. She wasn't a frightening stalker. Just a woman looking for her love.

"And you're trying to find Brooke here," I murmured.

Her chin tilted higher, forcing her to look at me down her nose. Despite my own wariness around Katrina/Lolo, I couldn't deny the real fear in her eyes.

"Yes." She swallowed. "It's been so long now. I don't want to live without an explanation any longer. I need closure. I've obsessed over this too long."

"Where do you live, Katrina?"

"New York or LA. I bounce between the two. I came here from New York."

"You came all that way?"

She nodded.

I sighed. "Have a seat," I murmured. "And I'll tell you what I can."

Relief, coupled with fear, filled her expression as she lowered into a nearby chair. The cagey energy she'd brought into the store subsided as I walked around the counter and sat down across from her. Now that her secret was out, she seemed a little more at ease. Terrified, but not so . . . odd.

The strangeness of this entire situation had set me off balance, and I struggled to pull my thoughts together. We sat there for several long moments. As if the world burning by fire outside wasn't enough, now Katrina had morphed into a lovesick woman seeking her lost mate.

A heart drawn underneath an author signature was hardly a rare idea, particularly in the romance world. Her timeline didn't really line up, either. Brooke had been looking for a publisher when it sounded like Jess's romance books were already out.

Somehow, Katrina allowed reality to line up in a deceptive way . . . or maybe her heart had just been so broken she *saw* the things she wanted to see. Either way, Bastian was not her Brooke.

All of this happened to be the whim of extraordinary circumstances that seemed almost too far to believe possible.

Somehow, I had to make her see that without outing Bastian.

My thoughts ran to Bastian and Inessa and his father and

the careful balance on which Bastian lived his life. Precarious, at best. Although things remained tenuous between me and Bastian, his secret wouldn't topple on my watch. Neither did Katrina have to be villainized either. Heartbreak drove people to dire straits. I remembered that.

"I do know Jess," I said quietly.

Her expression thrilled until I held up a hand.

"You are right. Jess does work here sometimes. Not a lot, but sometimes. I can tell you, however, that Jess is not Brooke."

The structure of her face slowly crumpled.

"You don't know Brooke," she said quickly. "Jess could really be Brooke but she'd been catfishing me. Remember? She was hiding. I just need to hear her voice and then I'll know. Then I'll ..." She choked up. "Then I'll *finally* know."

I reached out, put my warm hand on top of hers and said, "I'm sorry, Katrina. There is no way that Jess is really Brooke. There's nothing more I can say because Jess's story isn't mine to tell, but I can assure you that all of this is . . . mere happenstance. I'm sorry. Brooke broke your heart and that is the last of it."

Tears filled her eyes. Her nostrils flared. "You're trying to tell me that a total stranger wrote me into a book, gave me the same signature as my beloved Brooke used to do, and has no idea who I am? It's impossible. Jess *has* to be Brooke."

"What if she isn't?" I asked quietly.

"She must be!" Katrina cried. She shot to her feet, a mess of tears on her face now. "Because if Brooke *isn't* Jess, then she just left me. She let me go. She just . . . she just let me go. She was my person. How could she do that?"

Her stark whisper left a crater in my chest. I stood up slowly, matched her in height. "Katrina, I'm so sorry. Brooke is gone. You'll never find her by seeking Jess."

She breathed heavily now. Her hands trembled at her side

as a sob collapsed her chest. I held out my arms and she crumbled into a sob. I stroked her hair and murmured words that didn't make sense. She cried in my arms for several long minutes while I tried to puzzle my brain back together. My phone buzzed on the counter, incessant.

Outside, several people congregated at the windows. They didn't come in, just peered at us. The weird way they lingered outside so early in the morning set my hair on edge.

"Oh no," Katrina whispered. She pulled away, tear stained cheeks bright. Panic filled her gaze. "Oh no."

"What?"

She wiped her tears with shaky hands. "I might have . . . I wanted Brooke to reveal herself so I . . ."

"What?" I whispered.

More people appeared at the door. A crowd of twenty now, with others streaming from across the street. Where had they come from? From how far away? Katrina turned to look at me, apology in her eyes.

"I'm so sorry. I . . . I told everyone that Jess lived here."

My blood turned cold. "What?"

"In the social media group. The big one?" She hastily added, "So many women want to thank her! They just want her to know what it meant to them that she wrote those books. That's . . . that's all. I thought it would drive Brooke out of hiding so I could see her. If there were more people, maybe she'd reveal herself." Anguished now, she stepped back. "I'm sorry! It was wrong. I know that now, but I didn't then. I was just desperate to see Brooke and finish this documentary. I can't stop them now."

"Stop them?" I echoed softly.

Katrina paled.

"Jess's fans are *here*."

* * *

Horror tripled through me as I stared at the congregating crowd outside.

"Katrina," I hissed. "What have you done? There is an active fire here! They said last night that all of Pineville could be evacuated with all the wind today."

She stared outside, wide-eyed. "I don't know!" she cried. "I wasn't thinking. I just had to see Brooke."

Did none of these women care about the billowing inferno north of here? Granted, there was more than one way out of town, with a main exit opposite the fire, and several others around the other side of the reservoir.

Still, none of this felt very safe.

"Make this right!" I snapped.

"I don't know how!" she wailed.

I jabbed a hand to the porch. "Tell them the truth. Not that Jess is here, but that you were mistaken and you don't know where or who she is. All of that is true. Whatever you do, don't lead them to believe she *is* here."

"How do I do that?" she cried.

I stalked behind the counter again, shoving a chair under a table as I went. "I don't know! Get creative, but figure it out. They love Jess just like you, maybe you can send them somewhere else." I paused to glance outside. More women had appeared. Several of them chatted brightly. "Where did they come from?" I asked in growing astonishment.

Meanwhile, my phone vibrated again and again and again.

"Everywhere."

"When did you tell them?" I asked as another car stopped in the parking lot and dumped three more women.

The group had grown to barely surpassed thirty at the most. They must be coming from places other than Jackson City, because that highway had closed last night because of the fire.

"I told them to come today in the early morning and have

a sit-in outside." Katrina's lower lip blanched beneath her upper teeth bruising it. "I thought we could sit here all day and see if Jess would come! In the meantime, we'd be able to talk about all her books and I could get some filming done for the documentary I'm producing that covers this story. So many women are curious about her, it wasn't that hard!"

"And you planned to film the whole time?" I asked, livid. "To take advantage of Jess's obligation to show herself and spring a camera on her so you can get some accolades?"

Her expression dropped. "No," she snapped. "I might be a documentary filmmaker, but I wasn't using my love for Brooke as a career pedestal, thank you very much."

The coldness in her tone convinced me.

"Tell them," I muttered and grabbed my phone as it vibrated again.

Messages from the social media groups clogged my screen. Text messages from Lizbeth poured in after. I opened Lizbeth's message thread and scrolled to the first unread text at the top.

Lizbeth: Just saw a post in one of Jess's groups that she's been found! There's a group of women that took red-eyes and flew out last night to get her to reveal herself. Can you believe that?

"Can believe," I muttered.

Five minutes later, she'd sent another text.

Lizbeth: Shut up. A comment down the post says it's in Pineville. They're recruiting more people to come. As in PINEVILLE. Our Pineville.

My stomach started to hurt as I kept scrolling to the last message received less than one minute ago.

Lizbeth: WHAT. IS. HAPPENING. The comments said they're meeting at the Frolicking Moose. ARE PEOPLE THERE?

My phone began to ring. Lizbeth's name flashed across the screen. While Katrina stared outside, chewing a nail, I answered with a distracted, "Hello?"

"What's going on?" Lizbeth cried.

"It's . . . a long story."

"Does Jess live here? Are there people at the shop? Fill me in on everything. What is happening?"

"I can't explain right now. There are thirty people outside and more coming."

"I'm on my way!"

She hung up before I could ask how she'd get here. Lizbeth and JJ lived in Jackson City and the highway was closed. Katrina finally stepped outside and called out in a shaky voice, Hello, ladies. Thank you all for coming. I . . . I can't believe we were actually able to rally together in person to meet Jess."

"No," I sang under my breath, "you're not meeting Jess."

The door closed behind her, blunting the sound of her voice.

With a sharp breath, I pushed Katrina out of my mind and turned my back on the growing crowd. Ten seconds. I needed ten seconds to rally my thoughts back together. Once I couldn't see the massing people, I closed my eyes and drew in a deep breath.

Time to make a plan.

The last thing I wanted to do was draw Bastian here. Although the women would likely never assume he was someone important, it would be too risky. Because maybe they'd make that leap and he wouldn't be able to stop it and . . . . nope.

Not bringing him here.

But should I tell him?

This was *his* career on the line, not mine. Yet, how would I explain this? He left for the fire this morning around five. I saw the wildland truck leave. My gaze darted to the clock. He'd be out of cell range by now.

The weirdness between us yesterday gave me pause. He'd asked for time, so I hesitated over sending a text. Even though this was business related, what if he didn't respond? What if he did and he was upset? No, Bastian wouldn't get upset—not like that, anyway. I certainly couldn't send a video, and I wasn't about to call.

Finally, I just tapped out a text.

Dahlia: Some interesting developments on the Katrina front. Shoot me a text when you can? Would love to discuss.

Casual, non-hurried, but clear and concise. If Bastian knew me at all, it would probably make him panic even more. When was I cool and calm about any drama?

While I didn't want to hide this Jess-frenzy in the making, I also didn't want to stress him out. If he was stuck on a mountain fighting an inferno, he wouldn't be able to come down here anyway. He might be in the best possible spot ever—completely inaccessible. Knowing him, he'd stew on the situation and get stressed out.

At least, however, I'd contacted him. For a moment, I thought of calling Priyanka, but what could she do?

Time for *me* to handle this.

I whirled back around as more women crowded outside. Forty and counting. They seemed amiable enough. Some bounced on the balls of their feet, clapping. Others held onto bags stuffed full of what appeared to be books. A few males were interspersed among them, but they hung around the edges. Here with their wives, maybe? Not that men can't love a good romance novel.

Bastian proved that.

Several locals from the book club stood out amongst the rest of the crowd. That probably meant Lizbeth rallied them or they'd seen the post themselves. Or maybe they saw the chaos and decided to stop.

Either way, this could get interesting because the small mountain town of Pineville wouldn't know what hit it if the full power of the Jess fandom descended here.

While Katrina said something to the growing mass, my phone continued to chime with more alerts from the social media groups. Had Katrina noticed my phone getting blown up earlier? She'd looked at it suspiciously enough. Next thing I knew, she'd think *I* was Jess. The thought made me giggle.

A familiar head of red hair surfed through the crowd as I turned my phone to silent. Seconds later, Lizbeth stepped inside, her eyes wide. She pressed her back against the door and muttered, "Shut. Up. This. Is. Insane."

My throat tightened. Here came the reckoning. She darted toward me, moving deftly despite her belly.

"How are you here?" I asked, startled.

"Adventura evacuated last night because the firefighters were going to do a controlled burn to prevent the fire from crossing the highway."

A grim expression showed on her face.

"JJ and I drove to Adventura yesterday to help Mark and Stella clear out and prepare the camp just in case. Plus, I didn't want to be blocked from my family, so we're staying with them until the canyon opens back up."

"Scary."

"Very." She gulped. "It was a mess. Mark had to let the horses out of their pen and hope they find a safe place."

"But what if the horses get caught by the fire?" I squeaked.

She shrugged. "They'll run away. With any luck, they'll come back after things have settled down and not get hurt."

"What if they don't?"

She frowned. "Then," she murmured, "they don't."

"Macabre," I muttered.

"Very. We didn't have time to get a trailer and get them all out. For the record," she added with an upheld finger, "all of us told Mark *not* to get horses, but he had to follow through—"

"Lizbeth—"

"Back to the point." She nodded once. "I'm also here in Pineville to make sure Bethany and Mav are safe, because the fire could push close to their house up on the mountain. They're already ready to go in case they need to. And this?" Her finger twirled in a circle. "Is bananas."

"Right?" I croaked, brought back to the moment with a dose of reality. We had several things we needed to figure out.

"What is going on?"

She slipped behind the counter, but her gaze traveled wordlessly outside again. The fact that she didn't immediately drill me for answers or accuse me of harboring secrets calmed my nerves. All she knew about this situation came from social media.

Good enough.

For several long moments, we stared at the parking lot together. Women milled around, talking to each other after Katrina finished. Some of them kept an eye on the horizon. Others laughed, joining circles. Wind twisted by outside and ruffled their hair.

"Well," Lizbeth murmured, "they are calm."

"At least that," I sighed.

"So spill," she demanded. "What's going on?"

Lizbeth deserved as much of the truth as was mine to give. I wouldn't lie to her, but I also wouldn't betray Bastian either. I drew in a deep breath.

"Katrina, the girl that had been speaking out there, tracked Jess to the Frolicking Moose."

"Here?" she screeched.

I nodded. "Says she tracked Jess's IP."

Lizbeth's eyes narrowed to slashes. "Interesting," she murmured. "I never thought about that, to be honest. Bit . . . weird and maybe creepy and desperate at the same time. Is she stable?"

"I think so."

"This is the same girl that had been claiming to have found Jess?"

"The one. It *was* a desperate move. It's this big dramatic story," I said with a wave of my hand, "but she basically thought the real Jess was a girl she once met and dated online that catfished her. Katrina wanted to out her. So she told all these women that Jess worked from here and they all decided to come. Today. They were hoping that a sit-in or a big crowd would draw Jess out of hiding."

"Sweet baby pineapple," Lizbeth muttered. "It's mad or brilliant or both. If this is what other romance lovers are doing, I might need to step up my game. Where are all these people coming from?"

I shrugged. "I don't know. Everywhere? Local? Both? I haven't had a chance to ask."

"Some are local," she murmured, then waved to someone that called *hello*! through the window. "I recognize a few women from the library and book club, but . . . not all of them I'd wager. That's nuts."

"Yeah," I whispered.

"Think it'll work?" Her voice pitched a bit higher. "Do you think Jess will actually come?"

"No."

"When I walked in, Katrina was saying that they should just have a big discussion and book club inside in the back room, but that she was wrong about Jess. Katrina said that Jess isn't here."

My heart crinkled for Katrina. Well-enough intentioned of a motive, if not totally creeptastic, but not well thought out. I felt for her. Heartbreak sucked. Unrequited, unexpected heartbreak? That must *totally* suck.

"I don't know," I said.

Lizbeth reared back, hands in the air. "Hold the phone. How are we not talking about the fact that Jess *might freaking live in Pineville?*"

"According to Katrina," I squeaked. "She might have made it up!"

"Still." Lizbeth's face became a maze of concentration. "What if? That would be insane. What if she came into the shop all the time? What if I'd served her at the bakery? What if she vacations here at an old family cabin and I ran into her by accident on a frequent basis and *I never knew*? I read *while* I walk, you know? I know for a fact that I read three of her books while following JJ around the grocery store across the street. She could have seen that. Does that blow your mind?"

"The fact that you read while you walk blows my mind, yes."

"You bettah believe it," she murmured. "Saves a ridiculous amount of time and, c'mon! How did you set Rodrigo down? Anyway." Her expression brightened. "Think she could be that crazy lady that walks her dogs off leash by the river? No. Definitely not."

She continued to ramble to herself and I let her go. As long as she asked no questions, I had no obligation to provide answers. Before I could say another word, Katrina whirled around and came back inside. The wildness had calmed in her gaze, but uncertainty still lived there.

"Ah . . ."

She stopped a few paces into the room and chewed on her

bottom lip. Her gaze drifted to Lizbeth and then back to me. Lizbeth waved.

"How'd it go?" I asked carefully.

Katrina pulled in a deep breath. "Fine. I mean, they're not going to storm the coffee shop, but . . . they also aren't going to leave."

"What?" I asked.

"They want Jess. I told them I was wrong but . . . they didn't believe me. They're going to start taking pictures and spreading the word to see if we can get more people. One lady thinks Jess will show up if we fill all of Pineville with love and support from her fans."

"Sweet baby pineapple," Lizbeth whispered again.

"In the meantime," Katrina continued, "they want to start a round-table discussion about the latest launch. Someone thought about playing the audiobook out loud until Jess comes, but I told them no one could disturb the peace."

"Thank you," I sighed.

My face must have betrayed my annoyance because Katrina winced. "I'm so sorry. I don't know what to do now."

Lizbeth leaned against the counter. "Well, let's get them fed." She reached into her pocket for a ponytail holder. "We'll put them in the back room until we meet the person limit, then people can cycle in and out. No reason the Frolicking Moose shouldn't be put to work." She pointed to Katrina. "Any rowdiness or issues? It's coming back on you."

Katrina nodded.

"Sure. I'll let them know."

Chapter Twenty-Four

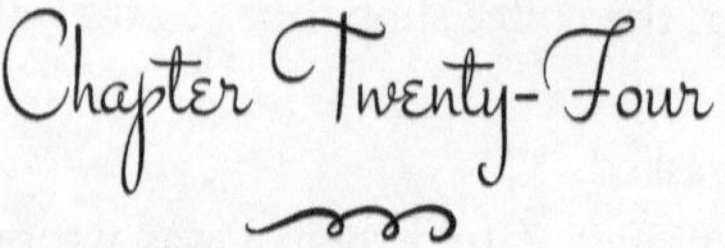

BASTIAN

Mack, the hotshot Superintendent, pointed to a map with a sooty finger.

"She's going to try to make a run."

A red line behind his finger indicated where the fire had last been mapped. Not far away lay the highway that ran from Pineville to Jackson City. The beast had definitely advanced.

Mack stood in front of our squad with a plug of tobacco puffed against his bottom lip, near his teeth. Smoke filtered through the forest around us, blocking out sunlight with a dull, orange haze.

"She's a real witch," muttered someone else.

Why, I wanted to ask, *are fires always referenced as female?*

"We shut down the highway between Jackson City and Pineville yesterday afternoon," Mack continued. "Last night, we did a controlled burn from the highway back toward the fire to get ahead of it. Squads have been patrolling through the night. No torching trees or sign of spotting on the other side of the highway yet, so it's doing its job so far."

A good sign. Burning before the fire arrived meant the fire would die down before it became out of control. Or so we hoped. Fire had a way of blasting through every expectation to do whatever the hell it wanted.

Mack pointed to the other side of the highway on the map, near Adventura. "We have structures at Adventura summer camp that were evacuated and protected last night." He spit a clear streak of juice. "It's empty."

Dahlia immediately came to mind. Because everything had to return back to her these days. The deep umber color of bark reminded me of her eyes. A restaurant she might like that we passed on the highway. A woman with long, wavy hair like hers. There was no simple act of forgetting a woman like Dahlia.

Not even when I tried.

With forced concentration, I turned my attention back to Mack's update for the tenth time. If Adventura was evacuated, then Sione would be safe. Dahlia would be tucked away in Pineville and I had no reason to worry over her.

Get out, I thought, *of my head.*

"The wind is blowing west to east and coming in fast," Mack continued. "We're anticipating growing gusts in the thirties to forties depending on slope and terrain. It's going to shift around mid afternoon and blow to the southeast and pick up speed, with gusts expected up to eighty miles at the higher altitudes."

"Right to Pineville," Nilla muttered.

I grimly agreed.

"Mandatory evacuations to the Pineville area should be going out soon," Mack continued. "We have volunteer fire departments and the Sheriff department working on local evacuations. In the meantime, you'll patrol the ground between the highway and Adventura summer camp to watch for candlesticks or spotting. Don't let the fire catch on that side of the canyon."

Mack nodded once, then faded back.

While the team broke apart to head back to the wildland truck, my fingers itched to send a quick text warning to Dahlia. I pushed the urge back. She'd sent a message but I hadn't read it yet.

Like the true coward I'd already shown myself to be when it came to women, I didn't want to read it. Didn't really want to know what it said inside. Probably something about the emails, which would be a disappointment and a relief. I wanted more even though I'd asked her for time.

Didn't deserve more, though.

My phone stayed safe in my pack while I loaded into the truck with the rest of the team, but my thoughts wandered far away.

Dad's neighborhood would be safe from the fire. The flames would have to drop into the valley, cross the river, and do impressive dancing to twist around to where he lived. I had no fear of that. He and Nessa both lived in Jackson City, which was a thirty minute drive north of the fire. They were safe.

Dahlia *wasn't*.

That hobbled RV was up on the mountainside and right in the path of the oncoming inferno. If it came as hot and fast as the weather conditions would allow today, she wouldn't have time to fix the stabilizer jack and get out of there. Or would she? She'd mentioned working on it yesterday. Maybe it was already done. Did she get the parts? Did she need help? With evacs going out, Hernandez would be too swamped to help if she needed it.

I muttered a swear word under my breath. She'd figure it out. Sione might have already helped her get unstuck if he'd evacuated to Pineville. No doubt Pineville was already anticipating evacuations. With so much uncertainty around the fire, the Frolicking Moose would be as slow and quiet as ever. Maybe they'd even close it to let Dahlia evacuate her RV.

I silently hoped that whatever happened, Dahlia would ditch the RV and get the hell out of there.

Chapter Twenty-Five

DAHLIA

A smoky haze settled over Pineville.

Sometime in between Lizbeth opening the floodgates to invite the swell of women into the back room and a group of ten more coming in a van from a state over, the wind picked up.

Gusts sprinted around the parking lot, whipping hair, leaves, and dirt into everyone's eyes. It slammed into the Frolicking Moose and sent whitecapped waves frothing on the lake. We crowded as many people as fire code would allow into the back room and interior. The empty loft upstairs became a book club discussion on books 1-6, which opened some space in the main area.

Still, women waited outside with excited, bright chatter.

"This is insane, don't you think?" I asked Lizbeth as I shoveled ice into a plastic cup. "All these women, at least a hundred now, want to meet an author that they all love. Meanwhile, an inferno rages north of here and no one can breathe all that well."

Lizbeth spread her hands. "Behold the power of romance."

"Do you think . . . I mean . . ."

My thoughts stuttered out before I could release them fully formed. My mind wrapped around an idea, but I couldn't say that I understood it yet. To let all this attention go unserved seemed like such a waste. I couldn't give them Jess, but maybe they could give something *to* Jess.

Twisting morsels of an idea began to spin together. All these women were here to meet and support Jess. Most of them had probably read all the books, maybe several times. They were peaceful, had a common bond, and wanted the same thing. Why *not* give them some satisfaction?

After all, hadn't they come all this way to form a connection with the author they loved? Maybe these women could get their goal after all. And benefit Bastian at the same time.

"Katrina," I called. "C'mere!"

She came around the corner, her bright cheeks a bit flushed. She couldn't hide her eager expression every time the door opened and she looked at it, as if she still hoped that Brooke would walk inside. Or maybe she really did want to meet Jess, and she thought that Jess might walk in and announce herself.

The panic and apology in her expression had faded into the warmth of mutual purpose and camaraderie.

"What's up?" she asked.

"I've been thinking about this whole situation. What if there's a way to make it so this isn't wasted? You know," I added hurriedly, "because Jess may not show up. All these women traveled so far to solve a mystery or to give their support, so I'd hate for that to feel misspent."

Could she hear the sudden nerves in my voice? Lizbeth didn't know that I'd confessed to knowing Jess. If possible, I wanted to keep it that way. So far, Katrina hadn't revealed me, but it would be an easy slip.

Katrina's gaze narrowed. "What do you mean?"

"Well, you're a filmmaker, right?"

"Right."

"And you've been filming this whole time anyway, right?"

"Yes."

"Do you have your equipment now?"

"Some. In my bag."

"Seems to me," I drawled, "that Jess might be kind of shy about who she is. Or maybe afraid that her fans won't like her? Or approve of her? Or maybe she has some kind of social anxiety or something? So maybe we can use this as an opportunity to show her how much her fans love her. No matter what," I tacked on.

"Oh," she murmured. Understanding illuminated her gaze. "Interesting."

My eyes widened. "Seems like a great opportunity to make something new that's never been done before. Might mean a *lot* to Jess, and also give these women an opportunity to confess their love for their favorite author? She might be more inclined to reveal herself if she has video proof of the kind of genuine readers she has."

Katrina's eyes glazed over. She blinked, came back into herself, and grinned. "That is an amazing idea."

Your best idea yet, Inner Me said.

Let's hope, I responded, *that Bastian doesn't hate me for it later.*

He could see it as a point of pressure, like I wanted to force him into revealing himself by showing fan support. That wasn't the intent, of course. Bastian had more support at his back than he thought.

Perhaps, if he saw it, he'd realize all the love his fans had for Jess and want to communicate with them more, even *as* Jess.

Katrina faded away. Another car parked in the grocery store parking lot across the street—our lot was long since packed—and four women rushed over. Lizbeth watched them with a sigh. Another round of titters came from the back room, then raucous laughter followed.

"Any updates?" Lizbeth asked quietly. Although she hadn't said the word *fire*, I could tell by the undertones of stress that's what she meant.

"Not that I've seen on my phone."

Lizbeth frowned.

The levity of all these Jess fans seemed to float around, nearly inextinguishable. Growing haze and smoke and wind made it impossible to forget what happened in the mountains north of us, no matter how much these women seemed immune to the fire. Although, I couldn't deny that the distraction felt nice.

I had intentionally avoided looking at the fire plume until I couldn't help myself anymore. By the time I glanced at the northern skyline, it was too late. Smoke had moved into the valley, obscuring anything more than 100 yards away.

Only the churn of the reservoir and the stores across the street were visible. My throat hurt. The scent of burning wood filled every single breath. The eerie light it created was like looking at the world through an orange glass. It lent a still, strange feeling to all of Pineville.

Meanwhile, the Jess crowd continued to mill inside and outside.

Some of them walked by and laughed the fire off. "We'll leave once Jess shows up," one woman reassured a friend as she headed out the door, probably to head to the loft entrance in the back. "I promise!"

The locals kept an eye out and muttered about animals at home. Everyone waited for something, but it wasn't the same tension.

In between orders, I checked my phone for new texts and worried over Bastian. Wind gusted outside from the northwest, as if driven from hell. It blasted the side of the coffee shop and sent leaves scuttling by.

What were the odds that such terrible weather could happen right when an epic fire waited to engulf us all? It felt as if the weather actively conspired to make everything worse.

Sometime around ten, my phone vibrated with a text.

Sione: We evacuated from camp last night.

Dahlia: Lizbeth mentioned that. Where are you staying?

Sione: At a hotel in Jackson City. Did you get the stabilizer jack fixed?

Dahlia: Not yet.

My RV was good and stuck at the campground. At this point, I'd have to hope the fire didn't come this far south because I couldn't move my trailer. If the fire came this far south and burned up the RV, I wouldn't be penniless thanks to insurance.

I would be homeless.

Sione: Sorry, cuz. We didn't have much time. We even had to let the horses loose.

My stomach flipped when another message came through right then, this one an alert. Red bars blinked on the top of my phone in warning, giving a low, annoying *bleep* with it.

Mandatory evacuations in progress for the Lower Pinegulch Area.

I blinked, read it again, and frowned.

A quick search for the local Pinegulch area made me gulp.

According to the map, Pinegulch was the canyon where the fire had originally started. Now it raced to the east.

My finger trailed along the canyon, which led right to a marked highway. Right across the highway lay Adventura. But there was more, because the whole Pinegulch area now under mandatory evacuation encompassed several miles south of there as well.

Including my campground.

Ugly.

This morning when I drove to the Frolicking Moose, I'd brought the most important essentials in my backpack. Computers. Hard drives. Pictures. My purse.

Walking away from my RV and not knowing if I'd ever see it again left a hollow spot inside me. Until now, I hadn't let myself think about it. Katrina and Jess and the shop had distracted me too much. Now, I felt the potential sorrow all the way in my gut.

My hands trembled when I opened up the text message to Sione again.

Dahlia: Glad you're safe.

Sione: Do you have access to a truck, by any chance?

My eyes flitted outside and off to the left. Not far away was the fire station, with the hotshots attached. Bastian's truck waited in the parking lot, barely visible through the smoke. A spare truck key was on the house key he'd given me.

Yes, I had access to a truck.

Whether I had permission to use said truck was another question entirely.

Dahlia: What do you need?

Sione: A truck to pull a horse trailer. A hotshot crew reported that some of the horses had returned to the stable at Adventura. No fire has spread that way yet, so they said Mark could get them if he hurries. He's in Pineville, so I can't help him. He's borrowing Maverick's truck and needs another one. Everyone else in Pineville is already loading up their stuff or using their trucks.

My breath caught. The hotshot crew might be Bastian's. To run to Adventura and help with the horses would give me a chance to see him. Maybe even clear the weird air between us.

I shook my head, brushing those thoughts aside. No, I had to focus on what was needed now. The horses, not affirmations from my crush.

Dahlia: Sure, but I've never driven horses before.

Sione: If you've pulled an RV, you can pull horses.

Dahlia: Done.

"Lizbeth!" I called.

She ducked out of the back room, eyebrows high. Noise from women laughing issued from the back room again.

"Sione just texted me."

Her face paled. "What is it? Something wrong with Adventura? The fire?"

I held up my phone. "Fine so far, I think. Some of the horses returned to the stable at Adventura, though. The hotshot crew said Mark could go get them, but he needs another truck and needs to leave now. Can I take Bastian's truck and go help him?"

Can I go see this guy I'm crazy about that I really want to like me? Inner Me tacked on, but I silenced her.

"Go. Yes. I got this."

"Pinegulch was just mandatory-evacuated." I ripped the apron strings off, balled it up, and tossed it onto the counter. "That includes the houses on the hills, up by my RV park and campground. Is that where Bethany lives?"

"Close, but not quite." Lizbeth gazed around, one hand on her hip. "Should we start kicking people out of here? If Pinegulch is evacuated, then Pineville will be next. I hate to send anyone home yet. Mav will be so happy to make up some lost revenue from this month being so slow, though, and we're safe with the reservoir right here . . ."

She trailed away. I couldn't help but wonder if Lizbeth found some solace in being around other people at a time like this.

"The evacuations aren't here yet," I said. "I'd wait until then and go from there." My gaze darted to Katrina, who had just fished some equipment out of a bag and started to fiddle with it. "Maybe give her a chance to get some video?"

Lizbeth glanced over, then nodded, lips pursed.

"Good idea. Besides, locals have started to come in and ask questions. They'll want somewhere to get updates and congregate anyway. The Frolicking Moose will stay open as a community support center."

"Sounds good. Thanks, Lizbeth."

A text vibrated in my hand. I glanced down.

Unknown number: Dahlia, this is Mark. I'm at the gas station at the corner of the highway with a trailer to hitch up to your truck. See you soon?

Dahlia: Be there in ten.

I grabbed my purse and tucked it under my arm.
"You good?"

Lizbeth shooed me away.

"A shop full of romance lovers gabbing about their favorite books and drinking coffee? Girlfriend, I got this."

The map on my phone displayed bright red lines around the active fire as I closed the browser and headed out the door.

To my eye, the fire appeared miles away from the highway still. Surely, enough time to drive up, help with the horses, see Bastian for a hot second if I got lucky, and head back down the mountain.

No problem.

I slipped into the smoke, my thoughts tangled up in fire.

Chapter Twenty-Six

BASTIAN

Years of wildland fire had trained me against bleak, dreary, soulless situations. Normally, charcoal-darkened hellscapes didn't bother me. Smoky terrains. Desperate animals fleeing their death. It all seemed so normal now.

Despite all that, a haunted feeling filled Adventura summer camp.

Maybe it had something to do with knowing what Adventura had been before the fire. Or knowing the owners and the people affected by the potential for harrowing loss.

For the first time in more than seven years as a wildland firefighter, I fought a fire on my home turf. The stakes of loss were personal now, even if Mark Bailey and I didn't have deep knowledge of each other.

Those thoughts accompanied me as I followed two other firefighters around the quiet camp. The ghosts of those that fled the danger seemed to lurk in the background.

Nilla checked a sprinkler set up on the main building while I veered toward the lake to check the hose access to water. Boot prints populated heavy tracks in the dirt around Adventura, indicating a broad bustle of movement as people scurried to get out. A volunteer fire department—probably Mark himself, too—had set most of this up.

They'd done well.

Not far from the lake lay a newish-looking stable. Three horses, skittish from the smoke, crowded the outside. Two of them pranced around, snorting when they saw me. I left a wide gap between us as I skirted the edge of the lake to head back.

When I returned to the main camp area, Nilla stared farther east. Rocky mountains jutted straight up behind Adventura, painted with slopes of evergreens in the steep faces. The mountains created a natural gorge, now filled with smoke, that led back. I'd hiked that gorge before.

Stunning, particularly in the summer, with the potential for frozen waterfalls climbing in the winter. A stream normally trickled out, but this dry summer had evaporated it to a muddy puddle now. Even the lake had lowered.

Much of Adventura was obscured now from smoke, but I recalled it from memory. The Merry Idiots and I had come this way before Mark Bailey purchased the land, back when it was nothing more than a forgotten tract that used to house sheep and some cattle. He'd turned it into something else all together, and I wasn't sure how I felt about the development of wild places.

"No sign of fresh starts," Nilla said. Her gaze scanned what we could see for fresh signs of smoke. I glanced behind us, to the west. Nilla searched the wrong trees for signs of spotting. They would come from west of Adventura and blaze over. Everything was so smoky, however, it was almost impossible to tell.

My neck itched.

I didn't like this at all.

"Bastian?"

My squad leader James' voice cut through my thoughts.

He approached from near the main building. Droplets of water sprinkled his shoulders. He probably checked the outbuilding sprinklers. I shook my head to clear my thoughts, and realized he'd asked me a question.

"Sorry, what?"

"How are the hoses?"

"Hoses are fine, not kinked. Appear to be working." The gentle *tch tch tch* of the sprinkler as it released water around the main building filled in the space between my words. James turned to Nilla.

"Everything else look good?"

"Cleared out," she murmured. "Buildings on the north side of camp are empty. Everything is set up appropriately. No historic structures to wrap."

"Empty on the south," I murmured, "except the stable near the lake. Some of the horses have returned."

"I radioed it into the Supervisor already," James said. "They let Bailey know. Mark's on his way to corral them. Ready to get on perimeter patrol here? We need to hike west, see if we find any signs of fresh starts."

I grunted. As if brought here by sheer thought, the sound of tires crunching on gravel followed. Nilla glanced up.

Two headlights shone out of the foggy orange haze, then a second pair followed. Round, globelike things in the smoke. Two trucks with attached horse trailers had driven past the main building and into camp to stop near us, one behind the other.

My breath caught in the back of my raspy throat when a familiar pair of strong legs and dark hair spilled out of *my* truck. Dahlia's gaze found me almost immediately, then widened. I fought the urge to swear.

What was she doing here?

Suddenly, all the excuses that I'd been telling myself disappeared. They dropped, settling like ash around me. One look at her lovely face and I lost all my determination to do everything myself.

I. Was. A. Total. Idiot.

Why was I holding Dahlia responsible for all the other women in my life? She deserved a chance. More importantly, I wanted her to have that chance.

Wind buffeted us as Mark Bailey stepped out of the truck next to Dahlia and came directly over. He held out a hand to James, who accepted it.

"Thank you all," Mark said, "for watching for new fire starts. You're my heroes."

"Lookin' good up here, Bailey." James let Mark's hand go. "We'll do our best to keep it safe. No sign of spotting so far, but if there is, we're on it."

Dahlia stepped up behind Mark, but kept her gaze on me. In it, I read a world of questions. My throat ached to speak, but I held back.

"Thank you," Mark said. "Let's hope it stays that way. Horses at the stable?"

"Yes." I nodded. "Just saw them there."

"If it's all the same," Mark clapped James on the shoulder as he shot us all a grin, "I'll grab them and get out of your way. Thank you again." He raised a stopping hand to Dahlia. "The horses are going to be skittish at best. They won't let you near them. I'll round them up and bring them over to load up."

"How can I help?" she asked.

"Wait until I'm here. I'll let you know if I need help to load them in the trailer."

Mark jogged away. He disappeared into the smoke like a wraith. With Mark and Dahlia here, James wouldn't want us to go on patrol just yet. My gaze lingered to the west as more wind surged. The radio crackled in James' hand.

"Give me a second?" I asked James and motioned toward Dahlia. He looked at her in surprise, to me, then shrugged.

With one last, inquiring glance, he called Nilla over and they headed toward the lake, radio in hand. I heard vague tones in the chatter, but purposefully tuned out the update.

The main fire would have likely advanced to the highway by now. We'd probably see fresh starts on our side of the canyon any moment.

Which meant Dahlia needed to get the hell out of here.

Once they were out of earshot, Dahlia stepped toward me.

"I hope it's okay I brought your truck," she blurted out. The first signs of stress appeared in her wrinkled forehead. "Mark needed help and couldn't find anyone that wasn't already evacuating their own animals. He's stupid fond of those horses, I hear."

"It's fine."

Her gaze skated over me, then back to my face. "Pretty intense get up you have here."

My bag strained at my shoulders and waist, filled with safety and survival gear and the most amount of water I could bear to carry and still hike fast. My clothes were grungy, the yellow almost faded to brown. Even though we'd just started work this morning, the grime of the smoky air had settled back into my skin. Never had I thought about what I'd look like in this get up until now.

"Yeah."

The lame word left an awkward silence between us. Unable to bear it I said, "Listen, about yesterday—"

Just as she said, "I'm sorry I pushed you too hard."

Dahlia rolled her lips together, giggled, and let out a long breath. "Let's start over. You first."

The tension broke between us, but I still felt it building inside. Here was my chance to make things right, but I wasn't really sure where I'd gone wrong. Or if I had. Or if I wanted it to be right after all. Things had been simpler before Dahlia shone light into my world. Before I willingly plunged her into it.

"I have no idea what to say, Dahlia."

Her curious expression softened. "Oh."

I lifted my hands in a helpless gesture. "I totally chickened out yesterday. I was excited to see you again, but I couldn't bring myself to visit after all I'd revealed to you the day before.

"I'd just spoken to my sister's hospice nurse, who was telling me about how they'd make her comfortable because she's dying. Also visited my father who is dying, but not really. I've never introduced my family to anyone before. Not when they've been unhealthy and . . . not themselves. I . . . I do things myself. I get them done. I don't invite other people into my world. So you . . . I couldn't . . . it all just . . . piled up."

Dahlia blinked. She didn't register utter terror on her face yet, so I took it as a good sign and kept going.

"I don't know the right thing to say. But I do want to say that I'm sorry. I should have come over to see you because it's what I wanted to do. Instead, I chickened out. Also, I struggle with anxiety and it's been so much worse since I met you. I'm in my head about all these things all the time, and women only make it worse. The ones that matter, anyway. I've been a mess since the moment I met you."

Another giggle peeped out of her. I stared at her, incredulous.

"I'm sorry," she whispered and put a hand on my arm. "I'm not laughing at you. Those are . . . those are just the most romantic words I've ever heard. *You give me anxiety.*"

Stated that way, they sounded utterly and completely ridiculous. They weren't wrong either, which only made it more funny. The warmth in her voice softened my fear, however, and I felt myself smile.

"It's true," I muttered.

She put a hand to her chest.

"I'm honored."

The sound of Mark talking to a horse came seconds before the *thud* of hooves followed. In the haze, Mark headed toward my truck and the horse trailer attached, one horse towed behind him. Dahlia held up a hand to me, then darted away. I closed my eyes, grateful for a moment to rally my thoughts back together.

Expecting a blast of self loathing for mucking things up *again*, I braced myself for the worst thoughts to follow. Then I blinked myself back to the moment when it didn't happen. In fact, right now I felt pretty good.

The things I'd wanted to admit about myself were finally out. Not having them locked inside removed the pressure. Which was just . . . stupid easy. Now the only things that remained were questions about her.

Was Jakob still around?

Did she want me?

Minutes passed. The sound of scuffling, a whinny of protest, and a few soothing words from Mark later, Dahlia reappeared.

Mark jogged away, back toward the lake. Dahlia stopped in front of me with a little cough. Wind made her hair dance around her shoulders. The blasts of air felt coarse and abrasive and too strong. She played with the bottom of a lock of hair as she reapproached. She blinked several times, her eyes no doubt irritated by the smoky air. She cleared her throat, and a semblance of the same awkwardness returned. In it, I fully comprehended that I had just told her she gave me anxiety.

Real smooth.

"You were saying?" she murmured, then tacked on with a quick grin, "You know, that I give you anxiety and make you spiral into a mental mess."

I chuckled. "Yes. That. Just that there's a lot of things I don't understand right now. Things I don't have the answer to, like Jess. But one thing that I *do* know is that I want to have a chance to get to know you better."

The words made me cringe. *Get to know you better* sounded so formal, like a stiff, awkward first date. Plus, they weren't right. They didn't hold the same amount of power as what I felt all the way in my bones.

The pressure of all the romance books that I'd written weighed on my shoulders. What would Adrick say? Derrick? Rodrigo? I shoved them all aside. They didn't matter right now.

Those words weren't enough.

"Ravage you." I cleared my throat. "That's what I meant. I want to kiss you until you can't find your breath ever again. I want to have my hands on you until you don't remember that other guy who broke your heart. I want to play with your hair all night while I hold you in my arms and we stare up at the stars."

Her eyes widened like globes. Dahlia sucked in a sharp breath and held it. Honoring the truth sent courage through me. Finally, I would lay it out there for a woman to decide what to do with.

"The only thing that held me back from kissing you the other day was the genuine sadness in your voice when you spoke about Jakob," I continued. "If I never heard his name again, I'd die a happy man. I want to do more than get to know you better, Dahlia. I want to test all my romance novels with you. Figure out how to give *you* butterflies. How to say your name so that you get goosebumps. I want to touch every inch of your body. I want to prove that maybe I don't have to do everything alone."

My throat knotted.

Being the son and the brother had sucked up all my bandwidth. Fire was the only choice I actively made. I hadn't let go of it, because then I really would have been lost. Lost in expectations and care. Lost in the miasma of medical issues and helplessness. Fire had been my only anchor, my tether, to me.

My life had always been sculpted by the people that didn't want me. By the people that left. My birth parents. My adopted Mom. Even the girlfriends that walked away from Dad because they didn't want to deal with his children.

Deep down, I finally understood what I'd avoided all along: that writing romance novels was my safest attempt to create the relationship I desperately wanted.

The relationships so honest and powerful they couldn't be real.

The ones that must be fiction.

Somewhere along the way, I believed that romantic novels had a guaranteed-happily-ever-afters that didn't apply to life in the same way. That had been a lie too.

Because now?

Now I had Dahlia, and everything had changed. With her, I stared down the path of an imperfect future with the perfect woman. A flawed woman, like me.

A woman that I wanted at my side so I could help her and she could help me.

"That's what I want," I finished, brought back to the moment. "And if that's totally freaked you out, I would understand and—"

Her soft lips cut me short. She collided into me. I took a step back to keep us both upright. On instinct, my hands grabbed her waist to keep her from falling. Her body pressed into me, her smell like smoke. Her touch like fire.

I fell to her blazing inferno.

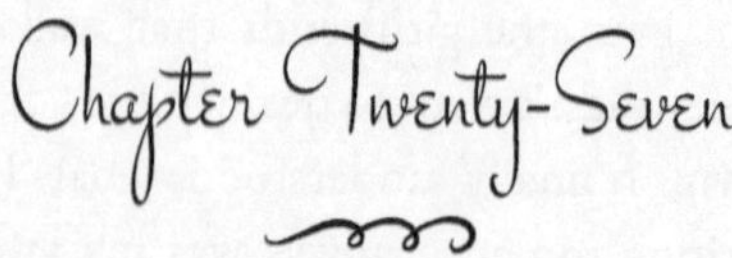

Chapter Twenty-Seven

He burned underneath me.

Bastian wrapped his arms around my back until I couldn't breathe. His chest pressed on mine, forcing our hearts together. The warmth of his mouth slanted over mine, equally intense and possessive. I tightened my hold around his neck and pulled us closer.

Just when the taste of smoke lingered at the back of my throat, he pulled away. Dazed, he blinked.

"Damn, Dahlia," he breathed.

I closed my eyes in silent agreement.

He didn't let go of me, but I loosened my hold on his waist. My feet returned to the ground, though my head played in the clouds. He kept me close, but his gaze darted to the spot where the other two firefighters had disappeared. My thoughts reeled around, consumed by his words.

Kiss you.

The burning intensity that I'd always sensed under him continued to play out now. My heart thudded wildly under my chest as Mark appeared again. I stepped away at the sound of a whinny.

"Just a sec," I murmured.

He nodded, dazed, as I slipped away. Mark led a white-and-brown colored horse that trotted a circle around him as he attempted to take her closer to the trailer. Her wild eyes glanced to me, then away. I stepped back, fading into the smoke as Mark crooned to her. She trotted in another circle, this one a little closer to the open trailer back.

"Stay back," Mark called. "She's nervous. She's the one that'll be hardest to get in. The easiest one will be last."

"How can I help?"

"Check the pins in the trailer behind your truck. You're just taking one horse, so make sure you're ready to go."

My mind spun while I stumbled toward the truck to check the trailer. How much time had passed while Bastian and I had been talking? Eternities? Two minutes? Mark was better at loading stressed-out horses than I expected.

Or maybe I couldn't fathom time now that Bastian had kissed me. While I double-checked the trailer in the thickening smoke alone, I forced my heart to comprehend what had just laid out.

Ravage you.

Maybe I don't have to do everything alone.

My mind wandered far from the smoky hills now. The outbuildings that had once been visible disappeared. Once finished with that task, I coughed and spun around to find Bastian. Questions to ask him streamed through my mind. Things I wanted to say. Apologies to make.

The sound of horses hooves on the trailer followed. A triumphant sound from Mark came next.

"Good girl," he crooned.

"Bastian?" I murmured tentatively.

He appeared out of the smoke, cheeks and face stained with a few streaks of soot. My breath caught as he closed the space between us. A step before he yanked me into his arms and laid another heart-stopping kiss on me, a voice called out, nearly muted by a blast of wind.

"Bastian! We have a new start that's taking off between here and the highway. The fire has crossed the road. We gotta get them out of here and join up with the other squad *now*. She's running."

Bastian stopped, nostrils flared.

The words sent a chill through me. Another gust of wind shuddered by, sending gravel onto my cheeks. Like a ghost, Mark hurried away from the trailer before they could tell him to leave the third horse alone.

Bastian swallowed. His gaze hadn't left mine. "On it," Bastian called to James.

We stood a foot apart now. The back of his hand touched my cheek.

"Get somewhere safe right now, Dahlia," he muttered, his voice hard. "The fire is coming and you will *not* be part of it, you hear me?"

I nodded.

"Get your stuff out of your RV. You can stay at my Dad's place for as long as you need to."

"Thank you. I'll be waiting for you," I said. "Text me as soon as you're safe. Don't do anything stupid. I don't need you, you big oaf, but I want you. There's a difference, and I'm not sure you've ever heard it before."

Surprise flickered in his eyes. He hesitated, then nodded once. "Thank you."

"Bastian!"

"I'm coming."

He grabbed my arm and towed me toward the truck. The door groaned when he shoved me inside. "Go now. Don't wait for Mark. Drive slower than usual, but don't take your time. This fire can take off in minutes."

I nodded, cranked the truck on. Mark materialized out of the smoke, coughing. The final horse hurried behind him.

"Go!" Mark waved me on, a bandana around his neck that he'd clearly had over his mouth and nose. "Take it easy. I'll meet you at the highway."

I nodded. Driving with the RV made me a pro at towing precious cargo. The back of my throat burned when I turned back to Bastian. He grabbed my jaw, pressed his lips to mine in a soul-lifting kiss, then pulled away.

"Be safe."

He faded back, disappearing into the smoke.

* * *

My phone resounded with an annoying *bleep bleep bleep* the moment I pulled into Pineville. A quick glance confirmed my nightmare.

Mandatory Evacuations for the North Pineville area.

A load of other text populated below that, dictating the urgency of escaping this mountain oasis.

Cars streamed out of town, heading toward the other exits, as I followed Mark to open land near the reservoir bed. Alone, our two trucks ambled out of the canyon and back toward Pineville.

My gaze darted up the mountain. The RV hid under a foamy, smoky blanket now. I turned my mind away from it, hopeful it would be spared. Smoke had thickened in Pineville as well. It skimmed over the surface of the reservoir, hovering just off the ground with a miasmic effect.

We crossed the highway south of the reservoir, then drove slowly down a dirt road until Mark stopped at a gate with a fence. Other horses littered the inside of a wide, fenced pasture. New bales of hay had been tossed inside. Horses with their faces covered lounged in the field. Others pranced, letting out irritated whinnies.

Bastian's truck slowed, then stopped. I shoved it into park, grateful that the drive was over with. Towing an RV had made it a simple task to get the horses down, but living cargo was very different from a touring home. Hardest of all had been putting space between me and Bastian.

Meanwhile, my lips still burned. My heart thrummed with the heady memory of Bastian. How safe would he be? Would he survive such an inferno?

He better.

Mark hopped out of his truck and hurried back. He grinned, the immediate stress of getting the horses out of the fire almost gone now.

"You're a lifesaver, Dahlia. I'll get her unloaded. Once we're done, just pull the truck around and we'll ditch the trailer here. We're safe now."

I nodded and obeyed his directions to pull off on a grassy side area. While he managed to safely back the horse out of the trailer, I worked on the hitch. By the time we had both horses unloaded and trailers pulled off to the side, I felt a modicum of relief. The horses were safe. Sione was safe. I was safe.

My belongings?

Not so much.

Bastian?

Definitely not so much.

Mark drew in a deep breath and looked north. Everything was obscured by smoke now, leaving the distant mountains an even more distant memory. Wind tried to push us around, like a bossy chess player coordinating the board. Mark clapped a hand on my shoulder.

"Appreciate you, Dahlia. You have somewhere to go now that evacs are going out?"

"Yes, thanks."

A knowing look came to his eyes. "Bastian's place?"

My lips twitched. "Yeah."

He nodded, patting my back. "He's a good one."

"Are you worried about Adventura?"

His expression dropped. Even beneath a manicured beard, I could see signs of stress. His brow lowered.

"Definitely. The buildings will probably be fine thanks to the sprinklers and the volunteers helping us set them up, but the forest? If that burns, what kind of summer camp do we have?" He shook that bleak thought off. "I'll be fine. We'll nurture it back to life if we have to. Can I do anything for you? Give you one of my horses as thanks?"

I laughed. "No, please don't. It was my pleasure to help."

And received that kiss of a lifetime, I silently added.

Inner Me applauded.

Twenty minutes later, women filled the parking lot of the Frolicking Moose when I drove by.

Forced to park all the way down the road, I walked back toward the coffee shop in utter disbelief. Chants of *We want Jess! We want Jess! We want Jess!* rang through the air. Sheriff deputies walked around the crowd, ushering them away from the coffee shop. Streams of cars took people away, and also brought others closer.

With deputies calling out commands to leave, reluctant people headed toward their cars, books in arms. Lizbeth's bright red hair bustled around the inside, which was also filled with people. I hurried through the cacophony to help her out. Several attempts to get through the crowd meant I had to skirt all the way around clumps of women, climb over a fallen chair, and duck inside.

Relief filled Lizbeth's expression when I hurried behind the counter. "You're back!" she called over the sound of chanting women. "The horses okay?"

"Yes, Mark too. What's going on?"

Her shoulders relaxed. "That's wonderful. JJ will be relieved. The mandatory evacuation order for north Pineville just went out and it's been nuts ever since. The women don't want to leave!" she cried. "So they're chanting for Jess to come out."

"She won't!"

Lizbeth shrugged. "They keep coming! The sheriff finally showed up to get them to leave in case they block evacuation routes for local people. They don't want to go without Jess. Katrina's been recording the whole thing. The local news showed up too. They're starting to trend on Tweetastic!"

Outside, Katrina wandered around with her camera. She popped into the bed of a truck, filmed from there, then hopped down. Books flew through the air as people tossed them high, like graduation caps. The chanting continued. Women inside began to rush outside when a deputy stepped in, barking orders for them to leave.

Hernandez appeared at the end of a surge of people that came from the back. Deep grooves formed in his brow. He shook his head, muttering something about *crazy gringos* under his breath.

He stopped, looked at me, and lifted one eyebrow. "You know where Bastian is?" he asked.

"On the fire," I said.

"Huh." Hernandez studied me. "How long have you had the hots for him?"

My cheeks didn't even heat up. This was one truth I could completely own. My gaze didn't waver as I met his.

"A few weeks."

Hernandez grinned a slow, beguiling smile. "That's a quick timeline for that Merry Idiot. He needs a strong woman like you." He nodded. "He okay on the fire? You heard from him?"

"He's fine."

Hernandez winked. "Watch out for him, will you?"

"You bet I will," I said firmly.

He grinned, then turned to the lingering women in the shop and called, "Everybody out!"

They rushed to the doors yet again. Bodies scattered everywhere. Deputies had to halt traffic to let them flow across the street and into their cars. The swirling smoke and alerts for more evacuations added to the chaos.

Thirty minutes later, the Frolicking Moose had finally emptied. I turned to Lizbeth, ragged at the edges from keeping all the pieces together.

She let out a long, long breath. "Well," she murmured. "That is that." She chucked me softly in the shoulder. "When were you going to tell me about you and Bastian?"

"When I knew more, myself," I murmured, and touched my lips.

A knowing gleam entered her eyes. "Ah," she murmured. "I see. Fresh as a new flower in spring?"

"Very fresh."

"It's good that way. He seems like a pretty tough nut to crack."

"Very."

Lizbeth sighed. "Romance is so wonderful, even when the world is threatening to burn down. Thanks for letting me relive it for a moment. Maverick told me to keep the place open, by the way. Their house is in the North Pineville mandatory evac zone, too. They're heading down the mountain to come here now. We're going to all pile into the loft here and leave the Frolicking Moose open. That way, locals and officials have a gathering spot if they need it. JJ's going to start batch making food on an outside grill."

The thought of going to Bastian's house and sitting there by myself felt interminable. With Sione in Jackson City and a closed highway between us, I'd have to be alone with my fears.

Right now, I wanted to be with the townspeople I'd come to love.

"Want some help?" I asked.

Lizbeth smiled, then nodded. "Yeah," she said quietly. "Let's wait here for news of your man, and our home."

Chapter Twenty-Eight

BASTIAN

The beast had finally arrived.

To the west, fire billowed plumes of smoke bigger than my eye could see. The roar of the fire came from not far away, darkening the world like a hellscape after all.

Heat and ash and wind flailed around us as we extinguished the new burn to stop the advancing fire from tearing through Adventura.

Grass and leaves curled in on themselves under the flames. Smoke stung my eyes as I walked the burning line. The lake would create a natural barrier to protect Adventura, not to mention the dirt roads and the gravel parking lot. But the trees could still ignite and spread and stop all our hard work.

So we constantly worked.

For the rest of the day, I strode around Adventura, shovel in hand, digging at the ground as I went. Embers flared in plumes of orange and red as the winds raged. Fire swirled. We dumped water, called commands, and tried to keep energy high.

All around us: smoke, smoke, smoke. All in my thoughts: Dahlia, Dahlia, Dahlia. This hungry beast that wanted to kill us had nothing on my Dahlia. Her lips pressed to mine burned hotter than the fires of Hades.

I wanted nothing more than to get back to her. No more flailing out here to make a point. From here on out, I would turn over a new leaf. New Bastian. New life. Time to embrace help, change, and the inevitable.

Dahlia was mine.

* * *

People lined the streets of Pineville.

Fire camp had been yanked back, repositioned in case a flank of fire left it in cinders. The mini-city took up the parking lot of the grocery store with their vans, tents, equipment, and supplies. It had doubled in size over the past twenty four hours, no doubt with new resources to fight the inferno.

I leaned my forehead against the cool windowpane and dreamed of popsicles. Ultra-cold ice cream to soothe my throat. Cold coffee. Ribs. Steak. Split potatoes dripping butter. Anything with so many calories they couldn't be counted. After twenty-four hours on the line, my stomach was so hungry it would gnaw itself open.

My eyes fluttered open and drifted to the north. Despite the darkness, I could see smoke lazily trailing heavenward. It didn't charge into the atmosphere like a bully anymore. Instead, it floated gently, barely visible in the building morning light.

Almost eighteen hours had passed since Dahlia left Adventura, but it felt like decades. My body creaked like an old man. I'd hiked through the forest, dug line, protected the summer camp, watched that earth, dug some more, poured an unholy amount of water over burning ground, and, somehow, arrived back here.

Winds gave way to calmer skies around 8:00 last evening.

With the onset of darkness and no harried gusts, the fire bedded down a bit. The still, quiet air felt heavy and odd in the wake of so much caterwauling.

A storm had blown in on the edge of the wind. It dropped little more than a drizzle, but the humidity helped calm the inferno. Thanks to the lake, manual labor, and a lot of line, Adventura and the forest around it had been saved. Except for a few areas where we fought the new fire start, very little burn marks would remain.

Brightness from the town startled me back to life.

I glanced over to see the Frolicking Moose illuminated with beckoning, buttery light down the road. My watch said 5:30. Behind the mountains, the dawning sun turned the edges of the sky to a rosy pink.

All day we'd bunk at the station until we were called out again for a night shift to keep a hold of the line at the highway. The fire would likely try to spread. Embers would dance to other spots. But such a wild storm wasn't present in the forecast tonight which gave us a big advantage.

No, this monster was just about to die out. It had charged hard, but now it lay down.

Time for us to win.

Several text messages from Dahlia downloaded to my phone after we left the canyon, all of them spaced about an hour apart, like she used a timer.

Her steady attention slipped through me like hot chocolate on a cold winter day.

Dahlia: Thinking of you.

Dahlia: Winds are still pretty fierce. Evacuations have cleared most people out of the north side of Pineville. Others are leaving the south side and flocking to the reservoir for camping. Since we're next to the lake, we're taking people who have

RVs or need a place to crash. Is this real life? It seems so strange.

Dahlia: Is Pineville the coolest community ever? I vote yes.

Dahlia: I had to stop checking Tweetastic for updates because the pictures of the fire were so ugly. How can a fire be so big? Mother Nature is a witch. Hoping you're safe. Can't stop thinking about that kiss.

Several other video messages followed, but I hadn't watched them yet. I'd save those for later, when I'd be back on the fire and a quick glimpse of her would fuel me.

The wildland truck slowed to a stop outside the fire station. All our weary bodies dragged themselves out of their seats and outside to the parking lot. My muscles had stiffened. Salt caked my skin and shook free as I made it down the steps. The only thing that propelled me forward was the thought of Dahlia so close.

Sleep even closer.

Two steps out of the truck, I halted.

A small chorus of clapping filled the air. Locals and visitors that had been evacuated from their homes and camping spots were bunking out in tents all the way down the main street of Pineville.

They stood sleepily nearby, applauding. Other people, up early, sat outside RVs with steaming cups of coffee. Dogs skittered their feet, running around, barking, pacing. Bustle inside the Frolicking Moose spilled into the parking lot like it was the beating heart of the town.

With the applause came more applause. Whistles. Shouts of gratitude. People stepped out of the Frolicking Moose to see us and call out their thanks. I blinked, dazed by the unexpected display.

Awkwardness filled me until I saw a familiar pair of dark eyes step out of the Frolicking Moose. Dahlia wore her usual shorts, tank top, and cream-colored apron over the front of her.

Fatigue and relief lingered in her gaze. Had she been up late? What had they been doing? If all the RVs, tents, and general bustle this early meant anything, she'd had a busy night.

That seemed about right.

The Frolicking Moose had always been the heart of Pineville, fishy smell or not.

James lifted a hand to acknowledge the praise. Nilla waved. Mack tried to act like he didn't hear it, but high color appeared on his cheeks. Slowly, the smatter died away. People turned back to the coffee shop or their tents.

Across the distance, Dahlia caught my gaze. Bodies slipped past her to go inside, murmuring. An old man approached James with a question about the fire and the rest of the crew filtered apart. The truck groaned as bags unloaded and fire fighters shuffled back to the station to crash and sleep until our next go-round. I started across the parking lot with long strides.

Dahlia hurried down the stairs and met me halfway. I wrapped my arms around her waist and lifted her up, relieved to see her safe. She tightened her hold around my neck and whispered, "I'm so glad you're here."

"Everything okay?" I asked.

"Fine now."

She held onto me for several long moments. When I could finally pull away, she stepped back. Her hands stayed on my arms. She had to tilt her head back a little to look up at me from this close. She'd fit perfectly under my arm. My gaze drifted to her lips. All I wanted to do was lock us together and forget everything else existed. I fisted my hand at my side to stop myself from touching her lips with my thumb.

Did fire live in those lips?

The smoky gaze?

Yes, it had to. I'd already been burned.

"There's a lot to update you on," she said, a little breathlessly. She smiled, the edges of her lips twitching, like she couldn't hold it back, even if she wanted to. "But let's just say that it's not what you'd ever imagine, and everything is fine."

My shoulders relaxed. "Good."

Her expression creased a little. I reached up to smooth the wrinkles away.

"I, uh . . . I hope it's okay," she continued, "but I called Inessa's care center to check on her. They said she was worried about the fire growing so big. Smoke in Jackson City was bad, and she heard the news. I spoke with her for a while. Several times, in fact. She's been calling when she's worried."

"Really?"

Dahlia nodded, swallowing. She squeezed my arm where her hand still rested.

"I've loved talking to her, and she calmed down as soon as we got on the phone together. Everything is fine. I just . . . I wanted them to have my number in case you were on a fire and they needed something. I'm sorry if it was presumptuous, maybe, but—"

I silenced her by kissing her. She quieted immediately, limp in my arms. It forced me to wrap an arm around her back to hold her weight, which pulled her even closer. The press of her chest against mine sent my stomach into a giddy whirl.

Breathless, I pulled away. She blinked, dazed.

"Oh," she whispered.

I pressed my forehead to hers. "Thank you," I murmured. "It means so much. It's going to take some practice for me not to feel like I have to do all of this alone, but I'm confident we can figure it out."

She smiled, flushed with relief. "Me too."

A sound from the station caught my ear. I glanced back, saw James waving for me, and reluctantly turned back to her.

"My two weeks is still just beginning. We'll be assigned here for that time. Maybe later it will be easier to connect, but I need you to assume you won't see me again."

"Can do."

"Just like that?" An incredulous smile spread across my face. "It's that easy for you? Two weeks and you're fine with it?"

"If you're the prize," she murmured with her bright grin, "then yes."

One last crushing kiss and I forced her away from me before I made an ass of myself in front of the squad. Dahlia stood there, toying with a strand of hair, while I yanked my bag out of the back of the buggy and headed for the station.

Meanwhile, smoky sunlight burst over the top of the mountains to the north like a welcome into better days ahead.

Chapter Twenty-Nine

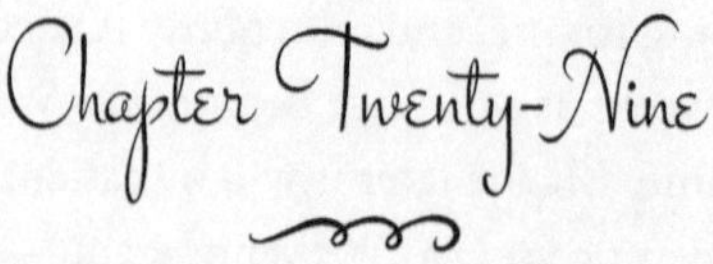

DAHLIA

Two weeks later

A breath of fresh air raced over my cheeks.

I lounged back against my foldout chair and closed my eyes. Misty vapor rolled by like dollops of pudding. The reservoir was obscured in a bank of clouds far below and rain threatened to fall at any moment.

Blessed, blessed water.

Not a single hint of smoke in the air. I would sit out here in the rain for as long as it lasted.

Next to me, Bastian grunted.

"85% containment," he murmured. "Good to hear."

He relaxed in the chair next to mine, his laptop propped on his legs despite the potential splash of falling rain. His two week rotation on the Pinegulch fire had officially ended this morning. The fog had welcomed them back home to the station.

So had my waiting arms.

He closed the laptop and looked at me. My breath caught in the back of my throat. Somehow, he still arrested my heart. The depth of his blue eyes, fathoms deep. The chiseled seriousness of his expression. Mist settled on top of his hair, darkening his blonde locks. I wanted to run my fingers through them.

Our relationship sprinted like fire—hot, fast, and intense. Now I felt a gentle smolder and burn. The gradual building up of a flame that would last forever.

I smiled.

He did too.

He reached over, fingers tangled in mine, then looked at the wisps ahead of us. They curled, toying with the trees, as they danced through the forest. My phone vibrated. I swallowed the last of my orange soda and reached for it in my pocket.

"So, there's something I still need to show you." I cleared my throat. A text message waited on my phone, just as I had expected.

"Oh yeah?" he drawled.

I cut an amused glare toward him when I heard the playful tone in his voice. "Not *that*."

He laughed, and the rolling sound sent a shiver through me. I couldn't wait to hear a lot more of that.

I turned my attention back to the phone, purposefully extricating myself from his touch so we didn't get distracted by kissing.

Again.

Katrina: Video is ready. Thought you'd like to see an advanced copy?

Dahlia: Yes please!

Katrina: Sent a link to your email.

The last six weeks had been a frenzy for many reasons.

Running the Frolicking Moose so residents had a safe place to congregate, sleep, and eat while the evacuations were underway. Dealing with my perpetual worry for Bastian while out on different fires, and diving deeper into my work with Bastian's career.

Not to mention helping Katrina finalize The Surprise.

She'd grabbed a ridiculous amount of footage from all the amassed women the day of the evacuation, but there was more work to be done.

As the project began, her vision for it expanded. She worked tirelessly on interviews of readers, fans, and footage of the social media groups. She'd stayed in Pineville to grab shots of the shop, where she'd stayed as she plotted the storyline. I'd held the camera while she narrated segments of her own heartbreak story.

In the end, Katrina still had no idea who Jess was.

But she didn't need to anymore.

"What is it?" Bastian asked. He leaned close, his breath warm on my neck like a gentle whiff of mist. I realized I'd been lost in my thoughts while the internet caught up with the video. Moments later, the video expanded to fill my screen. I scooted my chair closer and angled the phone toward him.

"A little surprise," I murmured.

The opening segment showed a barrage of screaming women chanting, "We want Jess! We want Jess! We want Jess!"

Bastian reared back slightly, blinking. I sucked in a sharp breath and studied his expression while the footage continued. The moment he recognized Pineville in the background of all these wild women sent a perplexed expression to his face. He glanced at me in a silent question.

"Keep watching," I said.

Bright, peppy music faded as Katrina began to narrate and the video cut to her in the shop. She'd edited in a chunky way.

The video frames ended abruptly as she spoke, but started again into her next sentence. It was funky and adorable.

She looked positively bright on the screen, not at all heartbroken. Books by Jess filled the bookshelf behind her—Lizbeth's idea—in a colorful menagerie. Her resemblance to Lolo was startling and uncanny and I wondered if he noticed it as quickly as I had.

While her story unfolded, Bastian remained riveted to the phone. Minutes of the documentary rolled by. Katrina strolling through the airport, filming in the loft of the Frolicking Moose, getting lunch at The Diner.

Overlaid in all of it was a pile of notes, shots of her computer while she spoke with women on social media, and images of her and her friends during the launch.

A timeline of the books unfolded in the documentary, as well as random facts taken from moments of time in Jess fandom. Blog posts. Fan hysteria. Articles. She even reviewed attempts to find Jess from other people that didn't work out.

Interspersed within all of this were small stories from readers whose lives had been changed by Jess's books. The story built and built in an expert way, funneling all to the same question: who is Jess?

When Katrina began her heartbreak story, Bastian took the phone from my hand, then sank deeper into the chair. I rested my cheek on his shoulder and wished I could peer into his mind.

Thirty minutes passed by the time that the footage of the Frolicking Moose on the evac day started. In the documentary, Katrina reviewed the fire, panned over the hazy northern skyline, showed footage of the Sheriff's deputies driving around with bull horns saying, "Mandatory evacuations in place for northern Pineville area!" The energy of the day replayed through the screen.

Meanwhile, Bastian didn't say a word. He opened his mouth, but shut it again several times.

His white knuckle grip began a seed of concern inside me. I hadn't considered that he'd be angry over all this. His privacy had remained intact the entire time, but he hadn't been here to see it unfold like me. I imagined there must be a sense of helplessness to this now. The documentary was Katrina's story, not Jess's, but they were intertwined. Just like Jess's life with so many other women.

Hopefully, he'd see that.

The documentary video wound down after forty-five minutes. Bright, chipper music continued as it had throughout, lending a peppy feel to the whole thing.

At the last of it, Katrina sat cross legged at the edge of the reservoir, not far from the Frolicking Moose. A crystal blue sky opened behind her, devoid of fire, and the whole thing felt like a new beginning.

"In the end," Katrina said, tortoise shell glasses perched on top of her head which held her dreadlocks away from her face. "I didn't meet Jess. Maybe I never really thought I would. When I realized how entangled Jess had been with Brooke for me, I also learned I didn't really *want* to meet Jess. I had built them both up as a certain person in my head. Meeting them could never be the same as the people I believed them to be." She smiled. "The mystery is the best part of the surprise."

The video rolled into text that told the final parts of Katrina's story as she moved on without Brooke. Once it ended, Bastian lowered the phone and stared at the ground. He appeared utterly lost in his thoughts. I took the phone from his hand, clicked it off, and set it aside.

For nearly fifteen minutes, we sat in the gentle silence. I sank down, tilted my head back, and closed my eyes to the frosting-like clouds. Rain began to slowly fall. Big, fat drops that stirred up pockets of dust with every *thud* on the ground.

They dropped into my hair and rolled down my scalp. It beaded on my shoulders.

A gentle touch on my face brought my eyes open. Bastian leaned close, studying me. He'd closed his computer and shoved it against his chest to protect it from rain. My stomach tightened, ready for one of his panty-melting kisses, but he stayed a tantalizing breath away. His lashes fluttered as he studied me.

"Why?" he asked quietly.

I struggled to wrap my mind around a response, even though I knew what he asked. *Why didn't I tell him?*

"It wasn't really my story to tell," I said. "She had her own ghosts to deal with, and she did that without disrespecting Jess's right for privacy and anonymity. I wanted to honor that for her . . . and for you."

His brow tightened as he thought about that, then nodded. The contemplation hadn't left his gaze yet.

"Thank you," he said.

I smiled.

The tips of his fingers drew a line down my cheek. He cupped my neck in his hand and pulled me close. Our lips crashed together like two fires converging. Seconds later, I sat in his lap, my hands in his hair. He pressed me close as the heavens opened up.

Blessed life-giving rain soaked us all the way through as I embraced the new future ahead of me.

Chapter Thirty

BASTIAN

"Bash!" Dahlia cried. "Do you want peppermint or vanilla?"

A little giggle followed the question.

Dahlia and Inessa conspired together on the other side of the room, near Inessa's microwave. Inessa sat on top of a walker/chair combination—she was too weak to stand for long—with her oxygen tubing trailing from her bed.

Dahlia had a bright pink mug set out that said *diva* for Inessa, and another one with a black and red flannel pattern with a cartoon picture of a frowning lumberjack.

That would be mine.

I held back a grin and called, "Peppermint hot chocolate. Always."

Inessa pealed with laughter. "I won!" she cried. "I said it's what he'd want!"

Dahlia held up two hands, conceding. "You absolutely won Inessa, fantastic call. You know your brother better than anyone." She glanced back, saw me staring at her, and winked.

My heart settled into a funky rhythm.

Snow fell outside in a gentle, latticed pattern. It collected on the windowsill in gentle puffs. Inessa's breathing rate had started to increase, so she'd have to go back to bed soon. The nurse would be in to get her settled with dinner. We'd already been here for three hours while Nessa taught Dahlia how to paint. Besides, we'd need to drive back to Dad's before the weather in the canyon turned sour.

Now that Leslie Miller had taken over running the Frolicking Moose, Bethany of Mercedy Realty would be putting Dad's house on the market in the morning.

Dahlia insisted she had to scrub the bathroom one last time before people came to walk through. Letting go of that piece of my life felt a bit like saying goodbye to the past—and hello to the future. Finally, I could part with the lonely place, because I'd found something infinitely better.

Thankfully, the fire hadn't pushed far enough south to burn up the RV park, so all Dahlia's belongings remained safe. That meant I needed to take my final round of donations to the local thrift store, because living in a trailer with my girlfriend while we plotted out more books—in addition to the next phase of our life together—meant a lot of downsizing.

But we still had a few more minutes here with Inessa.

Emails populated on my screen from Priyanka. Why she used email subjects like a text message, I would never understand.

The subject lines gave me pause, then made me laugh.

Priyanka Patel: Here's a new PR opportunity that doesn't reveal anything.

Priyanka Patel: I hate it, but you were right again.

Priyanka Patel: Another article about the mysterious Jess.

Priyanka Patel: Did you see sales? Soared after the video.

Priyanka Patel: Can we finally talk about the next launch date?

Priyanka Patel: Dahlia has been emailing me and I like her better than I like you.

Priyanka Patel: Can you have Dahlia call me?

My lips twitched. Everyone liked Dahlia better than they liked me. Who could blame them?

After the documentary aired, Priyanka had been oddly silent for days. When I finally got her back on the phone, she'd said something I never expected.

"You're right. We shouldn't reveal Jess."

For two hours, we unraveled my final decision. Yes, I could reveal myself as Jess. Now that I'd seen fandom at it's proudest moment, I was willing.

But in the end, it wasn't the right move.

Like Katrina said, these women really didn't want to solve the mystery. The mystery was half the fun. Jess needed to remain as just Jess.

Instead, I posted a thank you letter to Katrina, shared the documentary on social media, and made more time and space for interacting with my readers than I had before. Rumors circulated, but they always would. Some fans had even come to the Frolicking Moose and asked questions, but nothing dangerous.

Now that I lived my own romance, maybe I'd keep the books coming. My plans to not return to wildland fire meant I'd have the time to write, for sure.

The world was at *our* feet.

While Dahlia and Inessa made themselves comfortable on Inessa's bed so Dahlia could read her more from Rodrigo and

Amalia, I sank lower in the chair. Had life ever been happier than this?

No.

Dahlia had finally helped me see that things were better when I didn't bear it all myself. Thankfully, she had a soft spot for idiots that took too long to learn the right lesson and lips that tasted like fire.

I turned back to my computer, dismissed my emails, and pulled up a blank white page. Jagged words started to churn in my head again, ready to smooth out on the paper.

Months and months lay between me and my last writing session, but I'd bridge those easily enough now that I felt the power building in my mind again.

My fingers started to type.

Ah, oblivion.

When I sat down to write this novel, I faced three significant challenges.

First, writing a book about a wild forest fire that didn't read like a dirge, remained *mostly* true to life, yet still had significant tension.

Many wildfires are long hauls. They're slogs where the fire waxes, wanes, interrupts life, and crawls along. Yes, they can be blazing infernos, but not always.

My husband was a hotshot/wildland firefighter, so I can't tell you how convenient that was when writing this book. He, however, would apply a different word. :)

Inasmuch as feasibly possible, I kept true to the real experience these women and men go through as hotshots. I worked hard to keep analysis on the fire brief, but still paint a clear picture.

Obviously, the Pineville hotshots are not a real hotshot team—I took that liberty.

My husband approved how this plot laid out, and talked me down from a FAR more dramatic cliff with wild forest infernos and half-naked firefighters running to the aid of the lost protagonist in desperate need.

(Who am I kidding? I'd never write that book!)

The conditions these amazing people work through are no joke. The crappy pay is no joke. 16-24 hours digging line is no joke. In ten years of marriage, I'd never seen Husband as tired and haggard as that second summer we did wildland fire.

Go hug a wildland firefighter if they're cool with that— you wouldn't believe how hard they work, and under what conditions, to keep people and things safe.

Secondly, and also convenient to this book, is the fact that I almost lost my house to a historic wildland fire in Colorado. In the late summer/fall of 2020, the Cameron Peak fire raged across our mountains to eventually create a new record for the biggest wildfire in Colorado history.

The man-made start of the fire was only 10 or so miles as the crow flies from where I lived. One particularly bleak day with historically dry conditions and hurricane-like winds, it raced 17 miles. Over the course of months, it spurred two mandatory evacuations (one over two weeks long) and destroyed over 200,000 acres of forest.

We stayed in hotels, with family, traveled across states, lost school time, work time, parts of our forest, and had a sense of impending doom for months and months. The implications continue to rage now, a year later.

It's hard to quantify that experience beyond *awe-inspiring*. Until you see those pyrocumulus clouds in person, I'm not sure words do them justice. In the midst of it, I joked with my girlfriends that I should write a romance book about it one day because none of us could find a hotshot romance at the time that we loved.

So I did.

The third difficult pillar of this book was the inherent

challenge of tackling the world *from an author perspective.* Partly because Bastian's troubles involved a business slant.

The last thing I wanted my readers to assume is that Bastian and I are the same. In fact, I adore my readers. Trust them completely. Bastian's lack of sole focus on his writing career (which is so unlike me) startled me as I wrote the book. I don't know why his commitment wasn't 100% on Jess's career, but I decided to go with it.

If there's anything that I want for you, it's authentically written characters. Often, my characters puzzle me as well.

Also, I stewed and debated over the *should Bastian reveal himself as Jess* question for a very long time. I hope you enjoyed my final decision.

This book was really written out of fire itself. While writing SMOKE AND FIRE, my family had just moved states, I underwent surgery, we integrated together as a family after being apart for four or five months, my kids started a new school, and all the other normal crazies that go with normal life. These two characters eluded me almost more than any other couple I've written to date, just like smoke. I typed out Bastian and Dahlia in the midst of ever-changing circumstances outside my control, just like fire.

And how perfect is that?

To all of my beta readers and sensitivity readers, thank you so much for your hard work under a quick time pressure!

My team pulled together in these less-than-optimal manuscript conditions to save the book launch date and get you this novel. A round of applause to all of them and their unfaltering support.

Pele, your quick work was so appreciated. Thanks for having my back! Sione, you live in my past as one of my first proposals, yet on the beaches of Tonga. <3 May we meet again one day.

Warmly,

Katie Cross

Clean Sweep

A SNEAK PEEK INTO BOOK 8

LESLIE

Something fuzzy lived in the dish at the bottom of my fridge and it had been there for over a week now.

The old ceramic dish had a glass top so I could peer inside. At best, the contents appeared mushy and gray, with a slight green tint around the edges. Mold, for certain.

Never mind that my divorce had been final for over a year now, Mrs. Cortez still brought dinners for me and my son like we actively mourned my first marriage.

No, that thing *needed* to die. In fact, that marriage had died long before the divorce drove a wooden stake in its soul-sucking, vampiric heart.

Not for the first time, I regarded the moldy dish, shuddered, and closed the door.

"Not right now," I whispered, then crept away, like it would grow across the floor after me.

Coffee almost sloshed out of my mug as I set it on the table and called out, "Blake! You have five minutes before you have to leave. If you're tardy, you'll get detention and I am not saving you again."

An unintelligible, teenage grunt followed. I fought not to roll my eyes, but at least the thudding music quieted a little. I passed by a load of clothes that Blake still hadn't taken upstairs even though I'd graciously folded them in piles on the table. Most of the time these days, he dressed himself from the dining room.

Beneath the table lay carpet that needed a good vacuum a few weeks ago. Various parts of my kitchen and entryway boasted floorboards that weren't gray, but *appeared* to be from gathered dust. One wall collected cobwebs at the seam like an old lady would cats. Behind me, the dishwasher let out a groan as it attempted to clean an overly-full load I'd forgotten to start last night.

"Hello, Monday in the middle of November," I muttered, then sighed.

My phone chimed with a text from my oldest of four sons, Landon. At twenty-three and *almost* accepted into medical school, he currently finished up his last semester of his undergrad in Jackson City. It was a bigger—but still not big— mountain city forty-five minutes up the canyon from here in Pineville. He'd saved up all his online classes for his final semesters so he could move to Jackson City, work, get a hold of debt, and still graduate on time.

Sensible, this kid.

Landon soothed my Mama nerves every time I saw his name. Easy going. Hard working, but wasn't obnoxious about it. His latest girlfriend of four weeks showed real promise this time.

Not like all the others, anyway.

Landon: Can I come home Saturday for food?

Leslie: Sure. Your favorites?

Landon: You're the best. We'll be there at noon.

I paused.
Although he'd been idly mentioning a woman named Starla every now and then, there had never been a *we* attached to anything.
In fact, he'd almost disappeared since they started to officially date. Not only had I not met Starla yet, but I knew nothing else about her except her name and a vague mention of a *super awesome first date, Mom. Tell you about it later.*

Leslie: We?

Landon: Yeah, I'm bringing Starla. I proposed to her last night, thought you'd want to meet her. This seemed like a good time.

I blinked.
Wait, what?

Leslie: I'm sorry, you did what?

Landon: It's a conversation better to have in person, but didn't want to spring too much on you at once.

Leslie: Is this a joke?

Landon: No. It's a long story. Could we have BBQ instead of pasta?

"No," I murmured. "This . . . this has to be a joke."

Landon is not the son that would casually mention a proposal or break life-changing news to me over a text message without any contextual basis at all.

Certainly not after dating for four weeks!

This was something my second-oldest son Max would do, because he fell in and out of love every twenty seconds.

Not Landon.

Furious, I tapped the phone icon and listened to it ring in my ear. He denied the call, then texted back.

Landon: Can't talk now. At work. Later.

"You did not just decline me," I growled.

Blake descended the stairs, thudding like he stomped out cockroaches on his way down. He zoomed by, a blur that managed to snatch his car keys before disappearing out the kitchen door with a "Bye, Mom!" tossed over his shoulder.

I sent a vague wave in response.

With all my control, I stopped myself from calling Landon again. I settled on the most threatening I-brought-you-into-this-life-I-can-take-you-out-of-it message I could conjure with so little brain capacity left.

Leslie: We WILL talk later, young man.

Landon: Thanks, Mom!

Sensing that he must be nervous about this—or he would have told me about it already—I schooled my inner Mama Bear and gave a calm reply.

Leslie: We'll eat at six. See you then.

Then I set my phone down and screamed like a wild banshee.

* * *

Ready for more? **Please visit www.katiecrossbooks.com** to buy your paperback copy today.

Also by Katie Cross

The Health and Happiness Society

Bon Bons to Yoga Pants (Lexie)

I Am Girl Power (Megan)

You'll Never Know (Rachelle)

Hear Me Roar (Bitsy)

What Was Lost (Mira)

The Health and Happiness Society Collection

Finding Anna

Coffee Shop Series

Coffee Shop Girl

Lovesick

Runaway

Fighter

Shy Girl

Wild Child

Smoke and Fire

Clean Sweep

Protect Me

About the Author

Katie Cross is ALL ABOUT writing epic love stories and wild places. Creating new books is her jam.

When she's not hiking or chasing her two littles through the Montana mountains, you can find her curled up reading a book or arguing with her husband over the best kind of sushi.

Visit her at www.katiecrossbooks.com for free short stories, extra savings on all her books (and some you can't buy on the retailers), and so much more.

www.ingramcontent.com/pod-product-compliance
Lightning Source LLC
Chambersburg PA
CBHW021217220726
48287CB00015B/1675